John Doran

The Bentley Ballads

Containing the Choice Ballads, Songs and Poems Contributed to...

John Doran

The Bentley Ballads
Containing the Choice Ballads, Songs and Poems Contributed to...

ISBN/EAN: 9783744784498

Printed in Europe, USA, Canada, Australia, Japan

Cover: Foto ©Andreas Hilbeck / pixelio.de

More available books at **www.hansebooks.com**

THE

BENTLEY BALLADS.

CONTAINING

THE CHOICE BALLADS, SONGS AND POEMS CONTRIBUTED TO
" BENTLEY'S MISCELLANY."

LONDON:

RICHARD BENTLEY, NEW BURLINGTON STREET.

1862.

ADVERTISEMENT

TO THE NEW EDITION.

In introducing a New Edition to the public, the Publisher of " The Bentley Ballads" is desirous of calling attention to the new features which distinguish it from the former, and which, in reality, constitute it an entirely new Work.

The first edition was selected from only six volumes of " Bentley's Miscellany"—from 1837 to 1840; the present includes all the most famous Songs and Ballads contributed to that celebrated magazine during a period of eighteen years, from 1837 to 1855.

This Volume, it is believed, will be found worthy of a place in every library; for, perhaps, no single work in English modern literature exhibits such diversity of talent as these songs of love and sentiment, wit and humour, by the most popular authors of England, Scotland, Ireland,

and America. It is only necessary to mention the names of Prout, Maginn, Lover, Ingoldsby, Longfellow, and the Irish Whiskey-Drinker, to give an idea of the rich store of entertainment contained in the following pages.

LONDON,
February, 1861.

CONTENTS.

vi   CONTENTS.

CONTENTS.

CONTENTS.

BENTLEY BALLADS.

~~~~~~~~~~~~

OLD MORGAN AT PANAMA.

I.

In the hostel-room we were seated in gloom, old Morgan's
    trustiest crew ;
No mirthful sound, no jest went round, as it erst was
    wont to do.
Wine we had none, and our girls were gone, for the last
    of our gold was spent ;
And some swore an oath, and all were wroth, and stern
    o'er the table bent ;
Till our chief on the board hurl'd down his sword, and
    spake with his stormy shout,
" Hell and the devil ! an' this be revel, we had better arm
    and out.
        Let us go and pillage old Panama,
           We, the mighty Buccaneers !"

B

II.

Straight at the word each girt on his sword, five hundred
     men and more;
And we clove the sea in our shallops free, till we reach'd
     the mainland shore.
For many a day overland was our way, and our hearts
     grew weary and low,
And many would back on their trodden track, rather than
     farther go;
But the wish was quell'd, though our hearts rebell'd, by
     old Morgan's stormy roar,—
"The way ye have sped is farther to tread, than the way
     which lies before."
         So on we march'd upon Panama,
            We, the mighty Buccaneers!

III.

'Twas just sunset when our eyes first met the sight of the
     town of gold;
And down on the sod each knelt to his god, five hundred
     warriors bold;
Each bared his blade, and we fervent pray'd (for it might
     be our latest prayer),
" Ransom from hell, if in fight we fell,—if we lived, for a
     booty rare!"
And each as he rose felt a deep repose, and a calm o'er all
     within;
For he knew right well, whatever befell, his soul was
     assoil'd from sin.
         Then down we march'd on old Panama,
            We, the mighty Buccaneers!

IV.

The town arose to meet us as foes, and in order beheld us
  come ;—
They were three to one, but warriors none,—traders, and
  such like scum,
Unused to wield either sword or shield ; but they plied
  their new trade well.
I am not told how they bought and sold, but they fought
  like fiends of hell.
They fought in despair for their daughters fair, their
  wives, and their wealth, God wot !
And throughout the night made a gallant fight,—but it
  matter'd not a jot.
    For had we not sworn to take Panama,
      We, the mighty Buccaneers ?

V.

O'er dying and dead the morn rose red, and o'er streets of
  a redder dye ;
And in scatter'd spots stood men in knots, who would not
  yield or fly.
With souls of fire they bay'd our ire, and parried the hurl
  and thrust ;
But ere the sun its noon had won they were mingled with
  the dust.
Half of our host in that night we lost,—but we little for
  that had care ;
We knew right well that each that fell increased the
  survivor's share
    Of the plunder we found in old Panama,
      We, the mighty Buccaneers !

VI.

We found bars of gold, and coin untold, and gems which
    to count were vain;
We had floods of wine, and girls divine, the dark-eyed
    girls of Spain.
They at first were coy, and baulk'd our joy, and seem'd
    with their fate downcast,
And wept and groan'd, and shriek'd and swoon'd; but
    'twas all the same at last.
Our wooing was short, of the warrior's sort, and they
    thought it rough, no doubt;
But, truth to tell, the end was as well as had it been
    longer about.
              And so we revell'd in Panama,
                  We, the mighty Buccaneers!

VII.

We lived in revel, sent care to the devil, for two or three
    weeks or so,
When a general thought within us wrought that 'twas
    getting time to go.
So we set to work with dagger and dirk to torture the
    burghers hoar,
And their gold conceal'd compell'd them to yield, and add
    to our common store.
And whenever a fool of the miser school declared he had
    ne'er a groat,
In charity due *we* melted a few, and pour'd them down
    his throat.
              This drink we invented at Panama,
                  We, the mighty Buccaneers!

VIII.

When the churls were eased, their bags well squeezed, we
    gave them our blessing full fain,
And we kiss'd our girls with the glossy curls, the dark-
    eyed girls of Spain;
Our booty we shared, and we all prepared for the way we
    had to roam,
When there rose a dispute as to taking our route by land
    or by water home.
So one half of the band chose to travel by land, the other
    to travel by sea:
Old Morgan's voice gave the sea the choice, and I follow'd
    his fortunes free,
        And hasten'd our leaving old Panama,
            We, the mighty Buccaneers!

IX.

A bark we equipp'd, and our gold we shipp'd, and gat us
    ready for sea;
Seventy men, and a score and ten, mariners bold were
    we.
Our mates had took leave, on the yester-eve, their way
    o'er the hills to find,
When, as morning's light pierced through the night, we
    shook her sails to the wind.
With a fresh'ning breeze we walk'd the seas, and the land
    sunk low and low'r;
A dreary dread o'er our hearts there sped we never should
    see land more—
        And away we departed from Panama,
            We, the mighty Buccaneers!

X.

For a day or two we were busy enow in setting ourselves
    to rights,
In fixing each berth, our mess, and so forth, and the day's
    watch and the night's ;
But when these were done, over every one came the lack
    of aught to do,
We listless talk'd, we listless walk'd, and we pined for
    excitement new.
Oh ! how we did hail any shift in the gale, for it gave us
    a sail to trim !
We began to repent that we had not bent our steps with
    our comrades grim.
            And thus we sail'd on from old Panama,
                We, the mighty Buccaneers !

XI.

Day after day we had stagger'd away, with a steady breeze
    abeam ;
No shift in the gale ; no trimming a sail ; how dull we
    were, ye may deem !
We sung old songs till we wearied our lungs ; we push'd
    the flagon about ;
And told and re-told tales ever so old, till they fairly
    tired us out.
There was a shark in the wake of our bark took us three
    days to hook ;
And when it was caught we wish'd it was not, for we
    miss'd the trouble it took.
            And thus we sail'd on from old Panama,
                We, the mighty Buccaneers !

XII.

At last it befell, some tempter of hell put gambling in
    some one's head ;
The devil's device, the cards and the dice, broke the
    stagnant life we led :
From morn till night, ay, till next morn's light, we plied
    the bones right well ;
Day after day the rattle of play clatter'd through the
    caravel.
How the winners laugh'd, how the losers quaff'd ! 'twas
    a madness, as it were.
It was a thing of shuddering to hark to the losers swear.
        And thus we sail'd on from old Panama,
           We, the mighty Buccaneers !

XIII.

From morn till night, ay, till next morn's light, for weeks
    the play kept on :
'Twas fearful to see the winners' glee, and the losers
    haggard and wan ;
You well might tell, by their features fell, they would ill
    brook to be crost ;
And one morn there was one, who all night had won
    jeer'd some who all night had lost.
He went to bed—at noon he was dead—I know not from
    what, nor reck ;
But they spake of a mark, livid and dark, about the dead
    man's neck !
        And thus we sail'd on from old Panama,
           We, the mighty Buccaneers !

XIV.

This but begun: and those who had won lived a life of
    anxious dread;
Day after day there was bicker and fray; and a man now
    and then struck dead.
Old Morgan stern was laugh'd to scorn, and it worried his
    heart, I trow;
Five days of care, and his iron-grey hair was as white as
    the winter's snow:
The losers at last his patience o'erpast, for they drew
    their sword each one,
And cried, with a shout, "Hell take you! come out, and
    fight for the gold ye have won—
        The gold that our blood bought at Panama:
        We, the mighty Buccaneers!"

XV.

We never were slow at a word and a blow, so we cross'd
    our irons full fain;
And for death and life had begun the strife, when old
    Morgan stopp'd it amain,
And thunder'd out with his stormy shout,—"Dogs, ye
    have had your day!
To your berths!" he roar'd. "Who sheaths not his
    sword, Heaven grant him its grace, I pray!
For I swear, by God, I will cleave him like wood!" There
    was one made an angry sign;
Old Morgan heard, and he kept his word; for he clove
    him to the chine.
        So ended *his* exploits at Panama:
        He, the mighty Buccaneer!

XVI.

At this we quail'd, and we henceforth sail'd, in a
    smouldering sort of truce;
But our dark brows gloom'd, and we inward fumed for a
    pretext to give us loose:
When early one morn—" A strange sail astern!" we heard
    the look-out-man hail;
And old Morgan shout, " Put the ship about, and crowd
    every stitch of sail!"
And around went we, surging through the sea at our island
    wild buck's pace;
In wonderment what old Morgan meant, we near'd to the
    fated chase—
        We, the pillagers of old Panama,
            We, the mighty Buccaneers!

XVII.

She went right fast, but we took her at last. 'Twas a
    little brigantine thing;
With some four men for crew, and a boy or two—a bark
    built for trafficking;
Besides this crew were three women, too: her freight was
    salt-fish and oil:
For the men on board, they were put to the sword; the
    women we spared awhile.
And all was surmise what to do with the prize, when old
    Morgan, calling us aft,
Roar'd, " Ye who have fool'd yourselves out of your gold
    take possession of yonder craft,
        And go pillage some other Panama,
            Ye, the mighty Buccaneers!"

XVIII.

We were reckless and rude, we had been at feud till 'twas
    war to the very knife;
But it clove each heart when we came to part from
    comrades in many a strife:
Over one and all a gloom seem'd to fall, and in silence
    they pack'd their gear,
Amid curses and sighs, and glistening eyes, and here and
    there a tear.
We gave brooches and things for keepsakes and rings; and
    some truck'd the weapons they wore:
This Spanish gun was a token from one who had fought
    me a week before,
        While we diced for the spoils of old Panama,
            We, the mighty Buccaneers!

XIX.

Their traps all pack'd, there was nothing lack'd, but sharing
    the women three:
The odd one's choice was left to the dice, and she fell to
    the rich so free;
When the losers 'gan swear the dice were unfair, and
    brawl'd till our chief gat wild,
And, without more ado, cut the woman in two, as Solomon
    shared the child.
Then each of each band shook each old mate's hand, and
    we parted with hearts full sore;
We all that day watch'd them lessen away. They were
    never heard of more!
        We kept merrily on from old Panama,
            We, the mighty Buccaneers!

XX.

Their sufferings none know, but ours, I trow, were very,
    oh! very sore;
We had storm and gale till our hearts 'gan fail, and then
    calms, which harass'd us more;
Then many fell sick; and while all were weak, we rounded
    the fiery cape;
As I hope for bliss in the life after this, 'twas a miracle
    our escape!
Then a leak we sprung, and to lighten us, flung all our
    gold to the element:
Our perils are past, and we're here at last, but as penniless
    as we went.
           And such was the pillage of Panama
               By the mighty Buccaneers!

                        G. E. INMAN.

Morgan, who was the son of a Welsh Farmer, and who lived to be knighted, set out from Chagres with twelve hundred men, on the 18th August, 1670. In ten days he reached Panama, which he at once attacked and destroyed. The Buccaneers left the ruins with a hundred and seventy-five beasts of burden, laden with silver, gold, and other precious articles; and with six hundred unhappy prisoners, men, women, children, and slaves.—ED.

THE SABINE FARMER'S SERENADE.

BEING A NEWLY RECOVERED FRAGMENT OF A LATIN OPERA.

I.

Erat turbida nox
    Horâ secundâ man
Quando proruit vox
    Carmen in hoc inané;
Viri misera mens
    Meditabatur hymen,
Hinc puellæ flens
    Stabat obsidens limen;
    Semel tantum dic
Eris nostra LALAGÉ;
    Ne recuses sic
Dulcis Julia CALLAGÉ.

II.

Planctibus aurem fer,
    Venere tu formosior;
Dic, hos muros per,
    Tuo favore potior!
Voce beatum fac;
    En, dum dormis, vigilo,
Nocte obambulans hâc
    Domum planctu stridulo.

THE SABINE FARMER'S SERENADE.

I.

'Twas on a windy night,
　At two o'clock in the morning,
An Irish lad so tight,
　All wind and weather scorning,
At Judy Callaghan's door,
　Sitting upon the palings,
His love-tale he did pour,
　And this was part of his wailings :—
　　Only say
You'll be Mrs. Brallaghan ;
　　Don't say nay,
Charming Judy Callaghan.

II.

Oh ! list to what I say,
　Charms you've got like Venus ;
Own your love you may,
　There's but the wall between us.
You lie fast asleep
　Snug in bed and snoring ;
Round the house I creep,
　Your hard heart imploring.

Semel tantum dic
Eris nostra LALAGÉ;
Ne recuses sic,
Dulcis Julia CALLAGÉ.

III.

Est mihi prægnans sus,
　　Et porcellis stabulum;
Villula, grex, et rus[1]
　　Ad vaccarum pabulum;
Feriis cerneres me
　　Splendido vestimento,
Tunc, heus! quàm benè te
　　Veherem in jumento![2]
　　Semel tantum dic
Eris nostra LALAGÉ;
　　Ne recuses sic,
Dulcis Julia CALLAGÉ.

IV.

Vis poma terræ? sum
　　Uno dives jugere;
Vis lac et mella,[3] cùm
　　Bacchi succo,[4] sugere?
Vis aquæ-vitæ vim?[5]
　　Plumoso somnum sacculo?[6]
Vis ut paratus sim
　　Vel annulo vel baculo?[7]
　　Semel tantum dic
Eris nostra LALAGÉ;
　　Ne recuses sic,
Dulcis Julia CALLAGÉ.

Only say
You'll have Mr. Brallaghan;
  Don't say nay,
Charming Judy Callaghan.

III.

I've got a pig and a sow,
  I've got a sty to sleep 'em;
A calf and a brindled cow,
  And a cabin too, to keep 'em;
Sunday hat and coat,
  An old grey mare to ride on.
Saddle and bridle to boot,
  Which you may ride astride on.
  Only say
You'll be Mrs. Brallaghan;
  Don't say nay,
Charming Judy Callaghan.

IV.

I've got an acre of ground,
  I've got it set with praties;
I've got of 'baccy a pound,
  I've got some tea for the ladies;
I've got the ring to wed,
  Some whisky to make us gaily;
I've got a feather-bed
  And a handsome new shilelagh.
  Only say
You'll have Mr. Brallaghan;
  Don't say nay,
Charming Judy Callaghan.

V.

Litteris operam das ;
　　Lucido fulges oculo ;
Dotes insuper quas
　　Nummi sunt in loculo.
Novi quod apta sis[8]
　　Ad procreandam sobolem!
Possides (nesciat quis ?)
　　Linguam satis mobilem.[9]
　Semel tantum dic
Eris nostra LALAGÉ ;
　Ne recuses sic,
Dulcis Julia CALLAGÉ.

Conjux utinam tu
　　Fieres, lepidum cor, mî !
Halitum perdimus, heu,
　　Te sopor urget.　Dormi !
Ingruit imber trux—
　　Jam sub tecto pellitur
Is quem crastina lux[10]
　　Referet hùc fidelitèr.
Semel tandem dic
Eris nostra LALAGÉ ;
　Ne recuses sic,
Dulcis Julia CALLAGÉ.

FATHER PROUT.

V.

You've got a charming eye,
　You've got some spelling and reading ;
You've got, and so have I,
　A taste for genteel breeding ;
You're rich, and fair, and young,
　As everybody's knowing ;
You've got a decent tongue
　Whene'er 'tis set a-going,
　　Only say
You'll be Mrs. Brallaghan ;
　Don't say nay,
Charming Judy Callaghan.

VI.

For a wife till death
　I am willing to take ye ;
But, och ! I waste my breath,
　The devil himself can't wake ye.
'Tis just beginning to rain,
　So I'll get under cover ;
To-morrow I'll come again,
　And be your constant lover.
　　Only say
You'll be Mrs. Brallaghan ;
　Don't say nay,
*Charming Judy Callaghan.**

* The above English lines are a portion of a ballad by the late
Tom Hudson, grocer, publican, and vocalist.—ED.

<cm">18 THE SABINE FARMER'S SERENADE.

NOTULÆ.

NOTUL. 1.

1⁰ in voce *rus.* Nonne potiùs legendum *jus,* scilicet *ad vaccarum pabulum?* De hoc *jure* apud Sabinos agricolas consule *Scriptores de re rusticâ* passim. Ita *Bentleius.*

Jus imo antiquissimum, at displicet vox æquivoca; jus etenim *a mess of pottage* aliquando audit, ɔx. gr.

Omne suum fratri Jacob *jus* vendidit Esau,

Et Jacob fratri *jus* dedit omne suum.

Itaque, pace Bentleii, stet lectio prior.—*Prout.*

NOTUL. 2.

Veherem in jumento. Curriculo-ne? an ponè sedentem in equi dorso? dorsaliter planè Quid enim dicit Horatius de uxore sic vectâ? Nonne *" Post equitem sedet atra cura"?—Porson.*

NOTUL. 3.

Lac et mella. Metaphoricè pro tea; muliebris est compotatio Græcis non ignota, teste Anacreonte,—

ΘΕΗΝ, θεαν θεαινην,

Θελω λεγειν εταιρυι, κ.τ λ.

Brougham.

NOTUL. 4.

Bacchi succo. Duplex apud poetas antiquiores habebatur hujusce nominis numen. Vineam regebat prius; posterius cuidam herbæ exoticæ præerat quæ *tobacco* audit. Succus utrique optimus. —*Coleridge.*

NOTUL. 5.

Aquæ-vitæ vim, Anglo-Hybernicè, *" a power of whisky,"* ισχυς scilicet, vox pergræca.—*Parr.*

NOTUL. 6.

Plumoso sacco. Plumarum congeries certè ad somnos invitandos satis apta; at mihi per multos annos laneus iste saccus, Ang. *woolsack,* fuit apprimè ad dormiendum idoneus. Lites etiam *de lanâ* ut *aiunt caprinâ,* soporiferas per annos xxx. exercui. Quot et quam præclara somnia !—*Eldon.*

NOTUL. 7.

Investitura *" per annulum et baculum"* satis nota. Vide P. Marca de Concord. Sacerdotii et Imperii: et Hildebrandi Pont. Max. bullarium.—*Prout.*

Baculo certè dignissim. pontif. —*Maginn.*

NOTUL. 8.

Apta sis. Quomodo noverit? Vide Proverb. Solomonis cap. xxx. v. 19. Nisi forsan tales fuerint puellæ Sabinorum quales impudens iste balatro Cornelius mentitur esse nostrates.—*Blomfield.*

NOTUL. 9.

Linguam mobilem. Prius enumerat futuræ conjugis bona *immobilia,* postea transit ad *mobilia,* Anglice, *chattel property.* Præclarus ordo sententiarum !—*Car. Wetherall.*

NOTUL. 10.

Allusio ad distichon Maronianum, *"* Nocte pluit totâ, *redeunt spectacula manè."*—*Prout.*

κ. τ. λ.

LAUD YE THE MONKS!

Laud ye the monks!
  They were not men of a creed austere,
  Who frown'd on mirth, and forbade good cheer;
  But joyous oft were the brotherhood,
  In the depths of their sylvan solitude.
  The ruin'd abbey hath many a tale
  Of their gay conceits and deep wassail;
  The huge hearth, left to the wreck of time,
  Hath echoed of erst the minstrel's chime;
  The caves, despoil'd of their goodly store,
  Have groan'd 'neath their weight in days of yore!

Laud ye the monks!
  The wand'rer was their welcome guest,
  The weary found in their grey walls rest;
  The poor man came, and they scorn'd him not,
  Fro rank and wealth were alike forgot;
  The peasant sat at the plenteous board
  With the pilgrim knight and the feudal lord;
  The feast was spread, and the foaming bowl
  Gave freshen'd life to the thirsty soul;
  Round it pass'd, from the prince to the hind,
  The fathers adding their greeting kind!

Laud ye the monks!
    Many a blazon'd scroll doth prove
    The pains they took in their work of love ;
    Many a missal our thoughts engage
    With scenes and deeds of a bygone age ;
    Many a hallowing minster still
    Attests the marvels of olden skill !
    The broken shaft, or the altar razed,
    The mould'ring fane, where our sires have praised,
    Are beautiful, even amidst decay,
    Blessing the men who have pass'd away !

Laud ye the monks!
    For they were friends of the poor and weak.
    The proud man came to their footstool meek,
    And many an acre broad and good
    Was the forfeit paid for his curbless mood :—
    The penance hard, and the peasant's ban,
    Would make him think of his fellow-man ;
    The mass and dirge for his parting soul
    Would wring for the needy a welcome dole.
    The cowl bow'd not to the noble's crest,
    But kings would yield to the priest's behest !

Laud ye the monks!
    Tranquil and sweet was monastic life,
    Free from the leaven of worldly strife ;
    The desolate found a shelter there,
    A home secure from the shafts of care !
    Many a heart with sorrow riven
    Would learn to dream of a shadeless heaven !

And plenty smiled where the convent rose,
The herald of love and deep repose ;
The only spot where the arts gave forth
The hope of a glorious age to earth !

WILLIAM JONES.

THE LEGEND OF MANOR HALL.

BY THE AUTHOR OF " HEADLONG HALL."

OLD Farmer Wall, of Manor Hall,
   To market drove his wain:
Along the road it went well stowed
   With sacks of golden grain.

His station he took, but in vain did he look
   For a customer all the morn;
Though the farmers all, save Farmer Wall,
   They sold off all their corn.

Then home he went, sore discontent,
   And many an oath he swore,
And he kicked up rows with his children and spouse,
   When they met him at the door.

Next market-day he drove away
   To the town his loaded wain:
The farmers all, save Farmer Wall,
   They sold off all their grain.

No bidder he found, and he stood astound
   At the close of the market-day,
When the market was done, and the chapmen were gone
   Each man his several way.

He stalked by his load along the road ;
   His face with wrath was red :
His arms he tossed, like a good man crossed
   In seeking his daily bread.

His face was red, and fierce was his tread,
   And with lusty voice cried he,
" My corn I'll sell to the devil of hell,
   If he'll my chapman be."

These words he spoke just under an oak
   Seven hundred winters old ;
And he straight was aware of a man sitting there
   On the roots and grassy mould.

The roots rose high, o'er the green-sward dry,
   And the grass around was green,
Save just the space of the stranger's place,
   Where it seemed as fire had been.

All scorched was the spot, as gipsy-pot
   Had swung and bubbled there :
The grass was marred, the roots were charred,
   And the ivy stems were bare.

The stranger up-sprung : to the farmer he flung
   A loud and friendly hail,
And he said, " I see well, thou hast corn to sell,
   And I'll buy it on the nail."

The twain in a trice agreed on the price;
   The stranger his earnest paid,
And with horses and wain to come for the grain
   His own appointment made.

The farmer cracked his whip, and tracked
   His way right merrily on :
He struck up a song as he trudged along,
   For joy that his job was done.

His children fair he danced in the air ;
   His heart with joy was big ;
He kissed his wife ; he seized a knife,
   He slew a sucking pig.

The faggots burned, the porkling turned
   And crackled before the fire ;
And an odour arose that was sweet in the nose
   Of a passing ghostly friar.

He twirled at the pin, he entered in,
   He sate down at the board ;
The pig he blessed, when he saw it well dressed,
   And the humming ale out-poured.

The friar laughed, the friar quaffed,
    He chirped like a bird in May ;
The farmer told how his corn he had sold
    As he journeyed home that day.

The friar he quaffed, but no longer he laughed,
    He changed from red to pale :
" Oh, helpless elf ! 'tis the fiend himself
    To whom thou hast made thy sale !"

The friar he quaffed, he took a deep draught ;
    He crossed himself amain :
" Oh, slave of pelf ! 'tis the devil himself
    To whom thou hast sold thy grain !

" And sure as the day, he'll fetch thee away,
    With the corn which thou hast sold,
If thou let him pay o'er one tester more
    Than thy settled price in gold."

The farmer gave vent to a loud lament,
    The wife to a long outcry ;
Their relish for pig and ale was flown ;
The friar alone picked every bone,
    And drained the flagon dry.

The friar was gone ; the morning dawn
    Appeared, and the stranger's wain
Came to the hour, with six-horse power,
    To fetch the purchased grain.

The horses were black : on their dewy track
    Light steam from the ground up-curled ;
Long wreaths of smoke from their nostrils broke,
    And their tails like torches whirled.

More dark and grim, in face and limb,
    Seemed the stranger than before,
As his empty wain, with steeds thrice twain,
    Drew up to the farmer's door.

On the stranger's face was a sly grimace,
    As he seized the sacks of grain ;
And, one by one, till left were none,
    He tossed them on the wain.

And slily he leered as his hand up-reared
    A purse of costly mould,
Where, bright and fresh, through a silver mesh,
    Shone forth the glistering gold.

The farmer held out his right hand stout,
    And drew it back with dread ;
For in fancy he heard each warning word
    The supping friar had said.

His eye was set on the silver net ;
    His thoughts were in fearful strife ;
When, sudden as fate, the glittering bait
    Was snatched by his loving wife.

And, swift as thought, the stranger caught
    The farmer his waist around,
And at once the twain and the loaded wain
    Sank through the rifted ground.

The gable-end wall of Manor Hall
    Fell in ruins on the place:
'That stone-heap old the tale has told
    To each succeeding race.

The wife gave a cry that rent the sky
    At her goodman's downward flight:
But she held the purse fast, and a glance she cast
    To see that all was right.

'Twas the fiend's full pay for her goodman gray,
    And the gold was good and true;
Which made her declare, that "his dealings were fair,
    To give the devil his due."

She wore the black pall for Farmer Wall,
    From her fond embraces riven:
But she won the vows of a younger spouse
    With the gold which the fiend had given.

Now, farmers, beware what oaths you swear
    When you cannot sell your corn;
Lest, to bid and buy, a stranger be nigh,
    With hidden tail and horn.

And, with good heed, the moral a-read,
 Which is of this tale the pith,—
If your corn you sell to the fiend of hell,
 You may sell yourself therewith.

And if by mishap you fall in the trap,
 Would you bring the fiend to shame,
Lest the tempting prize should dazzle her eyes,
 Lock up your frugal dame.

THE "ORIGINAL" DRAGON.

A LEGEND OF THE CELESTIAL EMPIRE.

Freely translated from an undeciphered MS. of Con-fuse-us,* and dedicated to
Colonel Bolsover (of the Horse Marines), by C. J. Davids, Esq.

I.

A DESPERATE dragon, of singular size,—
   (His name was *Wing-Fang-Scratch-Claw-Fum,)—*
Flew up one day to the top of the skies,
   While all the spectators with terror were dumb.
The vagabond vow'd as he sported his tail,
   He'd have a *sky lark*, and some glorious fun :
For he'd nonplus the natives that day without fail,
   By causing a *total eclipse of the sun !*†
He collected a crowd by his impudent boast,
   (Some decently dress'd—some with hardly a rag on,)
Who said that the country was ruin'd and lost,
   Unless they could compass the death of the *dragon.*

* " Better known to illiterate people as *Confucius.*"—WASHINGTON
IRVING.

† In *China* (whatever European astronomers may assert to the con-
trary) an *eclipse* is caused by a *great dragon eating up the sun.*

To avert so shocking an outrage, the natives frighten away the monster
from his intended *hot* dinner, by giving a morning concert, *al fresco ;*
consisting of drums, trumpets, cymbals, gongs, tin-kettles, &c.

II.

The emperor came with the whole of his court,—
    (His Majesty's name was *Ding-Dong-Junk*)—
And he said—to delight in such profligate sport,
    The monster was mad, or disgracefully drunk.
He call'd on the army : the troops to a man
    Declared—though they didn't feel frighten'd the least—
They never could think it a sensible plan
    To go within reach of so ugly a beast.
So he offer'd his daughter, the lovely *Nan-Keen*,
    And a painted pavilion, with many a flag on,
To any brave knight who could step in between
    The *solar eclipse* and the dare-devil *dragon*.

III.

Presently came a reverend bonze.—
    (His name, I'm told, was *Long-Chin Joss,*)—
With a phiz very like the complexion of bronze ;
    And for suitable words he was quite at a loss.
But, he humbly submitted, the orthodox way
    To succour the *sun*, and to bother the foe,
Was to make a new church-rate without more delay,
    As the clerical funds were deplorably low.
Though he coveted nothing at all for himself,
    (A virtue he always delighted to brag on,)
He thought, if the priesthood could pocket some pelf,
    It might hasten the doom of this impious *aragon*.

IV.

The next that spoke was the court buffoon,—
    (The name of this buffer was *Whim-Wham-Fun,*)—

Who carried a salt-box and large wooden spoon,
  With which, he suggested, the job might be done.
Said the jester, " I'll wager my rattle and bells,
  Your pride, my fine fellow, shall soon have a fall :
If you make many more of your horrible yells,
  I know a good method to make you sing small !"
And when he had set all the place in a roar,
  As his merry conceits led the whimsical wag on,
He hinted a plan to get rid of the bore,
  By putting some *salt* on the *tail* of the *dragon !*

V

At length appear'd a brisk young knight,—
  (The far-famed warrior, *Bam-Boo-Gong*,)—
Who threaten'd to burke the big blackguard outright,
  And have the deed blazon'd in story and song.
With an excellent shot from a very *long bow*
  He damaged the dragon by cracking his crown ;
When he fell to the ground (as my documents show)
  With a smash that was heard many miles out of town.
His death was the signal for frolic and spree—
  They carried the corpse, in a common stage-waggon ;
And the hero was crown'd with the leaves of green tea,
  For saving the *sun* from the jaws of the *dragon.*

VI.

A poet, whose works were all the rage,—
  (This gentleman's name was *Sing-Song-Strum*,)—
Told the terrible tale on his popular page :
  (Compared with *his* verses, *my* rhymes are but rum !)

The Royal Society claim'd as their right
    The spoils of the vanquish'd—his wings, tail, and claws;
And a brilliant bravura, describing the fight,
    Was sung on the stage with unbounded applause.
" The valiant *Bam-Boo*" was a favourite toast,
    And a topic for future historians to fag on,
Which, when it had reach'd to the Middlesex coast,
    Gave rise to the legend of *"George and the Dragon."*

THE TEMPTATIONS OF ST. ANTHONY.

"He would have passed a pleasant life of it, in despite of the devil and all his works, if his path had not been crossed by a being that causes more perplexity to mortal man than ghosts, goblins, and the whole race of witches put together, and that was—a woman."—*Sketch-Book*

St. ANTHONY sat on a lowly stool,
   And a book was in his hand;
Never his eye from its page he took,
Either to right or left to look,
But with steadfast soul, as was his rule,
   The holy page he scanned.

"We will woo," said the imp, "St. Anthony's eyes
   Off from his holy book:
We will go to him all in strange disguise,
And tease him with laughter, whoops, and cries,
   That he upon us may look."

The Devil was in the best humour that day
   That ever his highness was in:
And that's why he sent out his imps to play,
And he furnished them torches to light their way,
Nor stinted them incense to burn as they may,—
   Sulphur, and pitch, and rosin.

So they came to the Saint in a motley crew,
   A heterogeneous rout :
There were imps of every shape and hue,
And some looked black, and some looked blue,
And they passed and varied before the view,
   And twisted themselves about :
And had they exhibited thus to you,
I think you'd have felt in a bit of a stew,—
   Or so should myself, I doubt.

There were some with feathers, and some with scales,
   And some with warty skins ;
Some had not heads, and some had tails,
And some had claws like iron nails ;
And some had combs and beaks like birds,
And yet, like jays, could utter words ;
   And some had gills and fins.

Some rode on skeleton beasts, arrayed
   In gold and velvet stuff,
With rich tiaras on the head,
Like kings and queens among the dead ;
While face and bridle-hand, displayed,
In hue and substance seemed to cope
With maggots in a microscope,
And their thin lips, as white as soap,
   Were colder than enough.

And spiders big from the ceiling hung,
   From every creek and nook :

They had a crafty, ugly guise,
And looked at the Saint with their eight eyes;
And all that malice could devise
Of evil to the good and wise
    Seemed welling from their look.

Beetles and slow-worms crawled about,
    And toads did squat demure;
From holes in the wainscoting mice peeped out,
Or a sly old rat with his whiskered snout;
And forty-feet, a full span long,
Danced in and out in an endless throng:
There ne'er has been seen such extravagant rout
    From that time to this, I'm sure.

But the good St. Anthony kept his eyes
    Fixed on the holy book;—
From it they did not sink nor rise;
Nor sights nor laughter, shouts nor cries,
    Could win away his look.

A quaint imp sat in an earthen pot,
    In a big-bellied earthen pot sat he:
Through holes in the bottom his legs outshot,
And holes in the sides his arms had got,
And his head came out through the mouth, God wot!
    A comical sight to see.

And he drummed on his belly so fair and round,
    On his belly so round and fair;

And it gave forth a rumbling, mingled sound,
'Twixt a muffled bell and a growling hound,
   A comical sound to hear :
And he sat on the edge of a table-desk,
   And drummed it with his heels ;
And he looked as strange and as picturesque
As the figures we see in an arabesque,
Half hidden in flowers, all painted in fresque,
   In Gothic vaulted ceils.

Then he whooped and hawed, and winked and grinned,
   And his eyes stood out with glee ;
And he said these words, and he sung this song,
And his legs and his arms, with their double prong,
Keeping time with his tune as it galloped along,
Still on the pot and the table dinned
   As birth to his song gave he.

" Old Tony, my boy ! shut up your book,
   And learn to be merry and gay.
You sit like a bat in his cloistered nook,
Like a round-shoulder'd fool of an owl you look ;
But straighten your back from its booby crook,
   And more sociable be, I pray.

" Let us see you laugh, let us hear you sing ;
   Take a lesson from me, old boy !
Remember that life has a fleeting wing,
And then comes Death, that stern old king,
   So we'd better make sure of joy."

But the good St. Anthony bent his eyes
　　Upon the holy book :
He heard that song with a laugh arise,
But he knew that the imp had a naughty guise,
　　And he did not care to look.

Another imp came in a masquerade,
　　Most like to a monk's attire :
But of living bats his cowl was made,
Their wings stitched together with spider thread ;
And round and about him they fluttered and played ;
And his eyes shot out from their misty shade
　　Long parallel bars of fire.

And his loose teeth chattered like clanking bones,
　　When the gibbet-tree sways in the blast :
And with gurgling shakes, and stifled groans,
He mocked the good St. Anthony's tones
　　As he muttered his prayer full fast.

A rosary of beads was hung by his side,—
　　Oh, gaunt-looking beads were they !
And still, when the good Saint dropped a bead,
He dropped a tooth, and he took good heed
To rattle his string, and the bones replied,
　　Like a rattle-snake's tail at play.

But the good St. Anthony bent his eyes
　　Upon the holy book ;
He heard that mock of groans and sighs,

And he knew that the thing had an evil guise,
    And he did not dare to look.

Another imp came with a trumpet-snout,
    That was mouth and nose in one:
It had stops like a flute, as you never may doubt,
Where his long lean fingers capered about,
As he twanged his nasal melodies out,
    In quaver, and shake, and run.

And his head moved forward and backward still
    On his long and snaky neck;
As he bent his energies all to fill
His nosey tube with wind and skill,
And he sneezed his octaves out, until
    'Twas well-nigh ready to break.

And close to St. Anthony's ear he came,
    And piped his music in:
And the shrill sound went through the good Saint's
        frame,
With a smart and a sting, like a shred of flame,
Or a bee in the ear,—which is much the same,—
    And he shivered with the din.

But the good St. Anthony bent his eyes
    Upon the holy book;
He heard that snout with its gimlet cries,
And he knew that the imp had an evil guise,
    And he did not dare to look.

A thing with horny eyes was there,
   With horny eyes like the dead ;
And its long sharp nose was all of horn,
And its bony cheeks of flesh were shorn,
And its ears were like thin cases torn
From feet of kine, and its jaws were bare ;
And fish-bones grew, instead of hair,
   Upon its skinless head.

Its body was of thin birdy bones,
   Bound round with a parchment skin ;
And when 'twas struck, the hollow tones
That circled round like drum-dull groans,
   Bespoke a void within.

Its arm was like a peacock's leg,
   And the claws were like a bird's :
But the creep that went, like a blast of plague,
To loose the live flesh from the bones,
And wake the good Saint's inward groans,
As it clawed his cheek, and pulled his hair,
And pressed on his eyes in their beating lair,
   Cannot be told in words.

But the good St. Anthony kept his eyes
   Still on the holy book ;
He felt the clam on his brow arise,
And he knew that the thing had a horrid guise,
   And he did not dare to look.

An imp came then like a skeleton form
　　Out of a charnel vault:
Some clingings of meat had been left by the worm,
Some tendons and strings on his legs and arm,
And his jaws with gristle were black and deform,
　　But his teeth were as white as salt.

And he grinned full many a lifeless grin,
　　And he rattled his bony tail;
His skull was decked with gill and fin,
And a spike of bone was on his chin,
And his bat-like ears were large and thin,
　　And his eyes were the eyes of a snail.

He took his stand at the good Saint's back,
　　And on tiptoe stood a space:
Forward he bent, all rotten-black,
And he sunk again on his heel, good lack!
And the good Saint uttered some ghostly groans,
For the head was caged in the gaunt rib-bones,—
　　A horrible embrace!
And the skull hung o'er with an elvish pry,
And cocked down its India-rubber eye
　　To gaze upon his face.

Yet the good St. Anthony sunk his eyes
　　Deep in the holy book:
He felt the bones, and so was wise
To know that the thing had a ghastly guise,
　　And he did not dare to look.

Last came an imp,—how unlike the rest !—
   A beautiful female form :
And her voice was like music, that sleep-oppress'd
Sinks on some cradling zephyr's breast ;
And whilst with a whisper his cheek she press'd,
   Her cheek felt soft and warm.

When over his shoulder she bent the light
   Of her soft eyes on to his page,
It came like a moonbeam silver bright,
And relieved him then with a mild delight,
For the yellow lamp-lustre scorched his sight,
   That was weak with the mists of age.

Hey ! the good St. Anthony boggled his eyes
   Over the holy book :
Ho ho ! at the corners they 'gan to rise,
For he knew that the thing had a lovely guise,
   And he could not choose but look.

There are many devils that walk this world,—
   Devils large, and devils small ;
Devils so meagre, and devils so stout ;
Devils with horns, and devils without ;
Sly devils that go with their tails upcurled,
Bold devils that carry them quite unfurled ;
   Meek devils, and devils that brawl ;
Serious devils, and laughing devils ;
Imps for churches, and imps for revels ;

Devils uncouth, and devils polite;
Devils black, and devils white;
Devils foolish, and devils wise;
But a laughing woman, with two bright eyes
  Is the worsest devil of all.

                                    T. H. S.

A TALE OF GRAMMARYE.

THE Baron came home in his fury and rage,
He blew up his Henchman, he blew up his Page;
The Seneschal trembled, the Cook looked pale,
As he ordered for supper grilled kidneys and ale,
Vain thought! that grill'd kidneys can give relief,
When one's own are inflamed by anger and grief.

What was the cause of the Baron's distress?
  Why sank his spirits so low?—
The fair Isabel, when she should have said "Yes,"
  Had given the Baron a "No."
He ate, and he drank, and he grumbled between:
First on the viands he vented his spleen,—
The ale was sour,—the kidneys were tough,
And tasted of nothing but pepper and snuff!
—The longer he ate, the worse grew affairs,
Till he ended by kicking the butler down stairs.

All was hushed—'twas the dead of the night—
  The tapers were dying away,
And the armour bright
Glanced in the light
  Of the pale moon's trembling ray;

Yet his Lordship sat still, digesting his ire,
With his nose on his knees, and his knees in the fire,—
All at once he jump'd up, resolved to consult his
Cornelius Agrippa de rebus occultis.

He seized by the handle
A bed-room flat candle,
And went to a secret nook,
Where a chest lay hid
With so massive a lid,
His knees, as he raised it, shook,
Partly, perhaps, from the wine he had drunk,
Partly from fury, and partly from funk ;
For never before had he ventured to look
In his Great-Great-Grandfather's conjuring-book.

Now Lord Ranulph Fitz-Hugh,
As lords frequently do,
Thought reading a bore,—but his case is quite new ;
So he quickly ran through
A chapter or two,
For without Satan's aid he knew not what to do,—
When poking the fire, as the evening grew colder,
He saw with alarm,
As he raised up his arm,
An odd-looking countenance over his shoulder.

Firmest rock will sometimes quake,
Trustiest blade will sometimes break,
Sturdiest heart will sometimes fail,
Proudest eye will sometimes quail ;—

No wonder Fitz-Hugh felt uncommonly queer
Upon suddenly seeing the Devil so near,
Leaning over his chair, peeping into his ear.

    The stranger first
    The silence burst,
And replied to the Baron's look:—
    " I would not intrude,
    But don't think me rude
If I sniff at that musty old book.
    Charms were all very well
Ere Reform came to Hell;
But now not an imp cares a fig for a spell.
    Still I see what you want,
    And am willing to grant
The person and purse of the fair Isabel.
Upon certain conditions the maiden is won;—
You may have her at once, if you choose to say ' Done!'

    " The lady so rare,
    Her manors so fair,
Lord Baron I give to thee:
    But when once the sun
    Five years has run,
Lord Baron, thy soul's my fee!"

Oh! where wert thou, ethereal Sprite?
    Protecting Angel, where?
Sure never before had noble or knight
    Such need of thy guardian care!
No aid is nigh—'twas so decreed;—

The recreant Baron at once agreed,
And prepared with his blood to sign the deed.

With the point of his sword
His arm he scored,
And mended his pen with his Misericorde ;
From his black silk breeches
The stranger reaches
A lawyer's leathern case,
Selects a paper,
And snuffing the taper,
The Baron these words mote trace :—
" Five years after date, I promise to pay
My soul to old Nick, without let or delay,
For value received."—" There, my Lord, on my life,
Put your name to the bill, and the lady's your wife."

*   *   *   *

All look'd bright in earth and heaven,
And far through the morning skies
Had Sol his fiery coursers driven,—
That is, it was striking half-past eleven
As Isabel opened her eyes.

All wondered what made the lady so late,
For she came not down till noon,
Though she usually rose at a quarter to eight,
And went to bed equally soon.
But her rest had been broken by troublesome dreams :—
She had thought that, in spite of her cries and her screams,
Old Nick had borne off, in a chariot of flame,
The gallant young Howard of Effinghame.

Her eye was so dim, and her cheek so chill,
The family doctor declared she was ill,
And muttered dark hints of a draught and a pill.

All during breakfast to brood doth she seem
  O'er some secret woes or wrongs;
For she empties the salt-cellar into the cream,
  And stirs up her tea with the tongs.
But scarce hath she finished her third round of toast,
  When a knocking is heard by all—
" What may that be?—'tis too late for the post,—
  Too soon for a morning call."
  After a moment of silence and dread,
      The court-yard rang
      With the joyful clang
  Of an armed warrior's tread.
Now away and away with fears and alarms,—
The lady lies clasped in young Effinghame's arms.

She hangs on his neck, and she tells him true,
How that troublesome creature, Lord Ranulph Fitz-Hugh,
Hath vowed and hath sworn with a terrible curse,
That, unless she will take him for better for worse,
  He will work her mickle rue!

" Now, lady love, dismiss thy fear,
Should that grim old Baron presume to come here,
We'll soon send him home with a flea in his ear;—
  And, to cut short the strife,
  My love! my life!
Let me send for a parson, and make you my wife!"

No banns did they need, no licence require,—
　　They were married that day before dark :
The Clergyman came,—a fat little friar,
　　The doctor acted as Clerk.

　　But the nuptial rites were hardly o'er,
　　Scarce had they reached the vestry door,
　　　　When a knight rushed headlong in ;
　　　　　From his shoes to his shirt
　　　　　He was all over dirt,
　　　　From his toes to the tip of his chin ;
But high on his travel-stained helmet tower'd
The lion-crest of the noble Howard.

By horrible doubts and fears possest,
The bride turned and gaz'd on the bridegroom's breast—
　　No Argent Bend was there ;
　　　　No Lion bright
　　　　Of her own true knight,
　　But his rival's Sable Bear !
The Lady Isabel instantly knew
'Twas a regular hoax of the false Fitz-Hugh ;
And loudly the Baron exultingly cried,
" Thou art wooed, thou art won, my bonny gay bride !
Nor heaven nor hell can our loves divide !"

This pithy remark was scarcely made,
When the Baron beheld, upon turning his head,
　　His Friend in black close by ;
He advanced with a smile all placid and bland,
Popp'd a small piece of parchment into his hand,
　　And knowingly winked his eye.

As the Baron perused,
His cheek was suffused
With a flush between brick-dust and brown;
While the fair Isabel
Fainted, and fell
In a still and death-like swoon
Lord Howard roar'd out, till the chapel and vaults
Rang with cries for burnt feathers and volatile salts.

"Look at the date!" quoth the queer-looking man,
In his own peculiar tone;
"My word hath been kept,—deny it who can,—
And now I am come for my own."
Might he trust his eyes?—Alas! and alack!
'Twas a bill ante-dated full five years back!
'Twas all too true—
It was over due—
The term had expired!—he wouldn't " renew,"—
And the Devil looked black as the Baron looked blue.

The Lord Fitz-Hugh
Made a great to-do,
And especially blew up Old Nick,—
" 'Twas a stain," he swore,
" On the name he bore
To play such a rascally trick!"—
A trick?" quoth Nick, in a tone rather quick,
It's one often played upon people who ' tick.' "
Blue flames now broke
From his mouth as he spoke,
They went out, and left an uncommon thick smoke,

E

Which enveloping quite
Himself and the Knight,
The pair in a moment were clean out of sight.
When it wafted away,
Where the dickens were they?
Oh! no one might guess—Oh! no one might say,—
But never, I wis,
From that time to this,
In hall or in bower, on mountain or plain,
Has the Baron been seen, or been heard of again.

As for fair Isabel, after two or three sighs,
She finally opened her beautiful eyes.
She coughed, and she sneezed
And was very well pleased,
After being so rumpled, and towzled, and teased,
To find when restored from her panic and pain,
My Lord Howard had married her over again.

MORAL.

Be warned by our story, ye Nobles and Knights,
Who're so much in the habit of " flying of kites ;"
And beware how ye meddle again with such Flights:
At least, if your energies Creditors cramp,
Remember a Usurer's always a Scamp,
And look well at the Bill, and the Date, and the Stamp:
Don't sign in a hurry, whatever you do,
Or you'll go the Devil, like Baron Fitz-Hugh.

DALTON.

THE RED-BREAST OF AQUITANIA.

AN HUMBLE BALLAD.

"*Are not two sparrows sold for a farthing? yet not one of them shall fall to the ground without your Father.*"—ST. MATTHEW, x. 29.

"Gallos ab Aquitanis GARUMNA flumen."—JULIUS CÆSAR.

"Sermons in stones, and good in everything."—SHAKSPEARE.

"GENIUS, left to shiver
On the bank, 'tis said,
Died of that cold river."—TOM MOORE.

I.

River trip from Thoulouse to Bourdeaux. Thermometer at ·0. Snow 1½ foot deep. Use of wooden shoes.

OH, 'twas bitter cold
As our steam-boat roll'd
Down the pathway old
   Of the deep GARONNE,—
And the peasant lank,
While his *sabot* sank
In the snow-clad bank,
   Saw it roll on, on.

II.

Yᵉ Gascon farmer hieth to his cottage, and drinketh a flaggonne.

And he hied him home
To his *toit de chaume;*
And for those who roam
   On the broad bleak flood

E 2

Cared he ? Not a thought ;
For his beldame brought
His wine-flask fraught
    With the grape's red blood.

III.

He warmeth
his cold
shins at a
wooden fire.
Good b'ye to
him.

And the wood-block blaze
Fed his vacant gaze
As we trod the maze
    Of the river down.
Soon we left behind
On the frozen wind
All farther mind
    Of that vacant clown.

IV.

Yᵉ Father
meeteth a
stray ac-
quaintance
in a small
bird.

But there came anon,
As we journey'd on
Down the deep GARONNE,
    An acquaintancy,
Which we deem'd, I count,
Of more high amount,
    it oped the fount
    Of sweet sympathy.

V.

Not yᵉ
famous alba-
tross of that
aincient ma-
riner olde
Coleridge,
but a poore
robin.

'Twas a stranger drest
In a downy vest,
'Twas a wee RED-BREAST,
    (Not an " *Albatross*,")

But a wanderer meek,
Who fain would seek
O'er the bosom bleak
   Of that flood to cross.

VI.

Ye sparrow
crossing ye
river mak-
eth hys half-
way house
of the fire-
ship.

And we watch'd him oft
As he soar'd aloft
On his pinions soft,
   Poor wee weak thing,
And we soon could mark
That he sought our bark
As a resting ark
   For his weary wing.

VII.

Delusive
hope. Ye
fire-ship
runneth 10
knots an
hour: 'tis
no go for ye
sparrow.

But the bark, fire-fed,
  On her pathway sped,
And shot far a-head
   Of the tiny bird,
And quicker in the van
Her swift wheels ran,
As the quickening fan
   Of his winglets stirr'd.

VIII.

Ye byrde is
led a wilde
goose chace
adown ye
river.

Vain, vain pursuit!
Toil without fruit!
For his forkèd foot
   Shall not anchor there,

Tho' the boat meanwhile
Down the stream beguile
For a bootless mile
    The poor child of air!

IX.

Symptomes
of fatigue.
'Tis mean-
cholie to fall
between
2 stools.

And 'twas plain at last
He was flagging fast,
That his hour had past
    In that effort vain;
Far from either bank,
Sans a saving plank,
Slow, slow he sank,
    Nor uprose again.

X.

Mort of y⁵
birde.

And the cheerless wave
Just one ripple gave
As it oped him a grave
    In its bosom cold,
And he sank alone,
With a feeble moan,
In that deep GARONNE,
    And then all was told.

XI.

Yᵉ old man
at yᵉ helm
weepeth for
a sonne lost
in yᵉ bay of
Biscaye.

But our pilot grey
Wiped a tear away;
In the broad BISCAYE
    He had lost his boy!

And that sight brought back
On its furrow'd track
The remember'd wreck
    Of long perish'd joy !

XII.

Condoleance
of yᵉ ladyes;
eke of 1
*chasseur
d'infanterie
légère.*

And the tear half hid
In soft BEAUTY's lid
Stole forth unbid
    For that red-breast bird ;—
And the feeling crept,—
For a WARRIOR wept ;
And the silence kept
    Found no fitting word.

XIII.

Olde Father
Proutte
sadly
moralizeth
anent yᵉ
birde.

But *I* mused alone,
For I thought of one
Whom I well had known
    In my earlier days,
Of a gentle mind,
Of a soul refined,
Of deserts design'd
    For the Palm of Praise.

XIV.

Yᵉ Streame
of Lyfe. A
younge man
of fayre
promise.

And well would it seem
Tha o'er Lifes dark stream,
Easy task for Him
    In hi flight of Fame,

Was the SKYWARD PATH,
O'er the billow's wrath,
That for GENIUS hath
    Ever been the same.

XV.

Hys earlie flyght across yᵉ streame.

And I saw him soar
From the morning shore,
While his fresh wings bore
    Him athwart the tide,
Soon with powers unspent
As he forward went,
His wings he had bent
    On the sought-for side.

XVI.

A newe object calleth his eye from yᵉ maine chaunce.

But while thus he flew,
Lo! a vision new
Caught his wayward view
    With a semblance fair,
And that new-found wooer
Could, alas! allure
From his pathway sure
    The bright child of air.

XVII.

Instabilitie of purpose a fatall evyl in lyfe.

For he turn'd aside,
And adown the tide
For a brief hour plied
    His yet unspent force,

And to gain that goal
Gave the powers of soul,
Which, unwasted, whole,
    Had achieved his course.

XVIII.

This is y*
morall of
Father
Prout's
humble
ballade,

A bright SPIRIT, young,
Unwept, unsung,
Sank thus among
    The drifts of the stream ;
Not a record left,—
Of renown bereft,
By thy cruel theft,
    O DELUSIVE DREAM !

THE SON TO HIS MOTHER.

THERE was a place in childhood that I remember well,
And there, a voice of sweetest tone bright fairy tales did
     tell;
And gentle words and fond embrace were given with joy
     to me,
When I was in that happy place, upcn my mother's knee.

When fairy tales were ended, "Good night!" she softly
     said,
And kiss'd and laid me down to sleep within my tiny
     bed;
And holy words she taught me there,—methinks I yet
     can see
Her angel eyes, as close I knelt beside my mother's knee.

In the sickness of my childhood, the perils of my prime,
The sorrows of my riper years, the cares of ev'ry time;
When doubt or danger weigh'd me down, then pleading,
     all for me,
It was a fervent pray'r to Heaven that bent my mother's
     knee!

And can I this remember, and e'er forget to prove
The glow of holy gratitude—the fulness of my love?
When thou art feeble, mother, come rest thy arm on me,
And let thy cherish'd child support the aged mothers'
    knee!

SAMUEL LOVER.

IMPROMPTU BY THE LATE GEORGE COLMAN.

ABOUT a year since, a young lady begged this celebrated wit to write some verses in her album : he shook
his head ; but, good-naturedly promising to try, at once
extemporised the following,—most probably his last
written and poetical jest.

> My muse and I, ere youth and spirits fled,
>   Sat up together many a night, no doubt ;
> But now, I've sent the poor old lass to bed,
>   Simply because *my fire is going out.*

THE MONKS OF OLD.

MANY have told of the monks of old,
   What a saintly race they were;
But 'tis more true that a merrier crew
   Could scarce be found elsewhere;
      For they sung and laugh'd,
      And the rich wine quaff'd,
And lived on the daintiest cheer.

And some they would say, that throughout the day
   O'er the missal alone they would pore;
But 'twas only, I ween, whilst the flock were seen
   They thought of their ghostly lore;
      For they sung and laugh'd,
      And the rich wine quaff'd
When the rules of their faith were o'er.

And then they would jest at the love confess'd
   By many an artless maid;
And what hopes and fears they have pour'd in the ears
   Of those who sought their aid.
      And they sung and laugh'd,
      And the rich wine quaff'd
As they told of each love-sick jade.

And the Abbot meek, with his form so sleek,
  Was the heartiest of them all,
And would take his place with a smiling face
  When refection bell would call ;
      And they sung and laugh'd,
      And the rich wine quaff'd,
  Till they shook the olden wall.

In their green retreat, when the drum would beat,
  And warriors flew to arm,
The monks they would stay in their convent grey,
  In the midst of dangers calm,
      Where they sung and laugh'd,
      And the rich wine quaff'd,
For none would the good men harm.

Then say what they will, we'll drink to them still,
  For a jovial band they were ;
And 'tis most true that a merrier crew
  Could not be found elsewhere ;
      For they sung and laugh'd,
      And the rich wine quaff'd,
  And lived on the daintiest cheer.

                            WILLIAM JONES.

OUR OPENING CHAUNT.

Written on the occasion of the First Publication of " Bentley's Miscellany."

I.

Come round and hear, my public dear,
    Come hear, and judge it gently,—
The prose so terse, and flowing verse,
    Of us, the wits of Bentley.

II.

We offer not intricate plot
    To muse upon intently ;
No tragic word, no bloody sword,
    Shall stain the page of Bentley.

III.

The tender song which all day long
    Resounds so sentimént'ly,
Through wood and grove all full of love,
    Will find no place in Bentley.

IV.

Nor yet the speech which fain would teach
　All nations eloquéntly ;—
'Tis quite too grand for us the bland
　And modest men of Bentley.

V.

For science deep no line we keep,
　We speak it reveréntly ;—
From sign to sign the sun may shine,
　Untelescoped by Bentley.

VI.

Tory and Whig, in accents big,
　May wrangle violéntly :
Their party rage shan't stain the page—
　The neutral page of Bentley.

VII.

The scribe whose pen is mangling men
　And women pestiléntly,
May take elsewhere his wicked ware,—
　He finds no mart in Bentley.

VIII.

It pains us not to mark the spot
　Where Dan may find his rént lie ;
The Glasgow chiel may shout for Peel,
　We know them not in Bentley

IX.

Those who admire a merry lyre,—
　　Those who would hear attent'ly
A tale of wit, or flashing hit,—
　　Are ask'd to come to Bentley.

X.

Our hunt will be for grace and glee,
　　Where thickest may the scent lie;
At slashing pace begins the chase—
　　Now for the burst of Bentley.
DR. MAGINN.

LINES

On seeing "The Young Veteran," JOHN BANNISTER,
toddling up Gower-street, after he had attained his
seventieth birthday.

WRITTEN BY SIR GEORGE ROSE, AND COMMUNICATED BY
J. P. HARLEY, ESQ.

WITH seventy years upon his back,
Still is my honest friend "Young Jack,"
Nor spirits check'd nor fancy slack,
　　But fresh as any daisy,
Though Time has knock'd his *stumps* about,
He cannot bowl his temper out;
And all the *Bannister* is stout,
　　Although the STEPS be crazy.

F

AD MOLLISSIMAM PUELLAM E GETICA
CARUARUM FAMILIA.

OVIDIUS NASO LAMENTATUR.

1.

HEU! heu!
   Me tædet, me piget o!
Cor mihi riget o!
Ut flos sub frigido...
   Et nox ipsa mî, tum
Cum vado dormitùm,
Infausta, insomnis,
Transcurritur omnis...
Hoc culpâ fit tuâ
Mi, mollis Carùa,
Sic mihi illudens,
Nec pudens.—
   Prodigium tu, re
Es, verâ, naturæ,
Candidior lacte;—
Plus fronte cum hâc te,
Cum istis ocellis,
Plus omnibus stellis
Mehercule vellem.—
Sed heu, me imbellem!
A me, qui sum fidus,
Vel ultimum sidus

TO THE HARD-HEARTED MOLLY CAREW,

THE LAMENT OF HER IRISH LOVER.

I.

Och hone!
  Oh! what will I do?
Sure my love is all crost,
Like a bud in the frost...
  And there's no use at all
In my going to bed;
For 'tis dhrames, and not sleep,
That comes into my head...
  And 'tis all about you,
My sweet Molly Carew,
And indeed 'tis a sin
And a shame.—
  You're complater than nature
In every feature;
The snow can't compare
With your forehead so fair:
And I rather would spy
Just one blink of your eye
Than the purtiest star
That shines out of the sky;
Tho'—by this and by that!
For the matter o' that—

Non distat te magis...
Quid agis!
   Heu! heu! nisi tu
Me ames,
Pereo! pillaleu!

II.

Heu! heu!
   Sed cur sequar laude
Ocellos aut frontem
Si NASI, cum fraude,
Prætereo pontem?...
   Ast hic ego minùs
Quàm ipse LONGINUS
In verbis exprimem
Hunc nasum sublimem...
   De floridâ genâ
Vulgaris camœna
Cantaret in vanum
Per annum.—
   Tum, tibi puella!
Sic tument labella
Ut nil plus jucundum
Sit, aut rubicundum;
Si primitùs homo
Collapsus est pomo,
Si dolor et luctus
Venerunt per fructus,
Proh! ætas nunc serior
Ne cadat, vereor,
Icta tam bello

You're more distant by far
Than that same.
   Och hone, wierasthrew!
I am alone
In this world without you!

II.

Och hone!
   But why should I speak
Of your forehead and eyes,
When your nose it defies
Paddy Blake the schoolmaster
   To put it in rhyme?—
Though there's one BURKE,
He says,
Who would call it *Snub*lime...
   And then for your cheek,
Throth 'twould take him a week
Its beauties to tell
As he'd rather:—
   Then your lips, O machree!
In their beautiful glow
They a pattern might be
For the cherries to grow.—
'Twas an apple that tempted
Our mother, we know;
For apples were scarce
I suppose long ago:
But at this time o' day,
'Pon my conscience I'll say,
Such cherries might tempt

Labello :
  Heu ! heu ! nisi tu
Me ames,
Pereo ! pillaleu !

III.

Heu ! Heu
  Per cornua lunæ
Perpetuò tu ne
Me vexes impunè ? ...
  I nunc choro salta
(Mac-ghìus nam tecúm)
Plantâ magis altâ
Quàm sueveris mecùm ! ...
  Tibicinem quando
Cogo fustigando
Ne falsum det melus,
Anhelus.—
  A te in sacello
Vix mentem revello,
Heu ! miserè scissam
Te inter et Missam ;
Tu latitas vero
Tam stricto galero
Ut cernere vultum
Desiderem multùm.
Et dubites jam, nùm
(Ob animæ damnum)
Sit fas hunc deberi
Auferri ?
  Heu ! heu ! nisi tu

A man's father!
   Och hone, wierasthrew!
I'm alone
In this world without you!

III.

Och hone!
   By the man in the moon!
You teaze me all ways
That a woman can plaze;
   For you dance twice as high
With that thief Pat Maghee
As when you take share
In a jig, dear, with me;
   Though the piper I bate,
For fear the ould chate
Wouldn't play you your
Favourite tune.
   And when you're at Mass
My devotion you crass,
For 'tis thinking of you
I am, Molly Carew;
While you wear ou purpose
A bonnet so deep,
That I can't at your sweet
Pretty face get a peep.
Oh! lave off that bonnet,
Or else I'll lave on it
The loss of my wandering
Sowl!
   Och hone, like an owl,

Coràm sis,
Cæcus sim: eleleu!

IV.

Heu! heu!
   Non me provocato,
Nam virginum sat, o!
Stant mihi amato...
   Et stuperes planè
Si aliquo manè
Me sponsum videres;
Hoc quomodo ferres?
   Quid diceres, si cum
Triumpho per vicum,
Maritus it ibi,
Non tibi!
   Et pol! Catherinæ
Cui vacca, (tu, sine)
Si proferem hymen
Grande esset discrimen;
Tu quàmvis, hìc aio,
Sis blandior Maio,
Et hæc calet rariùs
Quam Januarius;
Si non mutas brevi,
Hanc mihi decrevi
(Ut sic ultus forem)
Uxorem;
   Tum posthâc diù
Me spectrum
Verebere tu... eleleu!

FATHER PROUT.

Day is night,
Dear, to me without you!

IV.

Och hone!
  Don't provoke me to do it;
For there's girls by the score
That loves me, and more.
  And you'd look very queer,
If some morning you'd meet
My wedding all marching
In pride down the street.
  Throth you'd open your eyes,
And you'd die of surprise
To think 'twasn't you
Was come to it.
  And 'faith! Katty Naile
And her cow, I go bail,
Would jump if I'd say,
"Katty Naile, name the day."
And though you're fair and fresh
As the blossoms in May,
And she's short and dark
Like a cold winter's day,
Yet if *you* don't repent
Before Easter,—when Lent
Is over—I'll marry
For spite.
  Och hone! and when I
Die for you,
'Tis my ghost that you'll see every night!
                              S. LOVER

THE GRAND CHAM OF TARTARY,

AND

THE HUMBLE-BEE.

Abridged from the voluminous Epic Poem by Beg-beg,
(formerly a mendicant ballad-singer, afterwards Prin-
cipal Lord Rector of the University of Samarcand, and
subsequently Historiographer and Poet Laureate to the
Court of Balk,) by C. J. Davids, Esq.

I.

THE great Tartar chief, on a festival day,
Gave a spread to his court, and resolv'd to be gay;
But, just in the midst of their music and glee,
The mirth was upset by a humble-bee—
               A humble-bee—
They were bored by a rascally *humble-bee!*

II.

This riotous bee was so wanting in sense
As to fly at the Cham with malice prepense:
Said his highness, " My fate will be *felo-de-se*,
If I'm thus to be teas'd by a humble-bee—
               A humble-bee—
How *shall* I get rid of the humble-bee !"

III.

The troops in attendance, with sabre and spear,
Were order'd to harass the enemy's rear:
But the brave body-guards were forced to flee—
They were all so afraid of the humble-bee—
    The humble bee—
The soldiers were scar'd by the humble-bee.

IV.

The solicitor-general thought there was reason
For indicting the scamp on a charge of high-treason;
While the chancellor *doubted* if any decree
From the woolsack would frighten the humble-bee—
    The humble-bee—
So the lawyers fought shy of the humble-bee.

V.

The Cham from his throne in an agony rose,
While the insect was buzzing right under his nose:—
" Was ever a potentate plagued like me,
Or worried to death by a humble-bee !
    A humble-bee—
Don't let me be stung by the humble-bee !"

VI.

He said to a page, nearly choking with grief,
" Bring hither my valiant commander-in-chief;
And say that I'll give him a liberal fee,
To cut the throat of this humble-bee—
    This humble-bee—
This turbulent, Jacobin, humble-bee !"

VII.

His generalissimo came at the summons,
And, cursing the courtiers for cowardly *rum-uns,*
" My liege," said he, " it's all fiddle-de-dee
To make such a fuss for a humble-bee—
     A humble-bee—
I don't care a d—n for the humble-bee !"

VIII.

The veteran rush'd sword in hand on the foe,
And cut him in two with a desperate blow.
His master exclaim'd, " I'm delighted to see
How neatly you've settled the humble-bee !"
     The humble-bee—
So there was an end of the humble-bee.

IX.

By the doctor's advice (which was prudent and right)
His highness retired very early that night :
For they got him to bed soon after his tea,
And he dream'd all night of the humble-bee—
     The humble-bee—
He saw the grim ghost of the humble-bee.

MORAL.

Seditious disturbers, mind well what you're *arter*—
Lest, humming a prince, you by chance catch a *Tartar.*
Consider, when planning an impudent spree,
You may get the same luck as the humble-bee—
     The humble-bee—
Remember the doom of the humble-bee !

PADDY BLAKE'S ECHO.

A NEW VERSION FROM THE ORIGINAL IRISH.

"*Ecco* ridente," &c.

I.

There's a spot by that lake, sirs,
  Where echoes were born,
Were one Paddy Blake, sirs,
  Was walking one morn
With a great curiosity big in his mind!
    Says he, " Mrs. Blake
      Doesn't *trate* me of late
    In the fashion she did
      When I first call'd her Kate:
    She's crusty and surly,—
      My cabin 's the *dhiaoul*,
    My pigs and my poultry
      Are all cheek by jowl:
But what is the cause, from the *A*cho I'll find."

(Spoken.)

So up he goes *bouldly* to the *A*cho, and says, " The top

o' the mornin' t'ye, Misther or Missus *Acho*, for divil a know I know whether ye wear petticoats or breeches."

" Neither," says the *Acho* in Irish.

" Now, that being the case," says Paddy, turnin' sharp 'pon the *Acho*, d'ye see, " ye can tell me the stark-naked truth."

" 'Troth, an' ye may say that, with yir own purty mouth," says the *Acho*.

" Well, thin," says Paddy agin, " what the divil's come over Mrs. Blake of late ?"

" *Potcheen !*" says the *Acho*.

" Oh ! (*shouting*) by the pow'rs of Moll Kelly," says Paddy, " I thought as mich :—

" It wasn't for nothin' the taypot was hid,
Though I guess'd what was in it, by smelling the lid !"

II.

There's another suspicion
   Comes over my mind,
That with all his *contrition*
   And pray'rs, and that kind,
Ould Father Mahony's a wag in his way.
When a *station*, he says,
   Will be held at *my* house,
I must go my ways,
   Or be mute as a mouse.
For *him* turkey and bacon
   Is pull'd from the shelf;
Not so much as a cake on
   The coals for myself :
But what all this *manes*, why, the *Acho* will say.

(Spoken.)

Up he goes agin to the *A*cho, and says, "Tell me, aff ye plase, what is 't brings ould Father Mahony so everlastingly to my country seat in the bog of Bally Keeran?"

"Mrs. Blake!" says the *A*cho.

"Oh! hannimandhiaoul!" says Paddy, "I thought as mich—the thief o' the world—I thought as mich. Oh! tundher-a-nouns!

"I'll go home an' *bate* her, until my heart 's sore,
Then give her the key of the street evermore!"

W.

IMPROMPTU.

Who the *dickens* " Boz" could be
    Puzzled many a learned elf;
Till time unveil'd the mystery,
    And *Boz* appear'd as DICKENS' self!

C. J. DAVIDS.

HAROUN ALRASCHID.

O'ER the gorgeous room a luxurious gloom,
    Like the glow of a summer's eve, hung:
From its basin of stone, with rose-leaves bestrown
    The fountain its coolness flung;
Perfumes wondrously rare fill'd the eunuch-fann'd air,
    And on gem-studded carpets around
The poets sung forth tales of glory or mirth
    To their instruments' eloquent sound;
On a throne framed of gold sat their monarch the bold,
    With coffers of coin by his side,
And to each, as he sung, lavish handfuls he flung,
    Till each in his gratitude cried,
" Long, long live great Haroun Alraschid, the Caliph of
    Babylon old !"

Disturbing the feast, from the Rome of the East
    An embassage audience craves;
And Haroun, smiling bland, cries, dismissing the band,
    " We will look on the face of our slaves !"
Then the eunuchs who wait on their Caliph in state
    Lead the messenger Lords of the Greek.

Proud and martial their mien, proud and martial
  their sheen,
  But they bow to the Arab right meek;
And with heads bending down, though their brows
  wear a frown,
  They ask if he audience bestow.
"Yea, dogs of the Greek, we await ye, so speak!—
  Have ye brought us the tribute you owe?
Or what lack ye of Haroun Alraschid, the Caliph of
  Babylon old?"

Then the Greek spake loud, "To Alraschid the
  Proud
  This message our monarch doth send:
While ye play'd 'gainst a Queen, ye could mate her,
  I ween—
  She could ill with thy pieces contend;
But Irene is dead, and a Pawn in her stead
  Holds her power and place on the board:
By Nicephorus stern is the purple now worn,
  And no longer he owns thee for lord.
If tribute ye claim, I am bade in his name
  This to tell thee, O King of the World,
With these, not with gold, pays Nicephorus bold!"—
  And a bundle of sword-blades he hurl'd
At the feet of stern Haroun Alraschid, the Caliph of
  Babylon old.

Dark as death was his look, and his every limb
  shook,
  As the Caliph glared round on the foe—

G

" View my answer !" he roar'd, and unsheathing his
  sword,
 Clove the bundle of falchions right through.
" Tell my slave, the Greek hound, that **Haroun the**
  Renown'd,
 Ere the sun that now sets rise again,
Will be far on the road to his wretched abode,
 With many a myriad of men.
No reply will he send, either spoken or penn'd ;
 But by Allah, and Abram our sire,
He shall read a reply on the earth, in the sky,
 Writ in bloodshed, and famine, and fire !
Now begone !" thundered Haroun Alraschid, the Caliph
  of Babylon old.

As the sun dropt in night by the murky torch-
  light,
 There was gathering of horse and of man :
Tartar, Courd, Bishareen, Persian, swart Bedoween,
 And the mighty of far Khorasan—
Of all tongues, of all lands, and in numberless
  bands,
 Round the Prophet's green banner they crowd,
They are form'd in array, they are up and away,
 Like the locusts' calamitous cloud ;
But rapine or spoil, till they reach the Greek soil,
 Is forbidden, however assail'd.
A poor widow, whose fold a Courd robb'd, her tale
  told,
 And he was that instant impaled
By the stern wrath of Haroun Alraschid, the Caliph of
 Babylon old !

·On o'er valley and hill, river, plain, onwards still,
    Fleet and fell as the desert-wind, on !
Where was green grass before, when that host had
       pass'd o'er,
    Every vestige of verdure was gone !
On o'er valley and hill, desert, river, on still,
    With the speed of the wild ass or deer,
The dust of their tread, o'er the atmosphere spread,
    Hung for miles like a cloud in their rear.
On o'er valley and hill, desert, river, on still,
    Till afar booms the ocean's hoarse roar,
And amid the night's gloom are seen tower, temple,
       doom—
    Heraclea, that sits by the shore !
The doom'd city of Haroun Alraschid, the Caliph of
Babylon old.

There was mirth at its height in thy mansions that
       night,
    Heraclea, that sits by the sea !
Thy damsels' soft smiles breathed their loveliest wiles,
    And the banquet was wild in its glee !
For Zoe the fair, proud Nicephorus' heir,
    That night was betrothed to her mate,
To Theseus the Bold, of Illyria old,
    And the blood of the Island-kings great.
When lo ! wild and lorn, and with robes travel-torn,
    And with features that pallidly glared,
They the Arab had spurn'd from Damascus return'd,
    Rush'd in, and the coming declared
Of the armies of Haroun Alraschid, the Caliph of Babylon
    old·

A faint tumult afar, the first breathing of war,
    Multitudinous floats on the gale :
The lelie shout shrill, and the toss'd cymbals peal,
    And the trumpet's long desolate wail,
The horse-tramp of swarms, and the clangour of
      arms,
    And the murmur of nations of men.
Oh woe, woe, and woe, Heraclea shall know—
    She shall fall, and shall rise not again ;
The spiders' dusk looms shall alone hang her rooms,
    The green grass shall grow in her ways,
Her daughters shall wail, and her warriors shall
      quail,
    And herself be a sign of amaze,
Through the vengeance of Haroun Alraschid, the Caliph
    of Babylon old.

'Tis the dawn of the sun, and the morn-prayer is
      done,
    And the murderous onset is made ;
The Christian and foe they are at it, I trow,
    Fearfully plying the blade.
Each after each rolls on to the breach,
    Like the slumberless roll of the sea.
Rank rolling on rank rush the foe on the Frank,
    Breathless, in desperate glee ;
The Greek's quenchless fire, the Mussulman's ire
    Has hurled over rampart and wall.
And 'tis all one wild hell of blades slaughtering fell,
    Where fiercest and fellest o'er all
Work'd the falchion of Haroun Alraschid, the Caliph of
    Babylon old.

But day rose on day, yet Nicephorus grey,
    And Theseus, his daughter's betrothed,
With warrior-like sleight kept the town in despite,
    Of the Moslem insulted and loathed.
Morn rose after morn on the leaguers outworn,
    Till the Caliph with rage tore his beard;
And, terribly wroth, sware a terrible oath—
    An oath which the boldest ev'n fear'd.
So his mighty Emirs gat around their compeers,
    And picked for the onslaught a few.
Oh! that onslaught was dread,—every Moslem struck
    dead!
    But, however, young Theseus they slew,
And that gladdened fierce Haroun Alraschid, the Caliph
    of Babylon old.

Heraclea, that night in thy palaces bright
    There was anguish and bitterest grief.
" He is gone! he is dead!" were the words that they
    said,
    Though the stunn'd heart refused its belief:
Wild and far spreads the moan, from the hut, from
    the throne,
    Striking every one breathless with fear.
" Oh! Theseus the bold, thou art stark,—thou art
    cold,—
    Thou art young to be laid on the bier."
One alone makes no moan, but with features like
    stone,
    In an ecstacy haggard of woe,
Sits tearless and lorn, with dry eyeballs that
    burn,

And fitful her lips mutter low
Dread threatenings against Haroun Alraschid, the Caliph
of Babylon old.

The next morn on the wall, first and fiercest of all,
    The distraction of grief cast aside,
In her lord's arms arrayed, Zoe plies the death-
        blade,—
    Ay, and, marry, right terribly plied.
Her lovely arm fair, to the shoulder is bare,
    And nerved with a giant-like power
Where her deadly sword sweeps fall the mighty in
        heaps ;
    Where she does but appear the foe cower.
Rank on rank they rush on,—rank on rank are
        struck down,
    Till the ditch is choked up with the dead.
The vulture and crow, and the wild dog, I trow,
    Made a dreadful repast that night as they fed
On the liegemen of Haroun Alraschid, the Caliph of
    Babylon old.

This was not to last.—The stern Moslem, downcast,
    Retrieved the next morning their might ;
For Alraschid the bold, and the Barmecide old,
    Had proclaimed through the camp in the night,
That whoso should win the first footing within
    The city that bearded their power,
Should have for his prize the fierce girl with black
        eyes,
    And ten thousand zecchines as her dower.

It spurred them right well; and they battled and fell,
   Like lions, with long hunger wild.
Ere that day set the sun Heraclea was won,
   And Nicephorus bold, and his child,
Were captives to Haroun Alraschid, the Caliph of
   Babylon old.

To his slave, the Greek hound, roared Haroun the
   Renowned.
   When before him Nicephorus came,
"Though the pawn went to queen, 'tis checkmated,
   I ween.
   Thou'rt as bold as unskilled in the game.
Now, Infidel, say, wherefore should I not slay
   The wretch that my vengeance hath sought?"—
"I am faint,—I am weak—and I thirst," quoth
   the Greek,
   "Give me drink."   At his bidding 'tis brought;
He took it; but shrank, lest 'twere poison he drank.
   "Thou art safe till the goblet be quaffed!"
Cried Haroun. The Greek heard, took the foe at
   his word,
   Dashed down on the pavement the draught,
And claimed mercy of Haroun Alraschid, the Caliph of
   Babylon old.

Haroun never broke word or oath that he spoke,
   So he granted the captive his life,
And then bade his slaves bear stately Zoe the fair,
   To the warrior who won her in strife;
But the royal maid cried in the wrath of her pride,

She would die ere her hand should be given,
　Or the nuptial caress should be lavished to bless
　　Such a foe to her house and to Heaven.
Her entreaties they spurned, and her menace they
　　　scorned;
　But, resolute, spite of their power,
All food she denied, and by self-famine died;
　And her father went mad from that hour.
Thus triumph'd stern Haroun Alraschid, the Caliph of
　Babylon old!

G. E. INMAN.

TO THE HOT WELLS OF CLIFTON,

IN PRAISE OF RUM-PUNCH.

A Triglot Ode, viz.

1° Πινδαρου περι ρευματος ᾠδη.
2° Horatii in fontem Bristolii carmen.
3° A Relick (unpublished) of "the unfortunate Chatterton."

PINDAR.	HORACE.	CHATTERTON.
ηγη Βριστολιας	O fons Bristolii	I ken your worth
αλλον εν υαλῳ	Hoc magis in vitro	"Hot wells" of Bristol,
αμπουσ' ανθεσι συν	Dulci digne mero	That bubble forth
ικταρος αξιη	Non sine floribus	As clear as crystal;...
'αντλῶ	Vas impleveris	In parlour snug
υματι πολλῳ	Undâ	I'd wish no hotter
ισγων	Mel solvente	To mix a jug
αι μελιτος πολυ.	Caloribus.	Of Rum and Water.

β.	II.	2.
νηρ καν τις ερα̣ν	Si quis vel venerem	Doth Love, young chiel,
ιυλεται η μαχα̣ν	Aut prælia cogitat,	One's bosom ruffle ?
οι Βακχου καθαρον	Is Bacchi calidos	Would any feel
οι διαχρωννυσει	Inficiet tibi	Ripe for a scuffle ?
'οινῳ	Rubro sanguine	The simplest plan
᾽ αιματι νᾱμα·	Rivos,	Is just to take a
ροθυμος τε	Fiet protinus	Well stiffened can
αχ᾽ εσσεται.	Impiger !	Of old Jamaica.

γ.	III.	3.
Σε Φλεγμ' αιθαλοεν	Te flagrante bibax	Beneath the zone
Σειριου αστερος	Ore caniculâ	Grog in a pail or
Αρμοζει πλωτορι·	Sugit navita : tu	Rum — best alone —
Συ κρυος ηδυν εν	Frigus amabile	Delights the sailor.
Νησοις	Fessis vomere	The can he swills
Αντιλεσαισι	Mauris	Alone gives vigour
Ποιεις	Præbes ac	In the Antilles
Κ' αιθιοπων Φυλω.	Homini nigro.	To white or nigger.

δ.	IV.	4.
Κρηναις εν τε καλαις	Fies nobilium	Thy claims, O fount,
Εσσεαι αγλαη	Tu quoque fontium	Deserve attention :
Σ' εν κοιλω κυλακι	Me dicente ; cavum	Henceforward count
Ενθεμενην εως	Dum calicem reples	On classic mention.
Υμνησω,	Urnamque	Right pleasant stuff
Λαλον εξ ου	Unde loquaces	Thine to the lip is…
Σον δε ρευμα καβαλλεται.	Lymphæ	We've had enough
	Desiliunt tuæ.	Of Aganippe's.

THE DUMB WAITER.

I can not really understand,
  (Said Henry to his aunt,)
Why a dumb waiter this is called,—
  Upon my word, I can't ;
For I have heard you often say
  It *answers* very well.
Why, then, the waiter is called *dumb*,
  I cannot think, or tell.

Between you, boy, this difference know,—
  For once attention lending,—
While without *speaking* this *attends*,
  You *speak* without *attending*.

THE BOTTLE OF ST. JANUARIUS.

I.

In the land of the citron and myrtle, we're told
    That the blood of a MARTYR is kept in a phial,
Which, though all the year round, it lie torpid and cold,
    Yet grasp but the crystal, 'twill *warm* the first trial...
Be it fiction or truth, with your favourite FACT,
    O, profound LAZZARONI! I seek not to quarrel;
But indulge an old priest who would simply extract
    From your legend, a lay—from your martyr, a moral.

II.

Lo! with icicled beard JANUARIUS comes!
    And the blood in his veins is all frozen and gelid,
And he beareth a bottle; but TORPOR benumbs
    Every limb of the saint:—Would ye wish to dispel it?
With the hand of good-fellowship grasp the hoar sage—
    Soon his joints will relax and his pulse will beat quicker;
Grasp the *bottle* he brings—'twill grow warm, I'll engage,
    Till the frost of each heart lies dissolved in the LIQUOR!

Probatum est.

P. PROUT.

THE RISING PERIODICAL;

Being Mr. Verdant's Account of his last Aerial Voyage, *edited* by
Thomas Haynes Bayly.

WITHOUT apology, I'll trace
  Our airy flight across the sea,
Because at once we raised *ourselves*
  And public curiosity.

And well might those who saw us off,
  Our many perils long discuss,
Because, ere we were out of sight,
  'Twas certainly " all up with us !"

There might be danger, sure enough,
  On high, from thirst and hunger blending
But men are told they should *bear up*
  Against the danger that's impending.

So we bore up into the clouds,
  Of creature comforts ample store
And really coffee ne'er was known
  To rise so speedily before.

Our tongues, though salted, never halted ;
  Our game fresh-kill'd was very high ;
And, though all nicely truss'd and roasted,
  We saw our fowls and turkeys fly !

Our solid food rose like a puff,
  Hard biscuit seem'd a trifle, too ;
And our champagne was so much up,
  That e'en our empty bottles flew !

Our spirits rose ; in fact we were,
  When not a dozen miles from Dover,
Quite in a *state of elevation*,
  Indisputably " *half seas over*."

How like conspirators were we,
  So snug we kept our hour of rising ;
And when our movement once was made,
  All London cried, " Oh ! how surprising !"

If, when we soar'd above the great,
  They trembled, 'twas without occasion :
Our thoughts were turned to France ; in truth
  We meditated an invasion !

But over earth and over sea
  We went without one hostile notion
Our war on earth, a civil war ;
  The Channel,—our Pacific Ocean.

When passing over Chatham town
  We were just finishing a chicken ;

A soldier and a maiden fair
    I saw whilst I the bones was picking.

I threw a drumstick at the youth,
    Who all around the culprit sought;
And whilst the maiden laughed aloud,
    I struck her with a merry thought.

In darkness we the Channel cross'd,
    And left our fragile car to chance;
And, scorning customary rules,
    Without a passport enter'd France!

But on we went, and our descent
    Bewilder'd many a German gaper;
Until, to prove from whence we came,
    We show'd the last day's London paper!

We're told no good that is substantial
    Results from all we nobly dare;
What then?—We took a clever MASON
    To build us castles in the air.

We're not like certain *rising men*,
    Puff'd up with vain presumptuous thoughts;
We nothing boast of what we've done,
    And deem ourselves mere airy-noughts!

                                        T. H. B.

THE SONG OF THE COVER.

(NOT A SPORTING ONE.)

My dear Mr. Editor.—I have been for some time troubled by a slight longing to illustrate the title-page (or rather the Cover and its pretty *pages)* of the Miscellany. To-day I was taken suddenly worse with this desperate symptom of the *cacoethes scribendi*, but at length being safely delivered of the following doggrel, you will be glad to hear that I am now "as well as can be expected."

Ever, my dear Mr. Editor, yours truly,

R. J.

"Sing a song of half-a-crown—
   Lay it out this minute;
Buy the book, for half the town
   Want to know what's in it.
Had you all the cares of Job,
   You'd then forget your troubles,"
Cried Cupid, seated on the globe,
   Busy blowing bubbles.

Rosy Summer, pretty Spring,
   See them scattering flowers—
" Catch who can !" the song they sing ;
   Hearts-ease fall in showers.
Autumn, tipsy with the grape,
   Plays a pipe and tabor ;
Winter imitates the ape,
   Mocking at his neighbour.

Bentley, Boz, and Cruikshank, stand,
   Like expectant reelers—
" Music !"—" Play up !"—pipe in hand,
   Beside the *fluted* pillars !
Boz and Cruikshank want to dance,
   None for frolic riper,
But Bentley makes the first advance,
   Because he " pays the piper."

" 'Then sing a song of half-a-crown,
   And make a merry race on't.
To buy the book, all London town ;
   There's wit upon the *face* on't.
Had you all the cares of Job,
   You'd then forget your troubles,"
Cried Cupid, seated on the globe,
   Busy blowing bubbles.

WHO ARE YOU?

" Who are you ?—Who are you ?
  Little boy that's running after
Ev'ry one up and down,
  Mingling sighing with your laughter?"
" I am Cupid, lady belle,
  I am Cupid, and no other."
" Little boy, then pr'ythee tell
  How is Venus ?   How's your mother ?
Little boy, little boy,
  I desire you tell me true:
Cupid, oh ! you're alter'd so,
  No wonder I cry *Who are you ?*

II.

" Who are you ?—Who are you ?
  Little boy, where is your bow ?
You had a bow, my little boy."
  " So had you, ma'am, long ago."
" Little boy, where is your torch ?"
· " Madam, I have given it up :
Torches are no use at all ;
  Hearts will never now *flare up.*"

"Naughty boy, naughty boy,
 Such words as these I never knew:
Cupid, oh; you're alter'd so,
 No wonder I say
   "WHO ARE YOU?"

EPIGRAM.

ON Easter Sunday, Lucy spoke,
And said, "A saint you might provoke,
Dear Sam, each day, since Monday last;
But now I see your rage is past."
Said Sam, "What Christian could be meek!
You know, my love, 'twas *Passion Week;*
And so, you see, the rage I've spent
Was not my own—'twas only *Lent.*"

S. LOVER.

LEARY THE PIPER'S LILT.

This is the first o' the May, boys!
   Listen to me, an' my planxty pipe
Will show ye the fun o' the day, boys!
   I know for a spree that ye're always ripe,
And fond o' gingerbread while it is gilt.
" Hurroo! for Leary the Piper's Lilt!"

First, on the *first* o' the May, boys!
   Do as the birds did Valentine morn;
Find out a lass for the day, boys!
   And then together go *gether* the thorn—
I warrant she'll never be jade or jilt.
" Hurroo! for Leary the Piper's Lilt!"

Go where ye *may* for the May, boys!
   Folla yir nose, an' ye'll find it soon:
On every hedge by the way, boys!
   Ye'll hear it singin' its scented tune,
Unless by the breath o' your darlin' *kilt!*
" Hurroo! for Leary the Piper's Lilt!"

But isn't it betther the *May*, boys !
    All living to *lave* on its flow'ry tree,
Than wound it by *braking* away, boys !
    A branch that in blossom not long will be
When the rosy dew that it drank is spilt ?
" Hurroo ! for Leary the Piper's Lilt !"

An' when ye're all tir'd o' the May, boys !
    Come to the sign o' the Muzzle an' Can :
An' there, at the close o' the day, boys !
    Let ev'ry lass, by the side of her man,
Dance till the daisies are spreadin' their quilt.
" Hurroo ! for Leary the Piper's Lilt !"

W.

SONG OF THE MONTH.

(JANUARY.)

" Ille ego qui quondam," &c. &c.—*Æneid.*

I.

In the month of Janus,
When Boz to gain us,
Quite " miscellaneous,"
   Flashed his wit so keen,
One, (Prout they call him,)
In style most solemn,
Led off the volume
   Of his magazine.

II.

Though MAGA, 'mongst her
Bright set of youngsters,
Had many songsters
   For her opening tome ;
Yet she would rather
Invite " the Father,"
And an indulgence gather
   From the Pope of Rome.

III.

And, such a beauty
From head to shoe-tie,
Without dispute we
    Found her first boy,
That she detarmined,
There's such a charm in't,
The Father's *sarmint*
    She'd again employ.

IV.

While other children
Are quite bewilderin',
'Tis joy that fill'd her in
    This bantling; 'cause
What eye but glistens,
And what ear but listens,
When the clargy christens
    A babe of Boz?

V.

I've got a scruple
That this young pupil
Surprised its parent
    Ere her time was sped;
Else I'm unwary,
Or, 'tis she's a fairy,
For in January
    She was brought to bed.

VI.

This infant may be
A six months' baby,
But may his cradle
    Be blest! say I;
And luck defend him!
And joy attend him!
Since we can't mend him,
    Born in July.

VII.

He's no abortion,
But born to fortune,
And most opportune,
    Though before his time;
Him, Muse, O! nourish,
And make him flourish
Quite Tommy-Moorish
    Both in prose and rhyme!

VIII.

I remember, also,
That this month they call so,
From Roman JULIUS
    The " *Cæsarian*" styled;
Who was no gosling,
But, like this Boz-ling,
From birth a dazzling
    And precocious child!

GOD SAVE THE QUEEN!
                                    P. PROUT

SONG OF THE OLD BELL.

" In an old village, amid older hills,
  That close around their verdant walls to guard
  Its tottering age from wintry winds, I dwell
  Lonely, and still, save when the clamorous rooks
  Or my own fickle changes wound the ear
  Of Silence in my tower."—ANON.

For full five hundred years I've swung
  In my old grey turret high,
And many a different theme I've sung
  As the time went stealing by!
I've peal'd the chaunt of a wedding morn;
  Ere night I have sadly toll'd,
To say that the bride was coming, love-lorn,
  To sleep in the church-yard mould!
          Ding dong,
                  My careless song;
      Merry and sad,
              But neither long!

For full five hundred years I've swung
  In my ancient turret high,
And many a different theme I've sung
  As the time went stealing by!

I've swell'd the joy of a country's pride
   For a victory far off won,
Then changed to grief for the brave that died
   Ere my mirth had well begun!
        Ding-dong,
                My careless song
           Merry or sad,
                But neither long!

For full five hundred years I've swung
   In my breezy turret high,
And many a different theme I've sung
   As the time went stealing by!
I have chimed the dirge of a nation's grief
   On the death of a dear-loved king,
Then merrily rung for the next young chief;
   As *told*, I can weep or sing!
        Ding-dong,
                My careless song;
           Merry or sad,
                But neither long!

For full five hundred years I've swung
   In my crumbling turret high;
'Tis time my own death-song were sung,
   And with truth before I die!
I never could love the themes they gave
   My tyrannized tongue to tell:
One moment for cradle, the next for grave—
   They've worn out the old church bell!
        Ding-dong,
                My changeful song;
           Farewell now,
                And farewell long!

"BE QUIET—DO! I'LL CALL MY MOTHER!"

[Lest the author of the following should be accused of plagiarism, he thinks it right to state that in the second volume of the *Parnasse des Dames*, there is a song, the burden of which is, " *Tenez vous coi, j'appellerai ma mère.* It is, however, too gross for translation, and nothing of it has been preserved in the present lines, except the *refrain.*]

I.

As I was sitting in a wood,
　Under an oak-tree's leafy cover,
Musing in pleasant solitude,
　Who should come by, but John, my lover!
He pressed my hand, and kissed my cheek;
　Then warmer growing, kissed the other;
While I exclaimed, and strove to shriek,
　" *Be quiet—do! I'll call my mother!*"

II.

He saw my anger was sincere,
　And lovingly began to chide me;
And, wiping from my cheek the tear,
　He sat him on the grass beside me.

He feigned such pretty, amorous woe,
   Breathed such sweet vows one after other,
I could but smile while whispering low.
   " Be quiet—do ! I'll call my mother !"

III.

He talked so long, and talked so well,
   And swore he meant not to deceive me ;
I felt more grief than I can tell,
   When with a kiss he rose to leave me.
" Oh, John !" said I, " and must thou go !
   I love thee better than all other !
There is no need to hurry so,
   I never meant to call my mother !"

C. M.

OLD MOUNTAIN DEW.

Away with your port and your fine-flavour'd sherry,
  And fill up with toddy as high as you please ;
We men of the Northland should know ourselves better
  Than pledge her in liquors so paltry as these !
In whiskey, perfumed by the peat of the heather,
  We'll drink to the land of the kind and the true,—
      Unsullied in honour,
      Our blessings upon her !
  Scotland for ever ! and old mountain dew !
        Neish ! neish ! neish ! hurra !

Mountain dew ! *clear* as a Scot's understanding,
  Pure as his conscience wherever he goes,
Warm as his heart to the friend he has chosen,
  Strong as his arm when he fights with his foes !
In liquor like this should old Scotland be toasted ;
  So fill up again, and the pledge we'll renew—
      Long flourish the honour
      Her children have won her—
  Scotland for ever ! and old mountain dew !
        Neish ! neish ! neish ! hurra !

May her worth, like her lowland streams, roll on
    unceasing,—
Her fame, like her highland hills, last evermore,—
And the cold of her glens be confined to the climate,
    Nor enter the heart, though it creep through the door!
And never may we, while we love and revere her,
    As long as we're brave, and warm-hearted, and true,
        Want reason to boast her,
        Or whiskey to toast her—
Scotland for ever! and old mountain dew!
        Neish! neish! neish! hurra!

CHARLES MACKAY.

REV. SYDNEY SMITH.

The following anecdote of this witty Divine is too good to be lost.

At one of the Holland House Sunday dinner-parties many years ago, Crockford's Club, then forming, was talked of; and the noble hostess observed, that the female passion for diamonds was surely less ruinous than the rage for play among men; upon which Sydney Smith wrote the following *impromptu sermonet* most appropriately *on a card*:

Thoughtless that "all that's brightest fades,"
Unmindful of that *knave of spades*,
 The sexton and his subs :
How foolishly we play our parts !
Our *wives* on *diamonds* set their *hearts*,
 We set our *hearts* on *clubs*.

THE PIPER'S PROGRESS.

I

When I was a boy
  In my father's mud edifice,
Tender and bare
  As a pig in a sty;
Out of the door as I
  Looked with a steady phiz,
Who but Thade Murphy,
  The piper, went by;
Says Thady, "But few play
This music—can *you* play?"
Says I, " I can't tell,
  For I never did try."
So he told me that *he* had a charm
  To make the pipes purtily speak;
Then squeezed a bag under his arm,
  When sweetly they set up a squeak!
    Fa-ra-la la-ra-la loo!

Och hone!
How he handled the drone!
  And then the sweet music he blew
Would have melted the heart of a stone!

THE PIPER'S PROGRESS

I.

Pater me clauserat
Domi homunculum;
Grunniens sus erat
   Comes, ut mos:
Transibat tibicen
Juxta domunculam,
Quando per januam
   Protuli os;
Ille ait impromptu,
" Hâc tibiâ num tu,
Ut te sine sumptu
   Edoceam, vis ?"
Tum pressit amiculam
Sub ulnâ vesiculam
Quæ sonum reddidit
   Vocibus his :
     Fa-ra-la la-ra-la loo!

     Φευ, φευ!
Modo flens, modo flans,
   Magico ελελευ,
Cor et aurem vel lapidi dans!

             I

II.

" Your pipe," says I, " Thady,
　So neatly comes over me,
Naked I'll wander
　Wherever it blows;
And, if my poor parents
　Should try to recover me,
Sure it won't be
　By describing my clothes.
The music I hear now
Takes hold of my ear now,
And leads me all over
　The world by the nose."
So I follow'd his bagpipe so sweet,
　And I sung, as I leapt like a frog,
　Adieu to my family seat,
　So pleasantly placed in a bog!"
　　Fa-ra-la la-ra-la loo!
　Och hone!
　How we handled the drone!
　　And then the sweet music we blew
　Would have melted the heart of a stone!

III.

Full five years I follow'd him,
　Nothing could sunder us;
Till he one morning
　Had taken a sup,
And slipt from a bridge
　In a river just under us!
Souse to the bottom
　Just like a blind pup.

II.

Cui ego tum : " Tu sic, ah!
Me rapis musicâ,
Ut sequar nudulus
   Tibicen, te !
Et si pater, testibus,
Quærat me, vestibus,
Redibit, ædepol !
   Vacuâ re.
Sic melos quod audio
Me replet gaudio
Ut trahor campos et
   Flumina trans ;
Jam linquo rudibus
Hic in paludibus,
Patris tigurium
   Splendidè stans.
    Fa-ra-la la-ra-la loo !
     Dum tibicen, tu,
   Modo flens, modo flans,
    Iteras ελελευ
Cor et aurem vel lapidi dans.

III.

Ut arte sic magicâ
Egi quinquennium,
Magistro tragica
   Accidit res ;
Bacchi nam numine
Pontis cacumine
Dum staret, flumine
   Labitur pes !

He roar'd, and he bawl'd out;
And I also call'd out,
"Now, Thady, my friend,
　　Don't you mean to come up?" ...
He was dead as a nail in a door;
　　Poor Thady was laid on the shelf.
So I took up his pipes on the shore,
　　And now I've set up for myself.
　　　Fa-ra-la la-ra-la loo!
　　Och hone!
　　Don't I handle the drone,
　　　And play such sweet music? I too,
　　Can't I soften the heart of a stone?

" E sinu fluctuum,
O puer, duc tuum
(Clamat) didascalum,
   Fer opem nans !" . . .
Ast ego renuo ;
Et sumens denuò
Littore tibias
   Sustuli, fans,
     Fa-ra-la la-ra-la loo!
       Φευ, φευ !
     Modo flens, modo flans,
      Magico ελελευ
   Cor *et aurem vel lapidi dans !*

P. PROUT.

THE USEFUL YOUNG MAN.

" There's one of us in every family."

To make ourselves useful 's a duty we owe
To mankind and ourselves in our sojourn below;
To return good for evil, and always " to do
Unto others as you'd have them do unto you:"
So I bear all with patience, resolved, if I can,
To act well my part as a Useful Young Man!

But, alas! *entre nous*, 'tis a difficult task,
As seldom I'm left in life's sunshine to bask;
For I'm hurried, and worried, imposed on by all,
Who think I should run at their beck or their call:
" So obliging," folks say, " is their favourite Sam,
That he well earns the name of the Useful Young Man!"

Each morning at breakfast I'm doomed to peruse
" The Herald," and " Post," for " the family news,"
While the toast, eggs, and coffee, which fall to my lot,
Get a pretty considerable distance from hot:
Yes, such are the COMFORTS—deny it who can?—
That fall to the share of each Useful Young Man!

If Jane, or Maria, for work should agree,
The dear creatures invariably send down for me
To make myself useful, and read while they knit,
Paint, draw, or do anything they may think fit.
Thus Sam—poor pill-garlic!—they safely trepan:
Alack! what a life leads a Useful Young Man!

If the day 's rather wet, and they can't gad about,
They think nothing whatever, of sending me out:—
" Now, Sam, my good fellow, just pop on your hat;
Run to *Howell*'s for this thing, and *Holmes*'s for that;
You'll make yourself pleasant we know, if you can,—
What a comfort to have such a Useful Young Man!"

When John, our fat butler, or Bridget, the cook,
Have leisure for reading " some novelty book,"
They ne'er think of asking my leave to peruse,
But help themselves freely to just what they choose:
Making free with my novels is no novel plan,
For THEY own Master Sam 's such a Useful Young Man!

Once Thomas, the footman, kissed Anne on the stairs,
Who loudly squalled out, just to give herself airs;
When my father ran down, in great anger, to see
What the cause of the squeaking and squalling could be.
Tom had bolted; but not till they'd settled a plan
To throw all the blame on *the Useful* Young Man!

When the Opera we visit, I'm kept in the rear
Of our box, and can scarce get a glimpse, I declare,
Of the stage, or the audience;—so only remain,
To trot up to *Dubourg* for *punch à la Romaine*,
To run out for a book, or to pick up a fan:—
Alas! what a drudge is a Useful Young Man!

But sad is my fate when I go to a rout,
If a toothless old maid sits a partner without,
The beaux are looked o'er, but they always agree
To fix the *agreeable* task upon me;
For to dance with all *bores*, 'tis the province of Sam,
'Deed the fate of each victimised Useful Young Man!

If we're late at the dance, and no coach to be had,
There's Sam! the dear fellow! the exquisite lad!
He'll search all the stands in the town, but he'll gain
A coach for his friends—though it 's pelting with rain
Oh! such are the *pleasures*—deny it who can—
That fall to the lot of a Useful Young Man!

To be nice about trifles is not over wise;
Where's the churl that finds favour in woman's bright
     eyes?
To be nice about trifles, is trifling with folly,
For the right end of life is but left to be jolly;
So I'll make up. my mind just to stick to this plan,
And FAG *out* my *terms* as a Useful Young Man.

                       W. COLLIER.

MADRIGAL OF THE SEASONS.

SPRING MORN.

'Tis merry on a fair Spring morn,
When hush'd is ev'ry ruder wind,
And Nature, like a mother kind,
Smiles joyous on her babe just born:
When sparkling dew is on the ground,
And flowrets gay are budding round,
And Hope is heard in ev'ry sound,
'Tis merry, oh, 'tis merry!

SUMMER NOON.

'Tis merry on a Summer's noon,
When Zephyr comes with balmy kiss,
And wakes the drowsy earth to bliss,
By gently breathing Love's own tune:
When leaves are green, and skies are blue,
And waters of a golden hue,
And ev'ry glance brings beauties new,
'Tis merry, oh, 'tis merry!

AUTUMN EVE.

'Tis merry on an Autumn eve,
When birds sing farewell to the sun,
And, corn well sheaved, and labour done,
The fields the healthful reapers leave :
When those whom daylight keeps afar
May meet beneath the vesper star
Without one fear their joy to mar,
'Tis merry, oh, 'tis merry !

WINTER NIGHT.

'Tis merry on a Winter's night,
When fast descends the deep'ning snow,
And o'er the heath the shrill winds blow,
To watch the crackling faggot's light :
When spicy wine and nut-brown ale,
Give zest to each rare Christmas tale,
And song, and joke, and laugh prevail,
'Tis merry, oh, 'tis merry !

SIEGE OF BELGRADE.

An Austrian, army, awfully arrayed,
Boldly by battery besieged Belgrade ;
Cossack commanders cannonading come,
Dealing destruction's devastating doom.
Every endeavour engineers essay
For fame, for fortune,—fighting, furious fray :
Generals 'gainst generals grapple—gracious God!
How honours Heaven heroic hardihood !
Infuriate, indiscriminate in ill,
Kinsmen kill kinsmen,—kinsmen kindred kill !
Labour low levels loftiest, longest lives ;
Men march 'mid mounds, 'mid moles, 'mid murderous
    mines.
Now noisy, noxious numbers notice nought
Of outward obstacles opposing ought :
Poor patriots, partly purchased, partly pressed,
Quite quaking, quickly quarter, quarter quest.
Reason returns, religious right redounds,
Suwarrow stops such sanguinary sounds :
Truce to thee Turkey—triumph to thy train !
Unjust, unwise, unmerciful Ukraine !

Vanish vain victory! vanish victory vain!
Why wish we warfare? Wherefore welcome we
Xerxes, Ximenes, Xanthus, Xaviere?
Yield, ye youths! ye yeomen, yield your yell!
Zeno's, Zarpatus', Zoroaster's zeal,
And all attracting—arms against appeal.

THE DOUBLE BARREL.

SEPTEMBER the first on the moorland hath burst,
    And already with jocund carol
Each NIMROD of NOUSE hurries off to the grouse,
    And has shouldered his DOUBLE BARREL;
For well doth he ken, as he hies through the glen,
    That scanty will be *his* laurel
                Who hath not
                On the spot
        (Should he miss a first shot)
    Some resource in a DOUBLE BARREL.

'Twas the Goddess of Sport, in her woodland court,
    DIANA, first taught this moral,
Which the Goddess of Love soon adopted, and strove
    To improve on the " double barrel."
Hence her CUPID, we know, put two strings to his bow;
    And she laughs, when two lovers quarrel,
                At the lot
                Of the sot
        Who, to soothe him, han't got
    The resource of a DOUBLE BARREL.

Nay, the hint was too good to lie hid in the wood,
    Or to lurk in two lips of coral ;
Hence the God of the Grape (who his betters would ape)
    Knows the use of a DOUBLE BARREL.
His escutcheon he decks with a double XX,
    And his blithe *October* carol
               Follows up
               With the sup
        Of a flowing ale-cup
September's DOUBLE BARREL.

                                FATHER PROUT.

FRIAR LAURENCE AND JULIET.

Friar.

Who is calling Friar Laurence?
    —Madam Juliet! how d'ye do?
Dear me—talk of the—beg pardon—
    I've been talking about *you.*
Mistress Montagu, they tell me
    You on Thursday mean to wed!
It is strange you never told me
    That poor Mister M. was dead!

Juliet.

M.'s alive! yet County Paris
    I'm to marry, people say!
(I shall marry the whole county
    If I go on in this way:)
Once you've wedded me already,
    If I wed again, you see,
Though in *you* a *little* error,
    'Twill be very *big o' me.*

Friar.

'Pon my life, it's very awkward!
　I'll on some expedient hit;
If you'll find me ready money,
　I will find you ready wit:
I can't let you wed a second
　Ere I know the first has died;
Think of faggots! for such deeds, ma'am,
　Holy friars have been fried!

Juliet.

'Tan't my wish, sir, nor intention,—
　Any scheme of yours I'll hail;
To escape from County Paris,
　Put me in the county jail:
Kill me dead! and make me food for
　Earthworm, viper, toad, or rat;
Make a widower of Ro-me-
　-O,—('twill *hurt* me to do that!)

Friar.

If you've really resolution
　That your life-blood should be spilt,
I will save you, for I'll have you
　Not quite killed, but merely *kilt:*
Could you in a vault be buried—
　Horizontal—in a niche?
And of death so good a copy,
　None could find out which is which?

Juliet.

I would vault into a vault, sir,
  With a dead man in his shroud;
I'd do any dirty work, sir
  Though my family's so proud!
I'll do whatsoe'er you bid me,
  'Till you say I've done enough;
Nay, sir, much as I dislike it,
  I'll take 'poticary's stuff!

Friar.

Then go home, ma'am, and be merry;
  Say that Paris you will wed;
Tell your nurse you've got a headache,
  And go quietly to bed:
Ask for something warm,—some negus,
  Grog, or gruel, or egg-flip,
Put in this, and then drink quickly,—
  'Tis so nauseous if you sip.

Juliet.

Give, oh! give me quick the phial,
  From the trial I'll not shrink,—
Is it shaken when it's taken?
  Gracious me! it's black as ink!
There's no fear, I trust, of failure?—
  No—I doubt not its effect;
From your conversation's *tenor*
  No base phial I expect.

K

Friar.

You will have the bridegroom *follow*,
   Where he generally *leads;*
'Stead of hymeneal flowers,
   He will wear sepulchral weeds:
I to Romeo will quickly
   Write a letter by the post;
He will wake you, and should Paris
   Meet you,—say you are your ghost!

Juliet.

'Tis an excellent arrangement,
   As you bid me I will act;
But within the tomb, dear friar,
   Place a basket nicely pack'd;—
Just a loaf, a tongue, a chicken,
   Port and sherry, and some plums;
It will *really* be a comfort
   Should I wake e'er Romeo comes!

THE PHANTOM SHIP.

" My child! my child! come down to rest!
　　The day has long been past:
Sleep in thy mother's blessing blest,
　　The night is waning fast."

" Dear mother, let us linger here,
　　The moon shines forth so bright;
The starry sky is all so clear,
　　It does not look like night;

" And all around the waveless sea
　　In glassy smoothness lies,
And on it flows so silently,
　　It bids no murmur rise.

" And as I bend me o'er the side,
　　Methinks I trace below
The ocean's depths, their jewel'd pride,
　　A fair and goodly show;

" The beauties that the Mighty One
　　Hath lavish'd there from old;
The treasures that from earth have gone,
　　The diamond and the gold;
　　　　　K 2

" The glitt'ring and the sighed-for things
   Man seeks 'mid care and strife,
And ocean from him hardly wrings
   With wreck or loss of life ;

" The silver fish that gently glide,
   Or glance in gladsome play,
Filling with life the crystal tide,
   How fair and bright are they !

" And see ! and see ! approaching now,
   A ship of pride and cost ;
The weary crew asleep below,
   The helmsman at his post.

" No rushing wind compels her course,
   No tempest raves around ;
She moves as by some unseen force,
   Whilst all is still around.

" She ruffles not the glassy tide,
   Bends not her stately mast,
No fretful billows chafe her side,
   No foam is round her cast.

" She leaves no track upon the sea,
   No furrow in her wake;
But on, and on unmurmuringly
   Her silent way doth take."

" Come down to rest, my gentle child !
   Thou dost not see aright:
Thy words are as a sleeper's wild;
   There is no ship in sight."

"Yes, yes, the stately ship is near,
    And all my words are true;
A child looks on her mother dear,
    As I look up at you.

"And now I hear the soften'd tone,
    And gentle words of love;
And now they sound as though mine own,
    And now as thine they move."

"Hush! hush, my child! no ship is nigh,
    No voices canst thou hear:
A shadowy cloud is in thine eye,
    The breeze is in thine ear."

"No shadowy cloud is in mine eye;
    No breeze is in mine ear;
The stately ship is passing by,
    And gentle tones I hear.

"One walks the deck with weary pace,
    As though he sigh'd for sleep;
The steersman turns an anxious face
    Across the waveless deep.

"And two beside the steersman stand,
    A mother and her child:
One holds, as now, I hold your hand,
    One smiles as late you smiled."

"My child! my child! it cannot be!"
    Thus forth the mother broke;
And yet she answer'd shudd'ringly,
    And trembled as she spoke.

"My child! my child! it cannot be!
  Vessel save ours is none.
Look! o'er the still unbounded sea
  We take our way alone."

"Her words are true," the steersman said;
  To youth it has been given
To speak, without deceit or dread,
  The changeless will of Heav'n.

"Your child the phantom ship hath seen!
  Ere set to-morrow's sun,
No trace will rest where we have been,
  Our mortal course be run."

Before the morrow's sun went down,
  There was nor trace nor mark,
To show where o'er the sea had gone
  That strong and gallant bark.

No shatter'd spars, no riven mast
  Were floating o'er the waves:
None knew when those from life had past,
  Who slept in wat'ry graves.

Yet all she bore across the waves
  Had pass'd from human sight,
With none to weep above their graves,
  Or read the funeral rite.

                              ELLEN PICKERING.

POETICAL EPISTLE FROM FATHER PROUT TO BOZ.

I.

A RHYME! a rhyme! from a distant clime,—from the
    gulph of the Genoese:
O'er the rugged scalps of the Julian Alps, dear Boz!
    I send you these,
To light the *Wick* your candlestick holds up, or, should
    you list,
To usher in the yarn you spin concerning Oliver Twist.

II.

Immense applause you've gained, oh, Boz! through
    continental Europe;
You'll make Pickwick œcumenick; of fame you have a
    sure hope:
For here your books are found, gadzooks! in greater
    luxe than any
That have issued yet, hotpress'd or wet, from the types
    of GALIGNANI.

III.

But neither when you sport your pen, oh, potent mirth-
    compeller !
Winning our hearts " in monthly parts," can Pickwick
    or Sam Weller
Cause us to weep with pathos deep, or shake with laugh
    spasmodical,
As when you drain your copious vein for Bentley's
    periodical.

IV.

Folks all enjoy your Parish Boy,— so truly you depict
    him ;
But I, alack! while thus you track your stinted poor-
    law's victim,
Must think of some poor nearer home, poor who, unheeded
    perish,
By squires despoiled, by " patriots" gulled,—I mean the
    starving Irish.

V.

Yet there's no dearth of Irish mirth, which, to a mind
    of feeling,
Seemeth to be the Helot's glee before the Spartan
    reeling ;
Such gloomy thought o'ercometh not the glee of England's
    humour,
Thrice happy isle ! long may the smile of genuine joy
    illume her !

VI.

Write on, young sage! still o'er the page pour forth the
    flood of fancy;
Wax still more droll, wave o'er the soul Wit's wand of
    necromancy.
Behold! e'en now around your brow th' immortal laurel
    thickens;
Yea, SWIFT or STERNE might gladly learn a thing or
    two from DICKENS.

VII.

A rhyme! a rhyme! from a distant clime,— a song from
    the sunny south!
A goodly theme, so Boz but deem the measure not un-
    couth,
Would, for thy sake, that " PROUT" could make his bow
    in fashion finer,
" *Partant*" (from thee) "*pour la Syrie,*" for Greece and
    Asia Minor.

                          FATHER PROUT.

A SONG FOR A STORMY NIGHT.

THE winds without,
In their midnight rout,
Howl through our key-hole drearily;
But sweet is our mirth,
Round the social hearth,
When circles the wine-cup cheerily.
With a heigh ho ! nonnie no !
And a heigh ho ! nonnie nee !

Fill up the bowl,
And stir up the coal,
Let no hour languish wearily !
We've right good cheer,
And a welcome here,
And a big log crackling cheerily.
With a heigh ho ! nonnie no !
And a heigh ho ! nonnie nee !

Yet amid our glee
Perchance there be,
Hearts near us beating drearily;

All nipp'd by the cold,
Some traveller old,
May be trudging through snow-drifts wearily.
With a heigh ho! nonnie no!
And a heigh ho! nonnie nee!

Show then a light
From our window to-night,
Let it gleam to guide him cheerily:
We've a chair and a jug,
And a corner snug,
When he comes to our door so wearily.
With a heigh ho! nonnie no!
And a heigh ho! nonnie nee!

There let it burn,
While each in turn,
As he raises his full cup cheerily:
Drinks " Joy and zest,
" And a pleasant rest
" To all who wander wearily."
With a heigh ho! nonnie no!
And a heigh ho! nonnie nee!

Never shall it be said,
That we, well fed,
By our fire-side singing cheerily,
Could forget this night,
The bitter plight
Of the thousands pining wearily.
With a heigh ho! nonnie no!
And a heigh ho! nonnie nee!

Let us open the door
To the old and poor,
They shall all be welcome cheerily!
While there's bite or sup
On our board or cup,
They shall never pass by us wearily.
With a heigh ho! nonnie no!
And a heigh ho! nonnie nee!

CHARLES MACKAY.

SARDANAPALUS.

SARDANAPALUS was Nineveh's king;
And, if all be quite true that the chroniclers sing,
    Loved his song and his glass,
    And was given, alas!
    Not only to bigamy,
    Nor even to trigamy,
But (I shudder to think on't) to rankest polygamy :
For his sweethearts and wives were so vast in amount,
They'd take you a week or two *only* to count!

One morning his Majesty jump'd out of bed,
And hitting his valet a rap on the head,
By way of a joke, " Salamenes," he said,
    " Go, proclaim to the court,
    " 'Tis our will to resort,
    " By way of a lark,
    " To our palace and park
" On the banks of Euphrates, and there, with our wives,
" Sing, dance, and get fuddled, for once in our lives ;
" So, bid our state-rulers and nobles, d'ye see,
" Hie all to our banquet not later than three,
" And prepare for a long night of jollity."
" Very good," said the valet ; then eager and hot
On his errand, ducked thrice, and was off like a shot.

When the court heard these orders, with rapture elate,
They adjourn'd all the business of church and of state,
> And hurried off, drest
> Each man in his best;
> While the women, sweet souls,
> Went with them by shoals,
Some in gigs, some in cabs, some on horseback so gay,
And some in an omnibus hired for the day.—
(If busses in those days were not to be seen,
All I can say is, they *ought* to have been.)—
> Like a torrent, the throng
> Roll'd briskly along,
Cheering the way with jest, laughter, and song,
To the Banquetting Hall, where the last of the group
Arrived, by good luck, just in time for the soup.

The guests set to work in superlative style,
And his Majesty, equally busy the while,
Encouraged their efforts with many a smile.
> The High Priest was the first,
> Who seemed ready to burst;
> (For the ladies so shy,
> They swigged on the sly!)
But, proud of his prowess, he scorn'd to give o'er,
'Till at length with a hiccup he fell on the floor,
> Shouting out, 'mid his qualms,
> That verse in the Psalms,
Which saith (but it surely can't mean a whole can!)
That "Wine maketh merry the heart of a man."

While thus they sate tippling, peers, prelates, and all,
And music's sweet voice echoed light through the Hall;
> His Majesty rose,
> Blew his eloquent nose,

And exclaiming, by way of exordium, "Here goes!"
Made a speech which produced a prodigious sensation,
Greatly, of course, to the King's delectation:
One courtier, o'erpower'd by its humour and wit,
Held both his fat sides, as if fearing a fit;
While another kept crying, "Oh, God, I shall split!"
(So when a great publisher cracks a small joke,
His authors at table are ready to choke.)
And all, with the lungs of a hurricane, swore
They had ne'er heard so droll an oration before,
With the single exception of one silly fellow,
Who not being, doubtless, sufficiently mellow,
Refused to applaud, or to join in the laughter,
And was hang'd for a traitor just ten minutes after.

By this time Dan Phœbus in ocean had sunk,
And the guests were all getting exceedingly drunk,
 When, behold! at the door
 There was heard a loud roar,
And in rush'd a messenger covered with gore,
Who bawl'd out, addressing the Head of the State,
" If your Majesty pleases, the Foe's at the gate,
" And threaten to kick up the Devil's own din,
" If you do not surrender, and bid them come in;
 "The mob, too, has risen,
 "And let out of prison,
" With the jailor's own keys (but it's no fault of *his'n*),
" Some hundreds of burglars, and fences, and prigs,
" Who are playing all sorts of queer antics and rigs;
" Already they've fir'd up one church for a beacon,—
" Hocussed a bishop, and burked an archdeacon,
" And swear, if you don't give them plenty of grog,
" They'll all become Chartists, and go the whole hog!"

Scarce had he ended, when hark! with a squall,
A second grim herald pops into the Hall,
  And, " Woe upon woe!
  " The desperate foe,"
Quoth he, " Have forced open the gates of the town,
" And are knocking by scores the rich citizens down;
  " As I pass'd with bent brow,
  " By the Law Courts just now,
" Lo, sixty attorneys lay smash'd in a row,
" Having just taken wing for the regions below,
" (When lawyers are dead, none can doubt where they go,)
" 'Mid the cheers of each snob, who sung out, as he past,
" ' So, the scamps have gone home to their father at
   last!' "

Oh! long grew the face of each guest at this tale,
The men they turn'd red, and the women turn'd pale;
But redder and paler they turn'd when they heard
The more terrible tidings of herald the third!—
In he bounced with a visage as black as a crow's,
And a mulberry tinge on the tip of his nose;
  He'd a rent in his breeches,
  A tergo, the which is
(As Smollett has taught us long since to believe*)
Not the pleasantest sight for the daughters of Eve;
And he shook like a leaf, as thus hoarsely he spake
In the gruff and cacophonous tones of a drake—
  " The town's all on fire,
  " Hut, palace and spire
" Are blazing as fast as the foe can desire:
  " Such crashing and smashing,
  " And sparkling and darkling!

 * Vide Miss Tabitha Bramble, in Smollett's " Humphrey Clinker."

" Such squalling, and bawling, and sprawling,
" And jobbing, and robbing, and mobbing!
" Such kicking and licking, and racing and chasing,
" Blood-spilling and killing, and slaughtering and quar-
    tering !
" You'd swear that old Nick, with Belphegor his clerk,
" And Moloch his cad, were abroad on a lark !"

" Here's a go !" said the King, staring wild like a bogle
At these tidings, and wiping his eyes with his fogle;
    " 'Tis vain now to run for
    " Our lives, for we're done for ;
" So, away with base thoughts of submission or flight,
" Let's all, my brave boys, die like heroes to-night ;
" Raise high in this Hall a grand funeral pile,
" Then fire it, and meet our death-doom with a smile !"
He ceased, when a courtier replied in low tone,
" If your Majesty pleases, I'd rather live on ;
" For, although you may think me as dull as a post,
" Yet I can't say I've any great taste for a roast ;
" 'Tis apt to disorder one's system ; and so,
" Good night to your Majesty—D.I.O. !"
So saying, he made for the door and rush'd out,
While quick at his heels rushed the rest of the rout,
    Leaving all alone,
    The King on his throne,
With a torch in one hand which he waved all abroad,
And a glass in the other, as drunk as a Lord !

That night, from the Hall, late so joyous, there broke,
Spreading wide in 'mid air, a vast column of smoke ;
    While, higher and higher,
    Blazed up the red fire,
As it blazed from Queen Dido's funeral pyre !—

L

Hark to the crash, as roof, pillar, and wall
Bend—rock—and down in thunder fall!
Hark to the roar of the flames, as they show
Heaven and earth alike in a glow!
The hollow wind sobs through the ruins, as though
'Twere hymning his dirge, who, an hour ago,
Was a King in all a King's array;
But now lies, a blackened clod of clay,
In that Hall whose splendours have past away,
Save in old tradition, for ever and aye!

THE MEMORY OF THE POETS.

THE fame of those sweet bards, whose fancies lie,
  Like glorious clouds on summer's holiest even
  Fringing the west, upon the skirts of heaven,
And sprinkled o'er with hues of rainbow dye,
Is not of trumpet sound, nor strives to vie
With martial notes sublime.—From ages gone,
In most angelic strain it lengthens on,
  Earth's greenest bowers with fresh delight to fill,
Heard, breathing from the silence of the sky,
  Or trembling in the joy of gushing rill,
Or whispering o'er the lake's unrippled breast,
  Till its last earthly melodies are still ;—
Hush'd, 'mid the joys of immortality,
In the calm bosom of eternal rest.

T. N. TALFOURD.

BURNS AND BERANGER.

I.

Is there,
For honest poverty,
That hangs his head
   And a' that?
The coward slave
We pass him by,
   We dare be poor for a' that:
   For a' that, and a' that,
Our toils obscure,
   And a' that;
The rank is but
The guinea's stamp,
   The MAN's the gowd for a' that.

II.

What! though
On homely fare we dine,
Wear hodden grey,
   And a' that;
Give fools their silks,
And knaves their wine,
   A man's a MAN for a' that:
   For a' that, for a' that,

BURNS AND BERANGER.

I.

Quoi! Pauvre honnête
Baisser la tête?
Quoi! rougir de la sorte?
Que l'âme basse
S'éloigne et passe
Nous—soyons gueux! n'importe
Travail obscur—
N'importe!
Quand l'or est pur
N'importe!
Qu'il ne soit point
Marqué au coin
D'un noble rang—qu'importe!

II.

Quoiqu'on dût faire
Bien maigre chère
Et vêtir pauvre vêtement;
Aux sots leur soie,
Leur vin, leur joie;
Ca fait-il L'HOMME? eh, nullement!
Luxe et grandeur—
Qu'importe!

Their tinsel show,
    And a' that ;
The honest man,
Though e'er so poor,
    Is king o' men for a' that.

III.

Ye see
Yon birkie, ca'd a lord,
Wha struts and stares,
    And a' that ;
Though hundreds worship
At his word,
    He's but a coof for a' that:
    For a' that, for a' that,
His riband, star,
    And a' that ;
The man of
Independent mind
    Can look and laugh at a' that.

IV.

A king
Can make a belted knight,
A marquis, duke,
    And a' that ;
But an HONEST MAN
's aboon his might,
    Guid faith he manna fa' that.
    For a' that, for a' that,

Train et splendeur—
   Qu'importe !
Cœurs vils et creux !
Un noble gueux
Vaut toute la cohorte !

III.

Voyez ce fat—
   Un vain éclat
L'entoure, et on l'encense,
   Mais après tout
   Ce n'est qu'un fou,—
Un sot, quoiqu'il en pense ;
   Terre et maison,
     Qu'il pense—
   Titre et blazon,
     Qu'il pense—
   Or et ducats,
   Non ! ne font pas
La vraie indépendence !

IV.

Un roi peut faire
   Duc, dignitaire,
Comte et marquis, journellement ;
   Mais ce qu'on nomme
   Un HONNETE HOMME,
Le peut-il faire ? eh, nullement !
   Tristes faveurs !
     Réellement ;

Their dignities,
   And a' that;
The pith o' sense
And pride o' warth
   Are higher ranks than a' that.

V.

Then let us pray
That come it may—
As come it will
   For a' that—
That sense and warth,
O'er all the earth,
   May bear the gree, and a' that
   For a' that, and a' that,
It's coming yet,
   For a' that,
That man to man,
The warld a' o'er,
Shall brothers be, for a' that.

Pauvres honneurs !
   Réellement ;
Le fier maintien
Des gens de bien
Leur manque essentiellement.

V.

Or faisons vœu
   Qu'à tous, sous peu,
Arrive un jour de jugement ;—
   Amis, ce jour
   Aura son tour,
J'en prends, j'en prends, l'engagement.
   Espoir et en-
     couragement,
   Aux pauvres gens
    Soulagement ;
  'Lors sur la terre
  Vivrons en frères,
Et librement, et sagement !

FATHER PROUT.

THE VOICES OF THE NIGHT.

WHEN the hours of day are number'd,
  And the voices of the night
Wake the better soul, that slumber'd,
  To a holy calm delight.

Ere the evening lamps are lighted,
  And, like phantoms grim and tall,
Shadows from the fitful fire-light
  Dance upon the parlour wall,

Then the forms of the departed
  Enter at the open door!
The beloved ones, the true-hearted,
  Come to visit me once more.

He, the young and strong, who cherish'd
  Noble longings for the strife!
By the road-side fell, and perish'd,
  Weary with the march of life!

They, the holy ones, and weakly,
  Who the cross of suffering wore,
Folded their pale hands so meekly,
  Spake with us on earth no more!

And with them the being beauteous,
  Who unto my youth was given,
More than all things else to love me,
  And is now a saint in heaven.

With a slow and noiseless footstep
  Comes that messenger divine,
Takes the vacant chair beside me,
  Lays her gentle hand in mine.

And she sits and gazes at me,
  With those deep and tender eyes,
Like the stars, so still and saint-like,
  Looking downward from the skies.

Utter'd not, yet comprehended,
  Is the spirit's voiceless prayer;
Soft rebukes, in blessings ended,
  Breathing from those lips of air.

Oh ! though oft depress'd and lonely,
  All my fears are laid aside,
If I but remember only
  Such as they have lived and died.

                    H. W. LONGFELLOW.

THOUGHTS ON PATRONS, PUFFS, AND OTHER MATTERS.

IN AN EPISTLE FROM TOM MOORE TO SAMUEL ROGERS.

WHAT, *thou,* my friend! a man of rhymes,
   And, better still, a man of guineas,
To talk of " patrons," in these times,
   When authors thrive, like spinning-jenneys,
And Arkwright's twist and Bulwer's page
Alike may laugh at patronage !

No, no,—those times are past away,
   When, doom'd in upper floors to star it,
The bard inscribed to lords his lay,—
   Himself, the while, my Lord Mountgarret.
No more he begs, with air dependent,
His " little bark may sail attendant"
   Under some lordly skipper's steerage ;
But launched triumphant in the Row,
Or ta'en by Murray's self in tow,
   Cuts both *Star Chamber* and the Peerage.

Patrons, indeed ! when scarce a sail
Is whisked from England by the gale,

But bears on board some authors, shipp'd
For foreign shores, all well equipp'd
With proper book-making machinery,
To sketch the morals, manners, scenery,
Of all such lands as they shall see,
Or *not* see, as the case may be :—
It being enjoined on all who go
To study first Miss M*********,
And learn from her the method true,
To *do* one's books,—and readers, too.
For so this nymph of *nous* and nerve
Teaches mankind " How to Observe ;"
And, lest mankind at all should swerve,
Teaches them also " *What* to Observe."

No, no, my friend,—it can't be blink'd,—
The Patron is a race extinct ;
As dead as any Megatherion
That ever Buckland built a theory on.
Instead of bartering, in this age,
Our praise for pence and patronage,
We, authors, now, more prosperous elves,
Have learned to patronise ourselves ;
And since all-potent Puffing 's made
The life of song, the soul of trade,
More frugal of our praises grown,
Puff no one's merits but our own.

Unlike those feeble gales of praise
Which critics blew in former days,
Our modern puffs are of a kind
That truly, really *raise the wind ;*

And since they've fairly set in blowing,
We find them the best *trade*-winds going.
'Stead of frequenting paths so slippy
As her old haunts near Aganippe,
The Muse, now, taking to the till,
Has opened shop on Ludgate Hill,
(Far handier than the Hill of Pindus,
As seen from bard's back attic windows) ;
And swallowing there without cessation
Large draughts (*at sight*) of inspiration,
Touches the *notes* for each new theme,
While still fresh " *change* comes o'er her dream."

What Steam is on the deep,—and more,—
Is the vast power of Puff on shore ;
Which jumps to glory's future tenses
Before the present ev'n commences ;
And makes " immortal" and " divine" of us
Before the world has read one line of us.

In old times, when the God of Song
Drove his own two-horse team along,
Carrying inside a bard or two,
Book'd for posterity " all through ;"—
Their luggage, a few close-packed rhymes,
(Like yours, my friend,) for after-times,—
So slow the pull to Fame's abode,
That folks oft slept upon the road ;—
And Homer's self, sometimes, they say,
Took to his night-cap on the way.

Ye Gods ! how different is the story
With our new galloping sons of glory,

Who, scorning all such slack and slow time,
Dash to posterity in *no* time!
Raise but one general blast of Puff
To start your author,—that's enough.
In vain the critics, set to watch him,
Try at the starting post to catch him;
He's off—the puffers carry it hollow—
The critics, if they please, may follow.
Ere *they* 've laid down their first positions,
He's fairly blown through six editions!
In vain doth Edinburgh dispense
Her blue and yellow pestilence,—
(That plague so awful in my time
To young and touchy sons of rhyme,)
The Quarterly, at three months' date,
To catch th' Unread One, comes too late;
And nonsense, littered in a hurry,
Becomes " immortal," spite of Murray.

But, bless me!—while I thus keep fooling,
I hear a voice cry, " Dinner 's cooling."
That postman, too, (who, truth to tell,
'Mong men of letters bears the bell,)
Keeps ringing, ringing, so infernally
That I *must* stop,—

Yours sempiternally.

TOM MOORE.

RICHELIEU; OR, THE CONSPIRACY.

Cardinal Richelieu was Premier of France;
He was keen as a fox, and you read at a glance,
In his phiz so expressive of malice and trick,
That he'd much of the nature ascribed to Old Nick;
If a noble e'er dared to oppose him, instead
Of confuting his lordship, he whipped off his head:
      He fixed his grim paw
      Upon church, state, and law,
With as much cool assurance as ever you saw;
      With his satire's sharp sting
      He badgered the King,
        Bullied his brother,
        Transported his mother,
And (what is a far more astonishing case)
Not only pronounced him an ass to his face,
But made love to his Queen, and because she declined
His advances, gave out she was wrong in her mind!

Now the nobles of France, and still more the poor King,
Disliked, as was natural, this sort of thing;
The former felt shocked that plebeian beholders
Should see a peer's head fly so oft from his shoulders,

And the latter was constantly kept upon thorns
By the Cardinal's wish to endow him with horns;
    Thus rankling with spite,
    A party one night
Of noblemen met, and determined outright
    (So enraged were the crew)
    First, to murder Richelieu,
And, if needful, despatch all his partizans too:
    Next to league with the foes
    Of the King, and depose
The fat-pated monarch himself, for a fool
Rebellion ne'er uses, except as a tool.

On the night that Richelieu was thus marked out for
    slaughter,
He chanced to be tippling cold brandy and water
With one Joseph, a Capuchin priest—a sly dog,
And by no means averse to the comforts of grog,
As you saw by his paunch, which seemed proud to reveal
How exactly it looked like a fillet of veal.
They laughed and they quaffed, 'till the Capuchin's nose
('T was a thorough bred snub) grew as red as a rose;
And, whenever it chanced that his patron, Richelieu,
Cracked a joke, even though it was not very new;
And pointed his smart conversational squibs,
By a slap on Joe's back, or a peg in his ribs ;
The priest, who was wonderfully shrewd as a schemer,
Would bellow with ecstacy, "'Gad, that's a *screamer !*"
Thus they chatted away, a rare couple well met,
And were just tuning up for a pious duet,
    When in rushed a spy,
    With his wig all awry,
And a very equivocal drop in his eye,

M

Who cried (looking blue
As he turned to Richelieu)
" Oh, my lord, lack-a-day !
Here's the devil to pay,
For a dozen fierce nobles are coming this way ;
One of whom, an old stager, as sharp as a lizard,
Has threatened to stick a long knife in your gizzard ;
While the rest of the traitors, I say it with pain,
Have already sent off a despatch to Spain,
To state that his Majesty 's ceased to reign,
And order the troops all home again."

When his Eminence heard these tidings, " Go,"
He said, in the blandest of tones, to Joe,
" And if you can catch
The traitor's despatch,
I swear—no matter how rich it be—
You shall have, dear Joe, the very next see !"—
(*Nota bene*, whenever Old Nick is wishing
To enjoy the prime sport of parson-fishing,
He always, like Richelieu, cunning and quick,
Baits with a good fat bishoprick !)

No sooner had Joe turned his sanctified back—
I hardly need add he was off in a crack—
Than up the grand stairs rushed the murderous pack,
Whereon the sly Cardinal, tipping the wink
To the spy, who was helping himself to some drink
At a side-table, said,
" Tell 'em I'm dead !"
Then flew to his chamber, and popped into bed.
" What, dead ?" roared the traitors. " I stuck him myself,
With a knife which I snatched from the back-kitchen
shelf,"

Was the ready reply
Of the quick-witted spy,—

Who in matters of business ne'er stuck at a lie.
" Huzza, then, for office!" cried one, and cried all,
" The government's ours by the Cardinal's fall,"

And, so saying, the crew
Cut a caper or two,

Gave the spy a new four-penny piece and withdrew.

Next day all the papers were full of the news,
Little dreaming the Cardinal's death was a *ruse;*
In parliament, too, lots of speeches were made,
And poetical tropes by the bushel displayed ;
The deceased was compared to Ulysses and Plato,
To a star, to a cherub, an eagle, and Cato ;
And 't was gravely proposed by some gents in committee
To erect him a statue of gold in the city ;
But when an economist, caustic and witty,

Asked, " Gentlemen, pray,
Who is to pay ?"

The committee, as if by galvanic shock jolted,
Looked horrified, put on their castors, and bolted !

Meanwhile the shrewd traitors repaired in a bevy,
All buoyant with hope, to his Majesty's levee,
When, lo ! as the King with anxiety feigned,
Was beginning to speak of the loss he'd sustained,

In strutted Richelieu,
And the Capuchin too,

Which made each conspirator shake in his shoe ;
One whispered a by-stander, looking him through,

M 2

" By Jove, I can scarcely believe it! can you ?"
Another cried, " Dam'me, I thought 't was a *do !*"
And a third muttered faintly, o'ercome by his **fear,**
" Talk of the devil, and he's sure to appear ?"

When the King, who at first hardly trusted his eyes,
Had somewhat recovered the shock of surprize,
   He shook his thick head
   At the Cardinal, and said,
In tones in which something of anger still lurked,
" How 's this ? Why, God bless me, I thought you were
   burked !"
" Had such been my fate," quickly answered Richelieu,
" Had they made me a *subject*, the rascally crew,
My liege, they'd have soon made another of you.
Look here !" and he pulled out the nobles' despatch,
Who felt that for once they had met their match,
   And exclaiming, " 'Od rot 'em,
   The scoundrels, I've got 'em !"
Read it out to the King from the top to the bottom.

Next morning twelve scaffolds, with axes of steel,
Adorned the fore-court of the sprightly Bastille ;
And at midnight twelve nobles, by way of a bed,
Lay snug in twelve coffins, each *minus* a head—
A thing not uncommon with nobles, 't is said.
   Priest Joe got his see,
   And delighted was he,
For the bishoprick suited his taste to a T ;
And Richelieu, the stern, unforgiving, and clever,
Bullied king, church, and people, more fiercely than ever !

And the moral is this—if, conspiring in flocks,
Silly geese will presume to play tricks with a fox,
And strive by finesse to get rid of the pest,
' They must always expect to come off second best!

SONG OF A RIFLEMAN.

I.

I'D be a Rifleman, gallant and gay,
   Longest and last at the banquet or ball;
Waltzing, quadrilling, and flirting away,
   Constant to none, yet a favourite with all.
True to the opera, concert, or play,
   I'd never languish for wedlock's dull thrall;
I'd be a Rifleman, gallant and gay,
   Constant to none, yet a favourite with all.

II.

Oh! from a tailor some cloth could I wheedle,
   Some dark-coloured cloth of that beautiful green,
I'd set about, with my scissors and needle,
   As dashing a jacket as ever was seen.
What matter to me though I write or read ill,
   Though a truant at school, and at college I've been
Oh! from a tailor some cloth could I wheedle,
   I'd have a coat of that beautiful green.
I'd be a Rifleman, I'd be a Rifleman,
   Drest in a coat of that beautiful green.

III.

What though you tell me the jacket of scarlet
   Is forwarder seen when the battle's begun?
Yet the Rifleman sure you ought never to snarl at,
   For he'll safely return when that battle is done.
Others in conflict, while fighting may fall at
   The stroke of a sabre or shot of a gun;
But the Rifleman laughs at the jacket of scarlet,
   Perch'd in a tree till the battle is done.
I'd be a Rifleman, I'd be a Rifleman,
   Flirting in peace-time when battle is done.

            The Author of " VINCENT EDEN."

INVITATION TO AN EVENING WALK.

"There is hardly anything gives me a more sensible delight than the enjoyment of a cool still evening, after the uneasiness of a hot sultry day."—*Spectator*.

COME up the hill, to meet the moon—
She'll leave her daylight slumber soon,
And over mountain, over dale,
Weep her dewy lustre pale!

Come up the hill, and hear the flowers
Rustling in their heathy bowers;
Closing some, with close of day,
Waking more to moonlight ray!

Come up the hill, and list the breeze,
Full of mingled melodies,
Rising from the glens below,
Faintly sweet, as up we go!

Come up the hill, and smell the breath
Of the purple mountain-heath,
Sweeter than the painted flowers
Rear'd in artificial bowers!

Come up the hill, and joy with me,
In the mazy scenery
That below is sleeping calm,
Smiling beauty, breathing balm!

Come up the hill, and gaze with me
On the moon-besilver'd sea,
That so gently rocking moves
To cradle the young light it loves!

Come up the hill,—'tis nearer to
The fields of Heav'n, azure blue,
Where the spheral minstrels play
Music wild and sweet, for aye!

Come up the hill,—'t will give to thee
A view of deep eternity,
That in the valley's shorten'd ken
Is never known to minds of men!

Come up the hill—the waterfall
Is emblem, true to thee, of all:
'T is tranquil where it flows near Heaven—
'T is down, with Man,—its peace is riven!

J. A. WADE.

THE FOREST TREE.

Hail to the lone old forest tree,
　　Though past his leafy prime!
A type of England's past is he,—
　　A tale of her olden time.
He has seen her sons, for a thousand years,
　　Around him rise and fall;
But well his green old age he wears,
　　And still survives them all.
　　　　Then long may his safeguard the pride and care
　　　　　Of our children's children be;
　　　　And long may the axe and tempest spare
　　　　　The lone old forest tree!

The Norman baron his steed has rein'd,
　　And the pilgrim his journey stay'd,
And the toil-worn serf brief respite gain'd
　　In his broad and pleasant shade:
The friar and forester loved it well;
　　And hither the jocund horn,
And the solemn tone of the vesper bell,
　　On the evening breeze were borne.

Friar and forester, lord and slave,
　　Lie mouldering, side by side,

In the dreamless sleep of a nameless grave,
  Where revelling earthworms hide :
And Echo no longer wakes at the sound
  Of bugle or vesper chime ;
For castle and convent are ivy-bound
  By the ruthless hand of Time.

But gentle and few, with the stout old tree,
  Have the spoiler's dealings been ;
And the brook, as of old, is clear and free,
  And the turf beneath as green.
Thus Nature has scatter'd on every hand
  Her lessons, since earth began,
And long may her sylvan teacher stand,
  A check to the pride of man.
    And long may his safeguard the pride and care
      Of our children's children be ;
    Long, long may the axe and tempest spare
      The lone old forest tree !

                                        J. B. T.

THE EVENING STAR.

THE night is come, but not too soon ;
   And sinking silently,—
All silently,—the little Moon
   Drops down behind the sky.

There is no light in earth or heaven
   But the pale light of stars ;
And the first watch of night is given
   To the red planet Mars.

Is it the tender star of love ?
   The star of love and dreams ?
Oh no ! from that blue tent above
   A hero's armour gleams.

And earnest thoughts within me rise
   When I behold afar,
Suspended in the evening skies,
   The shield of that red star.

O star of strength ! I see thee stand
   And smile upon my pain ;
Thou beckonest with thy mailed hand,
   And I am strong again.

Within my soul there shines no light
   But the pale light of stars;
I give the first watch of the night
   To the red planet Mars!

The star of the unconquer'd will,
   He rises in my breast,—
Serene, and resolute, and still,
   And calm, and self-possess'd.

And thou, too, whosoe'er thou art,
   That readest this brief psalm,
As one by one thy hopes depart,
   Be resolute and calm.

O! fear not in a world like this,
   And thou shalt know ere long,
Know how sublime a thing it is
   To suffer and be strong!

                    H. W. LONGFELLOW.

SONG TO THE THAMES.

OF all the broad rivers that flow to the ocean,
   There's none to compare, native Thames! unto thee;
      And gladly for ever,
      Thou smooth-rolling river,
I'd dwell on thy green banks at fair Battersea.

'T was there I was born, and 't is there I will linger,
   And there shall the place of my burial be,
      If fortune, caressing,
      Will grant but one blessing,
The heart of the maiden of fair Battersea.

I seek not to wander by Tyber or Arno,
   Or castle-crown'd rivers in far Germanie;
      To me, Oh, far dearer,
      And brighter, and clearer,
The Thames as it rimples at fair Battersea.

Contentment and Hope, spreading charms all around
      them,
   Have hallow'd the spot since she smil'd upon me—
      O Love! thy joys lend us,
      O Fortune, befriend us,
We'll yet make an Eden of fair Battersea.

CHARLES MACKAY.

THE BLIND GIRL OF CASTEL CUILLE.

The sky was bright, the air was soft,
　　On good St. Joseph's eve,
When bursting from the orchard's stems
　　The snowy blossoms heave.

While, echoing from the mountain height
　　Of Castel Cuillé, rose
A strain of passing sweetness through
　　The valley's deep repose.

And loud and clear the cadence rung
　　As gay young voices bore
The burthen of that bridal hymn
　　Their fathers sang of yore.

" Pour your snowy blossoms forth,
　　Peach, and pear, and almond trees;
Hang your rosy garlands on,
　　Wave them with yon waving breeze.

" Mountain paths, and hedges wild,
　　Bloom, that never bloom'd before;
The bride of Castel Cuillé comes,
　　Fling your gifts her pathway o'er."

And now, where on that verging rock
　　Their careless steps alight,
A troop of fair and laughing girls
　　Arrest their giddy flight;

And, placed betwixt the earth and sky,
　　Like some bright angels sent,
They stood, and o'er the vale below
　　Their radiant glances bent.

But soon along the mountain's side
　　With joyous steps they bound,
Where tow'rds the woods of St. Amand
　　Their narrow pathway wound.

Why seek they thus with childish glee
　　St. Amand's laurel grove,
And poise their osier-baskets light
　　Their smiling heads above?

And why with youth's unsparing hand
　　Do these gay truants tear,
And hence in verdant heaps away
　　The shining foliage bear?

It is that Castel Cuillé's maids
　　Are ever wont to shed
Their leafy tribute o'er the path
　　Where bridal lovers tread :

And she, that laughing, blooming girl
　　Who, foremost, bounds along,
With dancing step and flying hair.
　　The thoughtless group among,

Is on the morrow's dawn in all
  The pomp of village pride,
To stand in Castel Cuillé's church
  Young Baptiste's willing bride.

And, wherefore, then, is Baptiste sad
  When all around is gay?
Was ever lover silent thus
  On eve of bridal day?

What ails thee, sullen bridegroom, say?
  Why wear so sad a brow?
Angèle is passing fair, and pure
  As yonder mountain snow.

Is it that near the mountain's foot,
  Where fast the streamlet glides,
The blind, the orphan Marguerite,
  The soldier's daughter, bides?

Baptiste had woo'd that gentle girl,
  Nor long had woo'd in vain,
The youth who fondly sought her love
  Full soon she loved again;

And much she loved him, deeply too;
  She cared for none beside,
Except her little brother Paul,
  Who never left her side.

Betroth'd they were, and Marguerite,
  His own affianced wife,
When came the dread disease that took
  Her sight, but spared her life.

Alas! for these young lovers now,
  Their earthly joys are o'er!
"My son the orphan shall not wed!"
  An angry father swore.

A lone and weary man, Baptiste
  His sadden'd home had left,
And, back returning, found that home
  Of love and peace bereft.

His father's prayers, his mother's tears,
  Extort a hasty vow,
And Baptiste to the rich Angèle
  His faith has plighted now.

But, hark! the bridal party shout
  With now redoubled glee,
"The witch! the witch! the lame old Jeanne
  Close by the fountain see."

And there she was, poor Jeanne, the witch,
  With snowy hair and cheek,
Whose shrivell'd skin, and furrows deep,
  Of age and sorrow speak.

Around her crowd the merry group,
  And laughingly pursue,
For nought that Jeanne had e'er foretold
  Had ever proved untrue.

Nor aught had maiden ever learnt,
  From Jeanne's prophetic lore,
But what her trembling heart had oft
  In secret wish'd before.

But stern is Jeanne the witch's eye,
   And wildly glares it now,
From underneath her wizen'd locks,
   On Baptiste's sullen brow.

For there he stood, and much, I ween,
   His colour went and came;
And cold as marble, statue-turn'd,
   The faithless lover's frame;

When, seizing on fair Angêle's hand,
   The aged sibyl made
The cross's blessed sign thereon,
   And thus address'd the maid:

" To-morrow's dawn the wedding sees
   Of perjured Baptiste's bride;
God send, Angêle, it may not see
   A maiden's grave beside !"

She hush'd, and moved away ; her words
   Have for one moment's space
O'ercast the sunny light of joy,
   On each bewilder'd face.

But can two troubled drops of rain
   The sparkling course obscure
Of yonder silver streamlet's wave,
   Or stain its surface pure ?

Oh, no ! for one short instant hush'd,
   The bridal voice of song
Burst forth anew, with louder glee,
   The joyous hills among.

The bridegroom follows pale as death,
　　Whilst up the path they bound;
And as they go their wild refrain,
　　Awakes the echoes round.

" Mountain paths and hedges wild
　　Bloom, which never bloom'd before,
The bride of Castel Cuillé comes,
　　Fling your gifts her pathway o'er."

Alone her cottage home within,
　　In broken accents sweet,
With pale fair face, and thoughtful brow,
　　Laments poor Marguerite.

" He's come, yet three long days are past
　　Since little Paul ran in,
And clapp'd his hands for joy, and cried,
　　' Baptiste is come again.'

" And knows he not that six long months
　　I've sat and watch'd alone,
And deem'd my dark night's single star,
　　For aye and ever gone.

" For what is day, and what is night,
　　To one whose aching brain
Has strain'd, and sought in agony,
　　One ray of light in vain.

" When others say the light is come
　　Then darkest 'tis to me,
For each returning day renews
　　The light I cannot see.

" One night of fearful gloom is all
　These burning eyelids know,
For other's light and joy, for me,
　All, all is darkness now.

" Ah me! my soul is sad, and dark
　My musing fancies grow,
But one sweet kiss from Baptiste's lip
　Would cool my fever'd brow.

" For light I yearn, and surely light
　Is but the sky so blue,
And Baptiste's beaming eyes reflect
　That deep unchanging hue.

" A heaven of love like that above
　Is mine, my loved one by ;
No more I care for fields and flowers,
　For earth, or sun, or sky ;

" But far from him, my spirit mourns
　The light of other days,
As ivy, rudely sever'd from
　The parent stem, decays.

" They say the love of those who mourn
　Has ever truest been ;
But, oh! such love as blindness feels
　Has never yet been seen.

" But will he come ? God only knows ;
　Perchance I wait in vain.
Oh, horrid thought! away, away!
　It scares my weaken'd brain !

"And, oh! 'tis wrong to doubt him thus;
  On holy cross he swore;
Hush, hush, my foolish heart! he'll come,
  And never leave me more.

"Perchance my lover's wearied, ill,
  And therefore tarries home;
But, hark! a hasty step! the latch!—
  My Baptiste, art thou come?"

Then open flew the garden-gate,
  And rose poor Marguerite,
With outstretch'd arms, and trembling pace,
  His welcome steps to meet.

But no; 'tis Paul who comes alone,
  And, bounding to her side,
"Come, sister, come; I fain would see
  Angêle, the pretty bride.

"And fain would I the laurel boughs
  Have borne from St. Amand:
Why came they not to fetch us here?
  Come, sister, take my hand."

"Angêle a bride! and hast thou seen
  The bridal party gay?
How secret was this wedding kept!
  And who the bridegroom, say?"

"Why, sister, 'tis thy friend Baptiste!"—
  A feeble cry was all
The poor blind orphan gave, and sunk
  Against her cottage wall.

Her heart well nigh had ceased to beat
  For some few seconds' space;
Whilst, half afraid, the startled child,
  Gazed on her alter'd face.

But now her ear has caught the sound,
  The well-known bridal strain,
And life returns, and with it, too,
  The icy grasp of pain.

"Now, hearken, sister, how they sing,
  And shout, and dance along;
To leave us out, sweet Marguerite,
  I can't but think it wrong.

"At early dawn the bells will ring
  To mark the wedding time;
How sad 'twill be, alone the while,
  To hear the merry chime."

"Hush, hush! and fret not, little Paul,
  Thou shalt not miss the show;
To this gay bridal, brother dear,
  Together we will go.

"And now run out awhile, and close
  The garden-gate;" but ere
The boy had left his sister's side,
  Old Jeanne, the witch, was there.

"Why, by my witchdom, ne'er did I
  So vile a racket know;
But, sure thy hand is icy cold,
  My child; what ails thee now?"

" There 's nothing ails me, Jeanne ; 'tis sweet
    For me to sit and hear
Those nuptial voices gay, and think
    My wedding day is near.

" When Easter comes, I too shall be
    A proud and happy bride ;
Thy fortune-telling cards, good Jeanne,
    Have never, never lied.

" And much, I ween, Baptiste and me
    Will praise thy wondrous lore,
And, oh ! 'twill be a blessed thing
    To hear his voice once more."

" Too dearly dost thou love him, child ;
    Too fondly dost thou lay
Thy hopes upon a broken reed :
    Kneel down, kneel down, and pray."

" The more I pray, the more I love,
    A sin it cannot be,
For surely, Jeanne, Baptiste is kind,
    And ever true to me ?"

No answer ; all is over then ;
    Her last faint hope is gone,
And true the fatal tale that turn'd
    Her tender heart to stone.

But wildly smiled poor Marguerite,
    And laugh'd, and questioned on,
The while a hectic flush arose
    Her pallid cheek upon.

And well till night, when Jeanne withdrew,
  The orphan play'd her part;
And little thought poor Jeanne she left
  Behind a breaking heart.

Alas! poor Jeanne the witch, 'tis clear
  No magic arts are thine;
Nor can thy simple skill the depths
  Of grief like hers divine.

Perchance this morn thy full heart found
  By yonder well side's brink
A clearer view of future woe
  Than even thyself could think.

Slow dawns the day; the clock has struck
  The hour of nine; meanwhile
Two maidens in their cottage homes
  The weary hours beguile.

Queen of the day, the one displays
  Her crown of orange flower;
The golden cross, and gay attire,
  Must grace the bridal hour.

And gazing on the lovely form
  Reflected in her mirror, smiles,
And, pleased, rehearses all her store
  Of beauty's playful wiles;

But no bright flowery wreath adorns
  The other maiden's brow;
And 'tis no golden cross, I ween,
  Her pale hands clasp e'en now.

As, tottering through her narrow room,
    Closer she draws the folds
Of her light vesture o'er the prize
    Her grasp securely holds.

With jest and song, a thoughtless group
    Around the one repair,
And she embraced, and flatter'd still,
    Omits her daily prayer.

The other kneels the while, and prays
    In murmured accents low,
Whilst cold her brow the death-drops stain,
    "Oh God! have mercy *thou!*"

And now they start, and, led by Paul,
    The orphan calmly wends
Her way the mountain path along,
    That towards the church ascends.

The day was foggy, damp the air,
    Perfumed with laurel came,
And with it deadly shivers brought,
    That wrung her feeble frame.

Not far from where the ruins stand
    Of Castel Cuillé's tower,
The little Gothic church erects
    Its weather-beaten spire;

Around whose cloud-enveloped height
    The ocean eagle sings,
Whilst underneath its time-worn roof
    Her brood the swallow brings.

"Hush, Paul!" the maiden cries ; "methinks
  The steep ascent we reach."
"Oh, yes! we're come, and, sister, hark,
  I hear the ospray screech.

"I hate that dark, ill-omen'd bird,
  Ill luck it surely brings,
And some misfortune follows still
  Whene'er it hoarsely sings.

"Dost thou remember, sister dear,
  What time our father died,
When, kneeling by his bedside, both
  The live-long night we cried.

"We cried all night, but chiefly when
  He kiss'd us both, and said,—
'Take care of Paul, my girl, for I
  To-morrow shall be dead.'

"Oh, how we wept! and, sure enough
  He died; and on the roof
The ospray sung—I marked it well—
  As now she sings aloof.

"Ah! sister, do not clasp me so;
  You hurt me, Marguerite!
You stifle me with kisses:—see,
  The bridal train we meet!

"But, pale thou art, and trembling too,
  I fear me thou wilt swoon."
And true it was, the maiden's strength
  O'ertask'd must fail her soon.

The chord her brother's words have wrung,
　　Has snapp'd with sudden pain;
Affrighted, back she starts, but Paul
　　Has urged her on again.

And when the poor bewilder'd girl
　　The laurel trod beneath
Her feet, and 'gainst her head had struck
　　The porch's hanging wreath,

A change came o'er her; on she rush'd
　　The moving crowd among—
As if to some gay festive scene,—
　　The narrow aisle along.

But, lo! with joyous peal, and loud,
　　The marriage-bells resound,
And, far and wide, through rock and vale
　　Awake the echos round.

The clouds have pass'd away, the sun
　　In splendour beams again,
As, winding through the portal gate,
　　Appears the bridal train.

But, gloomy still, as yester eve
　　The false one's cheek grew pale,
As in that nuptial hour he mused
　　On Jeanne's prophetic tale.

Whilst Angêle recks of little else
　　Her golden cross beside;
Enough for her, she moves along,
　　The fair and envied bride;

And shakes her pretty head and smiles,
    As all around her say,—
" Was ever bride as fair as her
    Whom Baptiste weds to-day ?"

And now high mass is said, and near
    The altar stood the priest ;
Betwixt his trembling fingers held
    The spousal ring, Baptiste.

But, while his bride's expecting hand
    The glittering pledge awaits,
He needs must speak the few short words
    That seal their mutual fates.

'Tis done ; and lo ! a voice has struck
    The bridegroom's ear, and chill'd
His heart's warm blood, and wildly through
    The wond'ring crowd has thrill'd,

Who from some dark, sequester'd shrine
    Behold, with sudden fear,
The waving arms, and face insane
    Of Marguerite appear.

" Baptiste has will'd my death !" she cried :
    " *This, this* shall set me free !
At this gay wedding blood must needs
    The holy-water be."

And as she spoke, a knife she drew
    That in her bosom lay ;
But ere the fearful deed was done
    Her spirit pass'd away.

And God in mercy call'd her home
   " Where those who mourn are blest,
Where the wicked cease from troubling,
   And the weary are at rest."

That eve, in place of bridal songs,
   The " De Profundis" rose,
As borne by weeping girls along
   A coffin churchward goes.

And village maids, in white attire,
   Around in silence drew,
And then, in murmur'd accents low,
   Their dirge-like chaunt renew.

"Peach, and pear, and almond trees,
   Away your snowy blossoms hide,
For death has woo'd the sweetest flower
   That grew on Castel Cuillé's side.

"Mountain paths, and hedges wild,
   Weep, that never wept before ;
Wave your darkest cypress boughs,
   Wave them yonder pathway o'er."

LADY GEORGIANA FULLERTON.

THE MOCKINGS OF THE SOLDIERS.

FROM ST. MATTHEW.

" Plant a crown upon his head,
Royal robe around him spread;
See that his imperial hand
Grasps, as fit, the sceptral wand:
Then before him bending low,
As becomes his subjects, bow;
Fenced within our armed ring,
Hail him, hail him, as our King!"

Platted was of thorns the crown,
Trooper's cloak was royal gown;
If his passive hand, indeed,
Grasp'd a sceptre, 'twas a reed.
He was bound to feel and hear
Deeds of shame, and words of jeer;
For he whom king in jest they call
Was a doom'd captive scoff'd by all.

But the brightest crown of gold,
Or the robe of rarest fold,
Or the sceptre which the mine
Of Golconda makes to shine,

Or the lowliest homage given
By all mankind under heaven,
Were prized by him no more than scorn,
Sceptre of reed, or crown of thorn.

Of the stars his crown is made,
In the sun he is array'd,
He the lightning of the spheres
As a flaming sceptre bears:
Bend in rapture before him
Ranks of glowing seraphim ;
And we, who spurn'd him, trembling stay
The judgment of his coming day.

Dr. Maginn.

A CLASSICAL ODE

WITH "A FREE TRANSLATION."

AD PŒTAM.

Quæ te sub tenerâ rapuerunt, Pœta, juventâ,
   O! utinam me crudelia fata vocent!

Ut linquam terras, invisaque lumina solis,
   Utque tuus rursùm, corpore, sim posito!

Te sequar: obscurum per iter dux ibit eunti
   Fidus Amor, tenebras lampade discutiens;

Tu cave Lethæo contingens ora liquore;
   Et citò venturi, sis memor, oro, viri!

TO PADDY.

Ah! Paddy, my darlin'! thin what has become o' ye?
   What spalpeen has darr'd to deprive ye of life?
Sure the thief o' the world might have left jest a crumb
   o' ye,
   To comfort the heart o' yer sorrowful wife!

o

Ochone! now ye 're gone, see how dreadful my fate is,
    Indeed, I can't bear it; I'll soon " cut my sticks :"—
I'll lave the bright sun, and the sweet land o' praties,
    And be off to look afther my Paddy " like bricks!"

Yes, I'll follow ye, Pat, though ye have got the start o'
    me,
For my love is so faithful, 'twill soon find ye out:
With a lamp, or a rushlight, I'll seek t'other part o' me,
    And as soon as I see ye, " Mavourneen!" I'll shout.

But don't drink of Lethe, or any sich stuff, my boy,
    If ye do, ye'll forget yer poor wife, mebbe hate her;
But if ye feel thirsty—the thought 's quite enough, my boy,
    By the pow'rs but I'll bring yiz a dhrop o' the cratur!

TO A FOUNTAIN IN HYMETTUS.

These infantine beginnings gently bear,
Whose best desert and hope must be your bearing.
PHINEAS FLETCHER.

O PURE and limpid fountain,
What snow on Alpine mountain,
   Sparkles like thee ?
While on thy turf reclining,
Our features soft and shining
   In thee we see.
The zephyrs flitting o'er thee,
O fount, methinks adore thee,
   And linger still,
With winglets light and tender
O'er thine eyes of splendour,
   And drink their fill.

A thousand sunny flowers
Their fragrance, like rich dowers,
   Around thee shed ;
And through the woodbine branches
No breeze its coldness launches
   On thy calm bed.

Sunshine upon thee slumbers,
As if thy rills' sweet numbers
 Lull'd it to rest;
The stars of night and morning
For ever are adorning
 Thy crystal breast.

About thy banks so fragrant,
That little rose-winged vagrant,
 Cupid, is seen;
And in thy silv'ry waters
Bathe the mild Goddess-daughters,
 In Beauty's sheen.
The Dryads rob'd in brightness,
With feet of fawn-like lightness,
 The Graces Three,
Beneath the golden glances
Of Hesper weave their dances,
 O fount! round thee.

Pan leaves his rosy valleys,
And by thy brightness dallies
 All day,—and wakes
Echo—the forest haunting—
Up with the notes enchanting
 His wild pipe makes.
Here, too, at times resorted,
Fair Venus, when she sported
 With am'rous Mars.
Their hearts with passion beating,
And none to view their meeting,
 But the lone stars.

Play on, thou limpid fountain
Eternal as yon mountain
   Olympus-crown'd :
Gush on—in light Elysian,
As Poet's shape-fill'd vision,
   Or Apollo's round.
The smiles of Heaven above thee,
And the stars to love thee,
   Fount, thou shalt glide
From thy crystal portal,
Strong, beauteous, and immortal,
   Whate'er betide.

EDWARD KENEALY.

WRECK OF THE HESPERUS.

It was the schooner Hesperus
  That sail'd the wintry sea;
And the skipper had ta'en his little daughter
  To bear him company.

Blue were her eyes as the fairy-flax.
  Her cheeks like the dawn of day,
And her bosom sweet as the hawthorn buds
  That ope in the month of May.

The skipper he stood beside the helm,
  With his pipe in his mouth,
And watch'd how the veering flaw did blow
  The smoke now west, now south.

Then up and spake an old sailór,
  Had sail'd the Spanish Main,
"I pray thee put into yonder port,
  For I fear a hurricane.

"Last night the moon had a golden ring,
  And to-night no moon we see!"
The skipper he blew a whiff from his pipe,
  And a scornful laugh laugh'd be.

Colder and louder blew the wind,
    A gale from the north-east ;
The snow fell hissing in the brine,
    And the billows froth'd like yeast.

Down came the storm, and smote amain
    The vessel in its strength ;
She shudder'd and paused, like a frighted steed,
    Then leap'd her cable's length.

" Come hither ! come hither ! my little daughter,
    And do not tremble so :
For I can weather the roughest gale
    That ever wind did blow."

He wrapp'd her warm in his seaman's coat
    Against the stinging blast ;
He cut a rope from a broken spar,
    And bound her to the mast.

" O father ! I hear the church-bells ring—
    Oh ! say, what may it be ?"
" 'Tis a fog-bell on a rock-bound coast !"
    And he steer'd for the open sea.

" Oh father ! I hear the sound of guns—
    Oh ! say, what may it be ?"
" Some ship in distress, that cannot live
    In such an angry sea !"

" O father ! I see a gleaming light—
    Oh ! say, what may it be ?"
But the father answer'd never a word,
    A frozen corpse was he.

Lash'd to the helm, all stiff and stark,
    With his face to the skies,
The lantern gleam'd through the gleaming snow
    On his fix'd and glassy eyes.

Then the maiden clasp'd her hands, and pray'd
    That savéd she might be;
And she thought of Christ, who still'd the wave
    On the lake of Galilee.

And fast through the midnight dark and drear,
    Through the whistling sleet and snow,
Like a sheeted ghost the vessel swept
    Toward the reef of Norman's Woe.

And ever the fitful gusts between
    A sound came from the land;
It was the sound of the trampling surf
    On the rocks and the hard sea-sand.

The breakers were right beneath her bows,
    She drifted a dreary wreck,
And a whooping billow swept the crew
    Like icicles from her deck.

She struck where the white and fleecy waves
    Look'd soft as carded wool;
But the cruel rocks they gored her side
    Like the horns of an angry bull.

Her rattling shrouds, all sheathed in ice,
    With the masts went by the board,
Like a vessel of glass, she stove and sank,
    Ho! ho! the breakers roar'd!

At daybreak, on the bleak sea-beach,
   A fisherman stood aghast
To see the form of a maiden fair
   Lash'd close to a drifting mast.

The salt sea was frozen on her breast,
   The salt tears in her eyes ;
And he saw her hair, like the brown sea-weed,
   On the billows fall and rise.

Such was the wreck of the Hesperus,
   In the midnight and the snow !
Christ save us all from a death like this
   On the reef of Norman's Woe!

H. W. LONGFELLOW.

"LIGHT."

"And God said, Let there be light, and there was light."—Gen. i. v. 2.

SPACE labour'd—quicken'd by Almighty word,
And from its shapeless womb unsightly voided
Chaos.   For on that great command, Matter,
Obedient to its great Progenitor,
Rush'd amain from all the corners
Of eternity.   Each atom jostling
Its fellow—in haste to pleasure *Him*—so form'd
A turgid lump, which surging to and fro
On a black sea of thickening vapour,
An unwholesome sweat oozed from the slimy depths
Of this miscarried mass.   Helpless—still with all
The germ of life, as in a new-born babe,
It lay upon the bosom of great Space,
Its mother, who could not help it into fair
Existence.   *   *   *   *   *
God said, "*Let there be light, and there was light.*"
The murky vault was split: Darkness was rent:
A golden orb sprung from the smile of God,
Stood, created,—Width oped her mighty jaws
To gape at this new wonder—for Space now
Had eyes to see her own immensity.

The Universe awoke, and dress'd in regal
Purple, stood in all the silent majesty
Of the interminable arch.   Empire
Of creation ! Night, so late a tyrant,
Shrank to some pit or grave within the bosom
Of its subject mass.   The infant Globe, smiling,
Stretched forth its cheek towards its novel nurse,
That sung, and soothed it with a gentle breeze.
Land sprung up to meet its benefactor,
And straight shot forth its trees and shrubs, which sent up
An odour,—the only language they could speak,
To kiss and greet the light that warmed them
Into life.   Syren myrtles woo the fickle
May-breeze with a rustling kiss filch'd of
The lagging wind; while ev'ry twinkling leaf
Whispers a lay of love-sick melody.
The airy multitudes, distilling
Sweetest music in their shrill tale of first
Affection, swell out the gentle tumult
Of this mellow choir, till beaming Nature
Seems one song of universal adoration.

" Light was—and God saw that it was good."

The Day went down, while Heaven blush'd at Evening's
Fickle flight.   Night crept from the caves, keeping
Far off the dreaded sun ; and as it came
With stealthy crawl, deserted Earth saw,
And its latest zephyr moan'd a wailing cry.
Twilight, the day's last warm embrace, turned back
From following the sun, and wept dew upon
The drooping flowers there, with a mother's slow
And struggling gait, with face o'er her shoulder

Bent, fixed a last fond gaze upon the mute-struck
Loveliness of recumbent Nature.   But
Ere she went she oped her jewel-box, and clad
The dingy darkness in a blaze of angel's tears,
Shed for the fallen seraphs,—a golden filter
For up-wending souls to strain out sin, and purge
Mortality withal.   Their sparkle does
Amuse her fright'ned offspring, who, half
Repelling, half accepting, sobs itself
To sleep.

DION L. BOURCICAULT.

THE FISHERMAN'S DWELLING.

TRANSLATED BY MARY HOWITT.

WE sate by the fisher's dwelling,
    And looked upon the sea;
The evening mists were gathering,
    And rising up silently.

Forth from the lofty lighthouse
    Streamed softly light by light,
And in the farthest distance
    A ship hove into sight.

We spoke of storm and shipwreck;
    Of seamen, and how they lay
Unsafe 'twixt heaven and water,
    'Twixt joy and fear each day.

We spoke of lands far distant;
    We took a world-wide range,
We spoke of wondrous nations,
    And manners new and strange.

Of the fragrant, glittering Ganges,
    Where giant trees uptower,
And handsome, quiet people,
    Kneel to the lotus flower.

Of Lapland's filthy people,
    Flat-headed, wide-mouthed, we spake ;
How they squat round their fires and jabber,
    And shriek o'er the fish they bake.

The maidens listened so gravely ;
    At length no more was said ;
The ship was in sight no longer,
    And night over all was spread.

HEINRICH HEINE.

THE ASCENTS OF MONT BLANC.

WHEN Jacques Balmat from his party was thrown,
He found out the summit untaught and alone,
And when he returned to his doctor with glee,
He said, " For your care you shall go up with me,"
    With your baton so sharp, tra la.

The next who tried was De Saussure, we're told,
Who climbed in a full suit of scarlet and gold:
Whilst poor M. Bourrit, four times driven back,
In dudgeon returned to Geneva—good lack!
    With his baton so sharp, tra la.

Woodley, Clissold, and Beaufoy, each thought it no lark,
And were followed by Jackson, and Sherwell and Clarke.
Then Fellowes and Hawes by a new passage went,
And avoided the dangers of Hamel's ascent,
    With their batons so sharp, tra la.

Brave Auldjo next was pulled over a bridge
Of ice-poles laid on the glacier's ridge;
You will see all his wonderful feats, if you look
At the views drawn by Harding, and placed in his book,
    And his baton so sharp, tra la.

Full forty gentlemen, wealthy and bold,
Have climbed up in spite of the labour and cold;
But of all that number there lives not one
Who speaks of the journey as very good fun.

With their batons so sharp, tra la.

ALBERT SMITH.

THE VILLAGE BLACKSMITH.

UNDER a spreading chestnut tree
   The village smithy stands ;
The smith a mighty man is he,
   With large and sinewy hands,
And the muscles of his brawny arms
   Are strong as iron bands.

His hair is crisp, and black, and long,
   His face is like the tan,
His brow is wet with honest sweat,
   He earns whate'er he can,
And looks the whole world in the face,
   For he owes not any man.

Week out, week in, from morn till night,
   You can hear his bellows blow,
You can hear him swing his heavy sledge
   With measured beat and slow,—
Like a sexton ringing the old kirk-chimes,
   When the evening sun is low.

And children coming home from school
   Look in at the open door ;
They love to see the flaming forge,
   And hear the bellows roar,
And catch the burning sparks that fly
   Like chaff from a threshing-floor.

P

He goes on Sunday to the church,
   And sits among his boys;
He hears the parson pray and preach,
   He hears his daughter's voice,
Singing in the village choir,
   And it makes his heart rejoice.

It sounds to him like her mother's voice,
   Singing in Paradise!
He needs must think of her once more,
   How in her grave she lies,
And with his hard, rough hand he wipes
   A tear from out his eyes.

Toiling, rejoicing, sorrowing,
   Onward through life he goes;
Each morning sees some task begin,
   Each evening sees it close;
Something attempted, something done,
   Has earned a night's repose.

Thanks! thanks to thee, my worthy friend
   For the lesson thou hast taught!
Thus at the sounding forge of Life
   Our fortunes must be wrought,
Thus on its sounding anvil shaped,
   Each burning deed and thought.

HENRY W. LONGFELLOW.

THE DONNYBROOK JIG.

Oh! 'twas Dermot O'Nolan M'Figg,
That could properly handle a twig,
    He wint to the fair, and kicked up a dust there,
In dancing a Donnybrook jig—with his twig.
Oh! my blessing to Dermot M'Figg.

Whin he came to the midst of the fair,
He was all in a paugh for fresh air,
    For the fair very soon, was as full—as the moon,
Such mobs upon mobs as were there, oh rare!
So more luck to sweet Donnybrook Fair.

But Dermot, his mind on love bent,
In search of his sweetheart he went,
    Peep'd in here and there, as he walked through the fair,
And took a small drop in each tent—as he went,—
Oh! on whisky and love he was bent.

And who should he spy in a jig,
With a meal-man so tall and so big,
    But his own darling Kate, so gay and so nate!
'Faith! her partner he hit him a dig—the pig,
He beat the meal out of his wig.

The piper, to keep him in tune,
Struck up a gay lilt very soon;
   Until an arch wag cut a hole in the bag,
And at once put an end to the tune—too soon—
Och! the music flew up to the moon.

The meal-man he looked very shy,
While a great big tear stood in his eye,
   He cried, "Lord, how I'm kilt, all alone for that jilt;
With her may the devil fly high in the sky,
For I'm murdered, and don't know for why."

"Oh!" says Dermot, and he in the dance,
Whilst a step to'ards his foe did advance,
   "By the Father of Men, say but that word again,
And I'll soon knock you back in a trance—to your dance,
For with me you'd have but small chance."

"But," says Kitty, the darlint, says she,
"If you'll only just listen to me,
   It's myself that will show that he can't be your foe,
Though he fought for his cousin—that's me," says she,
"For sure Billy's related to me.

"For my own cousin-jarmin, Anne Wild,
Stood for Biddy Mulroony's first child;
   And Biddy's step-son, sure he married Bess Dunn,
Who was gossip to Jenny, as mild a child
As ever at mother's breast smiled.

"And may be you don't know Jane Brown,
Who served goat's-whey in Dundrum's sweet town?

'Twas her uncle's half-brother, who married my mother,
And bought me this new yellow gown, to go down
When the marriage was held in Milltown."

" By the powers, then," says Dermot, " 'tis plain,
Like the son of that rapscallion Cain,
    My best friend I have kilt, though no blood is spilt,
But the devil a harm did I mane—that's plain ;
And by me he'll be ne'er kilt again."

DILLON.

TAGLIONI.

The universal admiration excited by the unrivalled grace and activity of Mademoiselle Taglioni produced the following poetical effusion from the pen of the Rev. Mr. Mitford. It struck me, however, upon reading it, that the frequent classical allusions, and the high strain of poetical metaphor pursued throughout the poem, might render it somewhat obscure to the general reader. I have, therefore, taken the liberty, by some slight alterations and additions, and by occasionally drawing the allusive imagery from more common-place scenery and circumstances, to render it a little more familiar, but, I trust, not less acceptable to the lovers of *Poetry* and *Motion.*—O. SMITH.

ONE moment linger! lo! from Venus' bowers
Descends the youngest of the roseate Hours:
She comes in all her blushing beauty, borne
From the far fountains of the purple morn,
Aurora's self! what time her brow resumes
The bright refulgence of its golden plumes.
Sylph of the earth! the sky! and oh! as fair
And beauteous as her sisters of the air.
In that sweet form what varied graces meet,
Love in her eye, and Music in her feet!
Light as the bounding fawn along the lea,
Or blythe bird glancing o'er the summer sea;
Light as the foam when Venus leaves the wave,
Or blossoms fluttering over April's grave.
Mark, on yon rose lights the celestial tread—
The trembling stalk but just declines its head;
Sweet Ariel floats above her as she springs,
And wafts the flying fair, and lends her wings.

TAGLIONI.

ꓳne moment linger!—lo! from Venus' bowers,
Painted by *Messieurs Grieve* with fruit and flowers,
She comes in all her blushing beauty, borne
On canvass clouds to represent the morn,
Aurora's self! what time her brow resumes
The wreath that 's scented with Delcroix' perfumes.
Sylph of the earth! the sky! and oh! as fair
As Op'ra dancers generally are.
In that sweet form what varied graces meet,
From sparkling eyes to tiny twinkling feet,
Light as the bounding fawn along the lea,
" *Ac-tive and spry*" as an industrious flea ;
Light as the foam when Venus leaves the wave,
Without a rag appearances to save :
Mark! on yon rose lights the celestial tread,
While agile carpenters decline its head ;
Sweet Ariel floats above her as she springs,
And wafts the flying fair with wires and strings.
Now wreathed in radiant smiles she seems to glide,
And in a well-greased groove is made to slide ;
Her light cymar in lucid beauty streams
'Mong fops and dandies crowding 'hind the scenes.
Round her small waist the zone young Iris binds,

Now wreathed in radiant smiles she seems to glide
With buoyant footsteps like Favonius' bride,
Or Psyche, Zephyr borne, to Cupid's blushing side.
Her light cymar in lucid beauty streams,
Of woven air, so thin the texture seems.
Round her small waist the zone young Iris binds,
And gives the sandals that command the winds.
A thousand voices challenge Music's throne,
Daughter of air! this empire is thine own!
Here Taglioni reigns unrivalled and alone!

REV. J. MITFORD.

And *Corset Parisien* her shape confines.
*Fille de Philippe!** the ballet is thine own :
When o'er the water'd stage the whit'ning 's strown,
A thousand fiddles scrape round Terpi's throne,†
All are on tip-toe till thy toe's tip 's shown.
When for thy farewell night Fame's trumpet 's blown,
Places are purchased at a price unknown
To any,—(but the box-keeper alone).
With weight unusual then the benches groan :
Into the 'bus‡ sixteen are cramm'd—ochone !
In fact it is the greatest house e'er known.

O. SMITH.

* The father of Mademoiselle Taglioni rejoices in the sponsorial
and patronymic appellation of Philippe.

† Terpsichore. Terpi for the sake of brevity, as we say Betsy for
Elizabeth.

‡ 'Bus for Omnibus. Mr. Farren says Omnibi. *Vide* Doctor Dil-
worth.

CUPID IN LONDON.

Young Cupid, grown tired of his wild single life,
  And the pranks he had long been pursuing,
Determined to marry a sweet little wife,
  So in earnest he set out a-wooing.

But disdaining to win her by magic or art,
  Or aught save his beauty and merit,
Away with contempt threw his bow and his dart,
  No longer their pow'r to inherit.

Then to London he came one fine morning in May,
  When the full tide of fashion was flowing;
His purse was brim-full, his heart light and gay,
  And his cheeks with fresh roses were glowing.

As a fine handsome youth he was soon known in town,—
  All the ladies his manners delighted;
Not a ball or a rout with the world would go down
  Unless Mr. Love were invited.

His cab was "*perfection*," his horse "*quite a love*,"
  And his *Tiger* "*the least of the little;*"
No one else ever wore such a hat or a glove,
  And his *Stultz* was a fit to a tittle.

The bride that he sought for was easy to find
  In the midst of such dazzling attraction;
And soon a fair maiden he met to his mind,
  Whom he loved at first sight to distraction.

'Twas at *Almack's* he met with the dear lovely girl,
  She was called " *the prize flower of the season;*"
And her exquisite form in the waltz to entwirl
  Was enough to deprive him of reason.

So he told her his love, and she whispered "Oh fie!"
  As she blushed and looked round for her mother;
And Cupid inquired, with a tremulous sigh,
  If her heart ever beat for another.

But her mind was as pure as her beauty was bright;
  And she told him no one e'er could win her
Who in frivolous pastime alone took delight—
  The *beau* of a ball or a dinner.

Ashamed and dejected, poor Cupid retired,
  Resolving to *cut*—cutting capers,—
And chambers next day in *the Temple* he hired,
  And filled them with law-books and papers.

Then to study the Law, like a man he went down,
  No scholar could ever be apter,
For he bought an arm-chair, with a wig and a gown.
  And in BLACKSTONE he read *a whole chapter.*

At the end of a fortnight he grew thin and pale,
  And he thought he should die without jesting;
So he dressed all in black, which he thought must prevail,
  For it made him look quite interesting.

Then he called on his love, looking grave as a judge,
    And to plead his first *suit* was beginning ;—
But she laughed in his face, said the law was all fudge,
    And *her* heart would never be winning.

Distracted he left her—transported with ire
    To think that his plan should miscarry ;
He tore up his gown—threw his wig in the fire—
    And kicked all his books to *Old Harry.*

Next morning to MELTON he rode like a dart,
    To adopt a new method to please her,
For he vow'd that he'd conquer her obdurate heart,
    Or break his own neck—just to tease her.

So he rode like a madman the wild *steeple chase,*
    And followed the hounds like a Tartar ;
And he galloped like wildfire at each *hurdle-race,*
    To win it or die like a martyr !

Then his fame got abroad as a sportsman of note,
    And he thought he was now quite a hero,
So he went to the maid in his bright scarlet coat,
    But his ardour soon tumbled to *zero.*

For she told him his deeds were unworthy of fame,
    (Her remarks were all true to the letter)
That a fox or a hare were but pitiful game,
    And the riding his groom could do better.

Poor *Love* now indulged in a grief without bounds,
    For a week or two " *sans intermission ;*"
Then he sold off his hunters, and gave up the hounds,
    And purchased a cornet's commission.

In a cavalry reg'ment to battle he went,
    And he said not a word of his going;
But resolved that in action his life should be spent,
    Or at least that his blood should be flowing.

And soon in a charge which he gallantly led
    At the enemy's troops in platoon,
He got a sad cut (while defending his head)
    In the arm from a heavy dragoon.

Disabled from duty, he homeward returned,
    The news of a victory bringing;
And now with affection his loved maiden burned,
    And the town with his praises was ringing.

One morning he called with his arm in a sling,
    And attired as a dashing young lancer;
To refuse him this time was a difficult thing,
    For she loved him, indeed,—when a dancer.

When he talked of his passion, she listened with pride,
    And her heart by assault was soon carried;
And she shortly appeared as the young soldier's bride,
    For in less than a month *they were married.*

R. More.

THE MISLETOE.

I.

A prophet sat in the Temple gate,
  And he spoke each passer by
In thrilling tones—with words of weight—
  And fire in his rolling eye.

" *Pause thee, believing Jew!*
  " *Nor make one step beyond*
  " *Until thy heart hath conned*
  " *The mystery of this wand.*"

And a rod from his robe he drew;—
  'Twas a withered bough
  Torn long ago
From the trunk on which it grew.
  But the branch long torn
  Showed a bud new born,
That had blossomed there anew :—
  That wand was " JESSE's rod,"
    Symbol, 'tis said,
    Of HER, the Maid—
  Yet mother of our GOD !

II.

A priest of EGYPT sat meanwhile
  Beneath his palm tree hid,
On the sacred brink of the flowing Nile,
  And there saw mirror'd, 'mid
Tall obelisk and shadowy pile
  Of ponderous pyramid,
One lowly, lovely, LOTUS plant,
  Pale orphan of the flood ;
And long did that aged hierophant
  Gaze on that beauteous bud ;
For well he thought, as he saw it float
  O'er the waste of waters wild,
On the long-remember'd cradle boat,
  Of the wond'rous Hebrew child :—
Nor was that lowly lotus dumb
Of a mightier Infant still, to come,
    If mystic skiff
    And hieroglyph
Speak aught in LUXOR's catacomb.

III.

A GREEK sat on Colonna's cape,
  In his lofty thoughts alone,
And a volume lay on PLATO's lap,
  For *he* was that lonely one ;
    And oft as the sage
    Gazed o'er the page
His forehead radiant grew,
  For in Wisdom's womb
  Of the WORD to come
A vision blest his view.—

He broached that theme in the ACADEME
　　Of the teachful olive grove—
And a chosen few that secret knew
　　In the PORCH's dim alcove.

IV.

A SYBIL sat in Cumæ's cave
　　In the hour of infant ROME,
And her vigil kept and her warning gave
　　Of the HOLY ONE to come.
'Twas she who culled the hallowed branch
　　And silent took the helm
When he the Founder-Sire would launch
　　His bark o'er Hades' realm :
But chief she poured her vestal soul
Thro' many a bright illumined scroll,
　　　By priest and sage,
　　　Of an after age,
Conned in the lofty CAPITOL.

V.

A DRUID stood in the dark oak wood
　　Of a distant northern land,
And he seem'd to hold a sickle of gold
　　In the grasp of his withered hand,
And he moved him slowly round the girth
　　Of an aged oak, to see
If an orphan plant of wondrous birth
　　Had clung to the old oak tree.
And anon he knelt and from his belt
　　Unloosened his golden blade,
Then rose and culled the MISLETOE
　　Under the woodland shade.

VI.

O blessed bough! meet emblem thou
  Of all dark EGYPT knew,
Of all foretold to the wise of old,
  To ROMAN, GREEK, and JEW.
And long, God grant, time-honor'd plant,
  Live we to see thee hung
In cottage small as in baron's hall
  Banner and shield among!
Thus fitly rule the mirth of Yule
  Aloft in thy place of pride,
Still usher forth in each land of the North
  The solemn CHRISTMAS TIDE!

L'ENVOY

TO MISS ADELAIDE KEMBLE.

Quam penès arbitrium est et jus et Norma canendi.

While thousands bless thee, DRUIDESS!
  Bright daughter of a gifted line,
From an aged priest of a distant hill,
  Firm friend to thee and thine,
    Take, take one blessing still!

FATHER PROUT.

THE GREEK POET'S DREAM.

Siate presenti   .   .   .   .
Tu madre d'Amor col tuo giocondo
E lieto aspetto, e 'l tuo figliol veloce
Co' dardi sol possente à tutto 'l mondo.

BOCCACCIO.

I dream'd a dream
  As fair—as bright
As the star's soft gleam,
  Or eyes of light.
At the midnight hour
  The Queen of Love,
From her fairy bower
  Of smiles above,
With Cupid came,
  And, with grace Elysian,
Yielded the god
  To the bard's tuition.
"This child hath come
  To learn from thee,
In thine own dear home
  Thy minstrelsy:
Teach him to sing
  The strains thou hast sung;
Like a bird of spring
  O'er its callow young."

She vanish'd in light,—
   That witching one,
Like a meteor of night,
   That shines, and is gone.
The Sprite of the skies
   Remain'd by me,
His deep-blue eyes
   Radiant with glee.
His looks were bright
   As roses wreathed.
A wild delight
   From his features breathed.
Legends I taught him
   Of nymph and swain;
Of hearts entangled
   In Love's sweet chain.
Fables that charm
   The soul from sadness;
Stories that warm
   The coldest to gladness:
Songs all glowing
   With passion and mirth,
Like music flowing
   From heaven to earth.
Such were the treasures
   Of wit and thought
I gave: yet dream'd not
   My task was nought.
Cupid listened,
   And clapp'd his hands,
And his wild eyes glistened
   Like burning brands.
Fanning the air

With snow-white wings,
   He seized my lyre,
      He swept the strings:
He look'd—he glitter'd
   Like golden morn,
As he chanted the loves
   Of the Heaven-born.
His voice was sweet
   And perfume-laden,
And light as the feet
   Of dancing maiden.—
"Hearts there are
   In Heaven above
Of wild desires,
   Of passionate love.
Hearts there are
   Divinest of mould,
Which Love hath among
   His slaves enroll'd;—
Love hath been,
   And ever will be:
The might of Heaven
   Shall fade ere he."
Then the Boy,—
   Nearer advancing,
The Spirit of Joy
   In his blue eyes dancing,
Told me such secrets
   Of Heaven as ne'er
Were before reveal'd
   But to poet's ear,
Revealings of beauty
   That make the soul

Like the stars, that on wings
  Of diamond roll.
In song—in splendour
  The god departed ;
The spell was o'er,
  From sleep I started.
Thoughts like sunbeams
  Around me hung,
And my heart still echoed
  What Love had sung.
Oh ! what could Heaven
  Deny to us,
To whom it hath given
  Its secrets thus ?

EDWARD KENEALY.

MY SOLDIER-BOY.

I give my soldier-boy a blade
   In fair Damascus fashioned well;
Who first the glittering falchion swayed,
   Who first beneath its fury fell,
I know not, but I hope to know,
   That for no mean or hireling trade,
To guard no feeling base or low,
   I give my soldier-boy a blade.

Cool, calm, and clear, the lucid flood,
   In which its tempering work was done,
As calm, as clear, as cool of mood,
   Be thou whene'er it sees the sun.
For country's claim, at honour's call,
   For outraged friend, insulted maid,
At mercy's voice to bid it fall,
   I give my soldier-boy a blade.

The eye which marked its peerless edge,
   The hand that weighed its balanced poise,
Anvil and pincers, forge and wedge,
   Are gone, with all their flame and noise—
And still the gleaming sword remains.
   So when in dust I low am laid,
Remember by these heart-felt strains
   I gave my soldier-boy a blade.

DR. MAGINN.

IT IS NOT ALWAYS MAY.

The sun is bright, the air is clear,
    The darting swallows soar and sing,
And from the stately elms I hear
    The blue-bird prophesying Spring.

So blue yon winding river flows,
    It seems an outlet from the sky,
Where, waiting till the west wind blows,
    The freighted clouds at anchor lie.

All things are new,—the buds, the leaves,
    That gild the elm tree's nodding crest,
And even the nest beneath the eaves:—
    There are no birds in last year's nest.

All things rejoice in youth and love,
    The fulness of their first delight;
And learn from the soft heavens above,
    The melting tenderness of night.

Maiden ! that read'st this simple rhyme,
  Enjoy thy youth—it will not stay.
Enjoy the fragrance of thy prime,
  For, oh ! it is not always May.

Enjoy the spring of love and youth ;
  To some good angel leave the rest ;
For time will teach thee soon the truth,
  There are no birds in last year's nest.

                              H. W. LONGFELLOW.

LINES ON GENEVA.

RUTHLESS ruin in cascades pouring,
Lightning echoing, torrents roaring;
Clouds obscuring every view,
Naught to see, and less to do.
Muse of muddled brains inspire me,
With a poet's rapture fire me,
Whilst I pen this careless lay,
Just to pass the hours away.

Fair Geneva! favoured city,
Bastions frowning, buildings pretty,
Crested by the high Saléve,
Mirror'd in thy lake's blue wave;
Ramparts, whence you rest your eyes on
Mont Blanc crowning the horizon;
And rich vineyards, growing poorer
As they climb ' the darken'd Jura.'

Then, thy bridge across the Rhone,
Built of wooden beams alone;
And thy verdant Isle des Barques,
Like an insulated park.

Steamers in thy harbour lying
To Lausanne and Villeneuve plying,
If a tour you choose to make
Round the margin of the lake.

Shops for watches very thin,
Gold without, and brass within.
Snuff-boxes to tinkle sonnets ;
Women in large flapping bonnets;
Milan voitures very crazy,
Kept by *vetturini* lazy,
Who will take two days to creep
O'er the mighty Simplon's steep.

Diligences coming in
With postillion's crack-whip din,
Pack'd with English all the way
From the Rue St. Honoré.
Touters to the *bureau* rushing,
Cards presenting, luggage crushing.
From these rhymes you may conceive a
Perfect picture of Geneva.

ALBERT SMITH.

LOVE AND CARE.

LOVE sat in his bower one summer day—
And Care, with his train, came to drive him away:
   " I will not depart," said Love !
And, seizing his lute,—with silvery words,
He ran his bright fingers along the chords,
And play'd so sweet, so entrancing an air,
That a grim smile lit up the face of Care.
   " *Away—away !*"—said Love !

" Nay, nay ! I have friends !" grim Care replied ;
" Behold, here is one—and his name is *Pride !*"
   " I care not for Pride," said Love !
Then touching the strings of his light guitar,
Pride soon forgot his lofty air ;
And seizing the hand of a rustic queen,
Laugh'd, gamboll'd, and tripp'd it o'er the green—
   " *Aha, aha !*" said Love !

" Away with your jeers !" cried Care, " if you please ;
" Here's another—lank, haggard, and pale *Disease !*"
   " I care not for him," said Love !
Then touch'd a strain so plaintive and weak,
That a flush pass'd over his pallid cheek ;

And Disease leap'd up from his couch of pain,
And smil'd, and re-echoed the healing strain—
   " Well done for Disease !" said Love !

" Pshaw ! pshaw !" cried Care—" this squalid one, see !
How lik'st thou the gaunt look of *Poverty ?"*
   " I care not for him," said Love !
Then struck such a sound from his viol's string,
That Poverty shouted aloud, *" I am King !—*
The jewell'd wreaths round my temples shall twine,—
For the sparkling gems of Golconda are mine !"
   " Ay, ay—very true !" said Love !

" Nay, boast not," said Care—" there is fretful *Old Age ;*
Beware of his crutches, and tempt not his rage !"
   " I care not for Age !" said Love !
Then swept the strings of his magic lyre,
Till the glaz'd eye sparkled with youthful fire ;
And Age dropp'd his crutches, and, light as a fay,
Laugh'd, caper'd, and danc'd, like a child at play !
   " Bravo, Sir Eld !" said Love !

" A truce," cried wrinkled Care, " with thy glee !
Now, look on this last one—'tis *Jealousy !"*
   " Ah me ! ah me !" said Love !
" Her green eye burns with a quenchless fire—
I die ! I die !" Then, dropping his lyre,
Love flew far away from his cherish'd bower,
And never return'd from that fatal hour !
   Alas for thee, blighted Love !

THE LASS OF ALBANY.

My heart is wae, and unco wae,
  To think upon the raging sea
That roars between her gardens green
  And the bonnie lass of Albany.

This lovely maid's of royal blood,
  That ruled Albion's kingdoms three;
But oh! alas! for her bonnie face!
  They've wrang'd the lass of Albany.

In the rolling tide of spreading Clyde
  There sits an isle of high degree;
And a town of fame, whose princely name
  Should grace the lass of Albany.

But there's a youth, a witless youth,
  That fills the place where she should be:
We'll send him o'er to his native shore,
  And bring our ain sweet Albany.

Alas the day, and woe the day,
  A false usurper wan the gree;
Who now commands the tower and lands,
  The royal right of Albany.

We'll daily pray, we'll nightly pray,
  On bended knees most fervently.
The time may come, with pipe and drum
  We'll welcome home fair Albany.

ROBERT BURNS.

ENDYMION.

THE rising moon has hid the stars
Her level rays, like golden bars,
   Lie on the landscape green,
   With shadows brown between.

And silver-white the river gleams,
As if Diana, in her dreams,
   Had dropt her silver bow
   Upon the meadows low.

On such a tranquil night as this,
She woke Endymion with a kiss,
   When, sleeping in the grove,
   He dreamed not of her love.

Like Dian's kiss, unasked, unsought,
Love gives itself, but is not bought;
   Nor voice nor sound betrays
   Its deep, impassioned gaze.

It comes,—the beautiful, the free,—
The crown of all humanity,—
   In silence and alone,
   To seek the elected one.

It lifts the boughs, whose shadows deep
Are life's oblivion,—the soul's sleep,—
   And kisses the closed eyes
   Of him who slumbèring lies.

O, weary hearts! O, slumbering ey
O, drooping souls, whose destinies
   Are fraught with fear and pain
   Ye shall be loved again!

No one is so accursed by fate,
No one so wholly desolate,
   But some heart, though unknown,
   Responds unto his own.

Responds, as if with unseen wings
A breath from heaven had touched its strings;
   And whispers in its song,
   "Where hast thou stay'd so long?"

               H. W. LONGFELLOW.

EVENING SONG OF

THE NORMANDY FISHERMEN.

" Priez pour nous, étoile de la mer !"

PRAY for us, star of the sea !
Through the mist of the even we call on thee:
Mother eternal! be thou our guide,
And light with thy beaming the dark flowing tide.
Pierce the dark clouds that o'ershadow the night,
And steal o'er our souls with a thrill of delight.
The winds murmur hoarsely, the waves rise in foam,
Shine forth, star of beauty, and lead us to home!

Pray for us, star of the sea !
As alone on the waters we worship thee!
Thou hast heard us, for lo! in the bright'ning west,
Adorable one! thou art showing thy crest,
A beacon of love to the weary and lone,
A symbol of mercy when all hope is gone.
The winds murmur hoarsely, the waves rise in foam,
Shine on, star of beauty, and lead us to home!

R

Pray for us, star of the sea!
And for those whom we love, not watching thee,
They offer their vows at the fisherman's shrine,*
And bless thee that o'er us thou deignest to shine!
Fondly they wait us by Seine's lovely shore,
With hearts that are throbbing to hail us once more.
The winds murmur hoarsely, the waves rise in foam,
Shine on, star of beauty, and lead us to home!

Pray for us, star of the sea!
Ave Maria! we glorify thee!
Soon, soon sl al we rest from our toil on the deep,
For dim in the distance is Heve's rugged steep;
Now Havre is seen, spreading forth 'neath the hill
That o'erlooks it in majesty, fair Ingonville!
The winds murmur hoarsely, the waves rise in foam,
Shine on, star of beauty, and lead us to home!

W. JONES.

---

* On the heights of Honfleur, a picturesque town on the borders of the Seine, (celebrated by Washington Irving in one of his most affecting tales, "Annette Delarbe,") is a small chapel situate amidst the most remote scenery. Before going on any perilous enterprise, the fisherman here places his votive offering, imploring the intercession of " Our Lady of Grace."

TO ********* *****.

In the green and leafy wood,
When the golden sisterhood
  Of stars are bright,
Wilt thou—wilt thou, lady fair,
Wander fondly with me there,
  By the pale star-light?

We shall stroll beneath the trees,
Through whose boughs' interstices
  The clear moon flings
Smiles as sweet and pure as thine,
Or the million rays that shine
  In a spirit's wings.

We shall wander by the stream,
Gazing on its water's gleam,
  Glassing the skies,
Hand entwined with hand the while,
And upon me bent the smile
  Of thy gentle eyes.

As its waters glide along,
We shall listen to its song,
  Whose melody,
Though it charm full many an ear,
Still is far—oh! far less dear
  Than thy voice to me.

On the turf we'll sit and pull
Flowers the most beautiful—
  A moonlight wreath;
Though their bosoms perfum'd be,
Have they, love, the fragrancy
  Thy kisses breathe?

When our garland is entwin'd,
I with it thy brows will bind—
  O garland blest!
Of this flowery diadem,
Every leaf is worth a gem
  On a monarch's breast.

Then, along the turf we'll walk,
Talking only Cupid-talk,
  And the sweet bond
Of affection, which, methinks,
Our two spirits closely links
  In *one* spirit fond.

Or, within our own dear grove
We shall sit and talk, my love,
  Thou, my sweet theme;
How I first before thee knelt,
Wildly, fondly lov'd, and felt
  Thee my life's dream

How thou wert within my heart
Long its bright Star ; how thou art
   Still—still mine own ;
How unto the paradise
Of thy face and shining eyes
   My whole life hath grown.

As our Eden moments fly
Thus beneath the purple sky,
   The stars shall shine
With a sweeter, lovelier light,
On that bower flower-dight,
   Where thou and I recline.

In the green and silent wood,
When the starry sisterhood,
   With footsteps bright,
Trip along the azure air,
Meet me, meet me, lady fair,
   By the pale star-light.

EDWARD KENEALY.

THE RAINY DAY.

The day is cold, and dark, and dreary; .
It rains, and the wind is never weary;
The vine still clings to the mouldering wall,
But at every gust the dead leaves fall,
    And the day is dark and dreary.

My life is cold, and dark, and dreary;
It rains, and the wind is never weary;
Memory clings to the mouldering past,
But the hopes of youth fall thick in the blast,
    And the days are dark and dreary,

Be still, sad heart, and cease repining;
Above the dark clouds is the sun still shining;
Thy fate is the common fate of all;
Into each life some rain must fall,
    Some days must be dark and dreary.

H. W. Longfellow.

TO ———

In Burlingtown, much honoured, tho' he bears his
  honours gently,
There lives a famous Barber, whom the public know as
  B——y.
The Queen herself, on whose fair head hath flowed the
  Lord's anointment,
Hath made him her Perruquier by a regular appoint-
  ment.
Since triple bob*tale*-scratch was first with *novel* wigs
  invented,
His *magazin de nouveautés* was brilliantly frequented,
In shaving, his performances were felt as smooth as
  vellum;
In sooth, he had certificates from Irving, Hook, and
  Pelham;
E'en men who wore of Mohammed the pagan beard and
  badge, he
Had shaved them all by turns, from Anastasius to
  Hadji.
Nay, ladies of a certain age no longer looked the Gorgon,
His art bedeckt the *front*ispiece of Trollope and of
  Morgan;
But Beauty, too, his style well knew as what would best
  become her,
So Norton said, and Blessington, and graceful Gore,
  and Romer.

Father Prout.

THE IDES OF MARCH.

I.

"BEWARE! beware!" said the Soothsayèr
    To the "noblest of the Romans;"
And well had it been for JULIUS, I ween,
    Had he lent an ear to the summons.
CALPHURNIA sighed, the screech-owl cried,
    The March gale blew a *burrasca,*
Yet, out he went to "meet Parliament,"
    And the dagger of "envious CASCA."

II.

"BEWARE how you land!" wrote old Talleyrand
    To his Elba friend, for, heigh O!
One bleak March day he would fain sail away
    In a hooker from *Porto Ferrajo.*
And, well had it been in the year "*fifteen,*"
    Had he *not* pursued that folly on,
Mad as any "March hare," though told to beware,
    But alas and alack for NAPOLEON!

III.

" BEWARE, beware! of the Black Frière,"
  So singeth a dame of Byron ;
Arouse not *him!* 'tis a perilous whim,—
  'Tis " meddling with cold iron."
E'en in crossing the ridge of BLACKFRIARS' bridge,
  When you come to the midmost arch,
While 'tis blowing hard,—be *then* on your guard,
Then carefully look to your hat and peruke,
  And " beware of the IDES OF MARCH !"

FATHER PROUT.

CUPID.

In the middle hour of night,
When the stars were shining bright,
  And the golden spell of sleep
Sat on ev'ry mortal eye.
  From a slumber sweet and deep,
Cupid rous'd me with a cry.

"Open, open."—"Tell me, pray,
Who art thou who com'st this way?"
  Straight the rosy God replied.
"Fear me not.   I am a child
  Wand'ring without friend or guide,
And the night is wet and wild.

From my couch I quickly rose,
My doors to Cupid to unclose,
  Seiz'd a lamp, and by its beam
Saw a Boy of beauty rare;
  On his shoulders arrows gleam,
And wings white and light as air.

By the hearth I plac'd the child.
His eyes on me softly smiled :
   Then his hands I chafed in mine,
And wrung his locks until a glow
   Of heat did o'er his features shine ;—
Suddenly he seiz'd his bow.

" Stranger, I must try," quoth he,
" If my bow-string injured be."
   Instantly he shot the shaft,
And transfixed me to the heart.
   " All is right," quoth he, and laugh'd,
" But I think thou'lt feel love's smart."

EDWARD KENEALY.

TO MY DAUGHTERS.

O my darling little daughters!
　O my daughters, lov'd so well!
Who by Brighton's breezy waters
　For a time have gone to dwell.
Here I come with spirit yearning,
　With your sight my eyes to cheer,
When this sunny day returning
　Brings my forty-second year.

Knit to me in love and duty
　Have you been, sweet pets of mine!
Long in health, and joy, and beauty
　May it be your lot to shine!
And at last, when God commanding,
　I shall leave you both behind,
May I feel with soul expanding
　I shall leave you good and kind!

May I leave my Nan and Pigeon*
　Mild of faith, of purpose true,
Full of faith and meek religion,
　With many joys, and sorrows few!
Now I part, with fond caressing,
　Part you now, my daughters dear—
Take, then take your father's blessing,
　In his forty-second year!

DR. MAGINN.

* A pet name for his youngest daughter.

MY NORA!

MY NORA—dear NORA, is dreaming,
The moon on her fair cheek is gleaming;
   Whilst the fairies unseen,
   Kiss her forehead serene,
As her eyes—through their lashes are beaming.

My NORA—sweet NORA is weeping,
The pearls through those lashes are peeping;
   Oh, the fairies, I fear,
   Have just breath'd in her ear
That my love from her bosom is creeping.

My NORA—loved NORA is waking,
Her heart with its anguish is breaking;
   NORA, come to thy rest
   On my fond, faithful breast—
Of thy soul's grief, love, mine is partaking.

                T. J. OUSELEY.

SONG OF ROLAND.

Say, whither are bound these illustrious knights,
   The pride and the glory of France?
In defence of his country, its laws, and its rights,
   Each paladin takes up his lance;
And foremost is Roland, whose scimitar keen
   The harvest of war prostrate leaves,
While, led to the slain by its glittering sheen,
   Death gathers them up in his sheaves.
        Shout! comrades, shout!
        Roland famous in story,
        And your war-cry give out
        For our country and glory!

On our frontier the Saracen armies extend
   Their legions in splendid array;
The unnumber'd bands from the hills that descend
   Their menacing banners display.
'Tis the foe! 'tis the foe! Sons of France spring to arms!
   And drive back the barbarous horde:
To them, not to us, will the fight bring alarms:
   Brave Roland has ask'd for his sword.
        Shout! comrades, shout! &c.

On—onward with Roland to honour and fame!
    Glory's waving her flag by his side,
And those who would gain an illustrious name
    Must follow his plume as their guide!
On—onward, to share in his glorious career.
    He stops not to number the foe,
Till, cleft by his sabre or pierced by his spear,
    Their bravest and best are laid low.
                Shout! comrades, shout! &c.

"How many? how many?" the coward may ask,
    As he lurks in his covert secure;
But perilous odds urge the brave to their task,
    And danger itself is a lure.
To Roland the number of foes is unknown;
    To count them he never is found,
Until at the close, by his might overthrown,
    They be stark and stiff on the ground.
                Shout! comrades, shout! &c.

Once more rings the blast of the paladin's horn
    As he rallies our wavering bands;
But, pierc'd by a shaft, to the earth he is borne,
    His life-blood is clotting the sands.
Still faithful to honour, he heeds not the pain,
    But smiles with a welcome to death;
While high o'er the tumult is heard the proud strain
    Which he shouts with unfaltering breath:
           Swell, comrades, swell
              The loud chaunt of my story;
           Sing how nobly I fell
              For my country and glory!"

                          W. COOKE TAYLOR.

LEATHER AWAY WITH THE OAK-STICK.

DESCEND, ye bright Nine, this grand scene to delight,
And in praise of Victoria my verses indite!
Och! she's Queen of the country, the say, and the sky,
For if they said 'black was the white of her eye,'
    She'd leather away with the oak-stick!

Of all the bould nations that's under the sun,
They're mighty polite to her, every one;
Bekaise, when she steps out in pride down the town,
Let them stand on the tip of the tail of her gown,
    She'd leather away with the oak-stick!

She set sail for France, for she laughs at the *say,*
In September, I mind me, 'twas near quarther-day;
The boatswain and saymen were all in fine glee,
And Lord Dolly Fitz-Clancy steered the ship, d'ye see
    And leathered away with the oak-stick!

Says brave Lewy Phil., 'Och you're welcome to me
As the flowers of May;' by bright Cushla ma Chree!—
He's a jolly ould chap, and, to see him, you'd say,
When they dish up the frogs, faith! he's not far away;
    But leathers away with the oak-stick!

Phil. politely and qui'tly slipp'd his arm round her waist,
And he gave three loud smacks, and three more, the
    ould *baste*.
But the blue-jackets cried, 'Mounseer Parly Voo,
Thry it on somewhere else, with your ' How do you do ?'
    And leather away with the oak-stick !

'Through the town she paraded in grandeur and pride,
To the great *Chapeau D'U*, where King Phil. does reside;
There the tents were all spread, like ould Donnybrook fair,
With *ceade mille failthe*, and plenty to spare,
    And leather away with the oak-stick !

We'd *consartos* by night, and *sham* shindies by day,
And the King trayted every mother's sowl to the play ;
' Ma'am,' says he to the Queen, ' you'll come home and take
    tay ;
Plaise your Majesty, 'tis all in the family way,
    And leather away with the oak-stick ?'

Och ! the fine town of Paris shines under the sky,
And a beautiful *skrimmage* took place there hard by ;
The sodgers fought shy, and the boys fought it out—
'Pon my sowl, I don't know what it all was about ;
    But they leather'd away with the oak-stick.

They jamm'd up the streets with hack-cars and pochaises,
' Fire again,' says the colonel, ' fire at them like blazes !'—
' Brave boys !' cries Fayette, ' don't stay here to be kilt,
But give them your tooth-pickers starch to the hilt,
    And leather away with the oak-stick !'

Then success to the stout roving boys of July,
And mate when they 're hungry and drink when they 're
      dry,
To drink Lewy's health, and the Queen's, d'ye see,
And the rest of the Frinch Royal Fam-i-lee,
    And leather away with the oak-stick!

When the *ruction* was quash'd, and the people was quiet,
Some blag-gaards in the North thought to kick up a riot;
Says Roossia to Spain, ' Sure, we won't stand all that!'—
' Arrah be aisy,' says England, ' and mind what ye're at,
    Or I'll leather away with the oak-stick!'

God save Queen Victoria, and bless her with joy!
Och! Albert, my jewel, you 're the broth of a boy!
Three cheers for ould Ireland, and Dan, and Saint Pat,
And Repayle, Father Mathew, and *send round the hat*,
    And leather away with the oak-stick.

THE IRISH WHISKEY-DRINKER.

EXCELSIOR.

THE shades of night were falling fast,
As through an Alpine village passed
A youth, who bore, 'midst snow and ice,
A banner with the strange device—*Excelsior!*

His brow was sad ; his eye beneath
Flashed like a falchion from its sheath,
And like a silver clarion rung
The accents of that unknown tongue—*Excelsior!*

In happy homes he saw the light
Of household fires gleam clear and bright ;
Above the spectral glaciers shone,
And from his lips escaped a groan—*Excelsior!*

"Try not the pass !" the old man said ;
"Dark lowers the tempest overhead ;
The roaring torrent is deep and wide !"
And loud that clarion-voice replied—*Excelsior!*

"O stay," the maiden said, "and rest
Thy weary head upon this breast !"
A tear stood in his bright blue eye,
But still he answered with a sigh—*Excelsior!*

s 2

" Beware the pine-tree's withered branch !
Beware the awful avalanche !"
This was the peasant's last good-night ;
A voice replied, far up the height—*Excelsior !*

At break of day, as heavenward
The pious monks of Saint Bernard
Uttered the oft-repeated prayer,
A voice cried through the frosty air—*Excelsior !*

A traveller, by the faithful hound,
Half buried in the snow was found,
Still grasping in his hand of ice
That banner with the strange device—*Excelsior !*

There, in the twilight cold and grey,
Lifeless, but beautiful, he lay,
And from the sky, serene and far,
A voice fell, like a falling star—*Excelsior !*

                                        H. W. LONGFELLOW.

ELEGY IN A LONDON THEATRE.

NOT BY GRAY.

THE curtain falls—the signal all is o'er,
   The eager crowd along the lobby throng,
The youngsters lean against the crowded door,
   Ogling the ladies as they pass along.

The gas-lamps fade, the foot-lights hide their heads,
   And not a soul beside myself is seen,
Save where the lacquey dirty canvass spreads,
   The painted boxes from the dust to screen,—

Save that, in yonder gallery enshrined,
   Some ragged girl complains in angry tone
Of such as, sitting in the seat behind,
   Had ta'en her shawl in preference to their own.

There where those rugged planks uneven lie,
    There on those dirty boards—that darken'd stage
Did Kean and Kemble fill the listener's eye,
    And add a lustre to the poet's page.

But they are gone—and never, never more
    Shall prompter's summons, or the tinkling bell,
Or call-boy crying at the green-room door,
    " The stage waits, gentlemen !"—their dreams dispel.

For them no more the coaches of the great
    Shall stop up Catherine Street—for them, alas !
No more shall anxious crowds expectant wait,
    Or polish up the gilded opera-glass.

Oft did the vicious on their accents hang,
    Their power oft the stubborn heart hath bent,
And, whilst the spacious house with plaudits rang,
    They sent the harden'd homewards to repent.

There, in that empty box, perchance, hath swell'd
    A heart with Romeo's burning passion rife,
Hands that " poor Yorick's " skull might well have held,
    Or clutch'd at Macbeth's visionary knife.

Full many a pearl of purest ray serene
    The rugged oyster-shell doth hold inside,
Full many a vot'ry of the tragic queen
    The dingy offices of London hide.

Some Lear, whose daughters never turn'd his head,
    Nor changed to gall the honey of his life ;
Some white Othello, who with feather-bed
    Had smothered not, his unoffending wife.

The applause of listening houses to command,
    The critic's smile and malice to despise,
To win reward from lord and lady's hand,
    And the approval of the thundering skies,

Their parents hindered, and did thus o'erthrow
    The brilliant hopes that in their bosom rose,
To tear Macready's laurels from his brow,
    And put out Charley Kean's immortal nose.

Of one of these I heard a drummer say,
    " Oft have I seen him from the muddy street,
Across the crimson benches make his way,
    To gain his well-loved and accustomed seat.

" There, where yon orchestra uprears its rail,
    On which I hang my drumsticks, many a night
I've seen him, with a dirty shirt, and pale,
    Watching the motley scene with wild delight.

" There, upon yonder seat, which now appears
    To have rent its robe for grief he is not here,
Oft have I seen him sit, dissolved in tears,
    Veiling his grief in draughts of ginger-beer.

" One night I missed him from his favourite seat.
    I wondered strangely where the boy could be.
Another night—I gazed—in vain my gaze—
    Nor in the *pit*, nor in the *house* was he!

" Come here ! I saw him carried to that tomb,
    With drunken mutes, and all their mock parade.
Just read—I've left my spectacles at home—
    The epitaph a friend has kindly made."

The Epitaph.

Here lieth one beneath the cold damp ground,
  A youth to London and the stage unknown,
Upon his merits stern Macready frowned,
  And ' Swan and Edgar' marked him for their own.

' Large was his bounty, unto aught wherein
  The stage did mingle, and the cost was sweet.
He gave the drama all he could—his " tin,"
  And gained—'twas all he could—his favourite seat.

" No father had he who could interfere
  To check his nightly wanderings about,
And from the best authority we hear,
  His mother never dreamt that he was out!"

HOTSPUR.

UNFINISHED LINES UPON MY LIBRARY.

My days among the dead are past;
  Around me I behold,
Where'er these casual eyes are cast,
  The mighty minds of old:
My never-failing friends are they,
With whom I converse day by day.

With them I take delight in weal,
  And seek relief in woe;
And when I understand and feel
  How much to them I owe,
My cheeks have often been bedew'd
With tears of thoughtful gratitude.

My thoughts are with the dead; with them
  I live in long past years,
Their virtues love, their faults condemn,
  Partake their hopes and fears;
And from their lessons seek and find
Instruction with a humble mind.

My hopes are with the dead ; anon
  My place with them will be,
And I with them shall travel on,
  Through all futurity ;
Yet leaving here a name, I trust,
That will not perish in the dust.

ROBERT SOUTHEY.

THE WAR-SONG OF THE GALLANT
EIGHTY-EIGHTH.

COME now, brave boys, we're on for marching,
Where there's fighting and divarsion;
Where cannons roar, and men are dying,
March, brave boys, there's no denying!
      Love, farewell!

Hark! 'tis the Colonel gaily crying,
"March, brave boys, there's no denying,
Colours flying, drums are bayting,
March, brave boys, there's no retrayting!"
      Love, farewell!

The major cries, "Boys, are yez ready?"
"Yes, your honour, firm and steady;
Give every man his flask of powdher,
And his firelock on his shouldher!"
      Love, farewell!

The mother cries, "Boys, do not wrong me,
Do not take my daughters from me!
If you do, I will tormint yez!
After death my ghost will haunt yez!"
      Love, farewell!

"Oh, Molly, dear, you 're young and tinder,
And when I'm gone you won't surrinder,
But howld out like an auncient Roman,
And live and die an honest woman."
   Love, farewell!

"Oh, Molly, darling, grieve no more, I
'M going to fight for Ireland's glory;
If I come back, I 'll come victorious;
If I die, my sowl in glory is!"
   Love, farewell!

      THE IRISH WHISKEY-DRINKER.

269

THE EXPEDITION TO PONTARLIN.

TRANSLATED BY W. COOKE TAYLOR.

Oh long, very long Winter lengthens his day;
We hear not the song of the birds from the spray;
They are silent and sad in the groves and the bowers,
Awaiting the coming of spring-time and flowers!

But when the first birds on the branches were seen,
And the hedge changed its brown for a mantle of green,
The trumpet of war blew its blast o'er the land,
And summon'd the brave to the patriot band!

There was arming and bustling, confusion and haste,
Ere battalions were form'd, and line-of-march traced;
But when once in the field, the proud duke we defied:—
At peasants no longer he laugh'd in his pride.

We came on so proudly through Burgundy's states,
That we soon forced Pontarlin to open its gates;
And the women, at morn dress'd in colours so bright,
Were making the dark weeds of widows ere night.

The foreigners, frantic, came forward in force ;
They number'd twelve thousand of foot and of horse :
They assaulted us fiercely to gain back the town,
But their vaunts and their boastings were soon cloven down!

Our Swiss sprung upon them with blow upon blow,
Till never was seen such a wide overthrow ;
From the ramparts their banners and pennons were thrust,
And lay all unheeded, defiled in the dust !

The wild bear of Berne put forth his sharp claws,
And bristled his mane up, and grinded his jaws ;
He came with his cubs, who of thousands were four,
And the foreigners trembled on hearing his roar!

Be warn'd, duke of Burgundy ! timely beware,
Nor venture to mate thee with Berne's fierce bear ;
See his teeth, see his claws, his cubs eager for prey ;
Haste ! haste ! save your lives, and get out of his way.

They would not take warning; the bear rose in wrath,
And soon through their ranks forc'd a terrible path,
And, though the Burgundians were full four to one,
The bear and his cubs soon compell'd them to run !

And still the bear roar'd, until, borne on the gale,
Its echo had reach'd the brave burghers of Basle ;
And they said, since the bear is come out of his den,
We must go and assist him with all of our men.

Then prais'd be the warriors of Basle and of Berne,
Nor pass we in silence Soleure and Lucerne ;
They came without summons our dangers to share,
And bravely they fought by the side of the bear !

Thus .trengthen'd, to Grandson our armies were led,
As the knights and the nobles of Burgundy fled.
We girdled the town, and our musketry's din
Never ceas'd night or day, the proud fortress to win!

On the morning of Sunday the place we assail'd;
Its gates were forced open, its ramparts were scal'd;
The banner of freedom soon stream'd from its towers,
And announc'd to the duke that proud Grandson was
    ours!

THE SIEGE OF HENSBURGH.

Brave news! brave news! the Emperor
  Hath girded on his sword,
And swears by the rood, in an angry mood,
  And eke by his knightly word,
That humbled Hensburgh's towers shall be,
With all her boasted chivalry.

The brazen clarion's battle note
  Hath sounded through the land;
And brave squire and knight, in their armou₁ dight
  Ay, many a gallant band,
Have heard the summons far and near,
And come with falchion and with spear.

"Ho! to the rebel city, ho!
  Let vengeance lead the way!"
And anon the sheen of their spears was seen,
  As they rushed upon the prey.
Beneath where Hensburgh's turrets frown'd
Great Conrade chose his vantage ground.

Far stretching o'er the fertile plain
  His snow-white tents were spread;
And the sweet night air, as it linger'd there,
  Caught the watchful sentry's tread.
Then o'er the city's battlement
The tell-tale breeze its echo sent.

Day after day the leaguer sat
  Before that city's wall,
And yet, day by day, the proud Guelph cried "*Nay*,"
  To the herald's warning call;
Heedless, from morn to eventide,
How many a famish'd mother died.

Weak childhood, and the aged man,
  Wept—sorely wept for bread;
And pale Hunger seem'd, as his wild eye gleam'd
  On the yet unburied dead,
As if he longed, alas! to share
The night dog's cold, unhallow'd fare.

  * * * * *

  * * * * *

No longer Hensburgh's banner floats;
  Hush'd is her battle-cry,
For a victor waits at her shatter'd gates,
  And her sons are doom'd to die.
But Hensburgh's daughters yet shall prove
The saviours of the homes they love!

T

All glory to the Emperor,
　　The merciful and brave ;
Sound, clarions, sound, tell the news around,
　　And ye drooping banners wave !
Hensburgh's fair daughters, ye are free ;
Go forth, with all your "*braverie !*"

" Bid them go forth," the Emperor cried,
　　" Far from the scene of strife,
Whether matron staid, or the blushing maid,
　　Or the daughter, or the wife ;
For ere yon sun hath left the sky,
Each rebel-male shall surely die.

" Bid them go forth," the Emperor said,
　　" We wage not war with *them ;*
Bid them all go free, with their '*braverie,*'
　　And each richly valued gem ;
Let each upon her person bear
That which she deems her *chiefest* care."

The city's gates are open'd wide ;
　　The leaguer stands amazed ;
'Twas a glorious deed, and shall have its meed,
　　And by minstrel shall be praised,
For each had left her *jewell'd tire ;*
To bear a *husband,* or a *sire.*

With faltering step each laden'd one
　　At Conrade's feet appears ;
In amaze he stood, but his thirst for blood
　　Was quench'd by his falling tears ;
The victor wept aloud to see
Devoted woman's constancy.

All glory to the Emperor,—
   All glory and renown !
He hath sheath'd his sword, and his royal word
   Hath gone forth to save the town ;
For woman's love is mightier far
Than all the strategies of war.

JOHN RYAN, LL.D.

BRYAN O'LYNN.

In Dalkey a king of great weight,
   Though his deeds are not *blarney'd* in story,
For he rose, and he *rowl'd* to bed late,
   Lived Bryan O'Lynn in his glory.
With a nate spanchel'd* cawbeen† so gay,
He was crown'd by Queen Sheelah each day
       They say.
   Bryan's praise let us sing!
   What a jolly good king
Was rattling bowld Bryan O'Lynn!
       Hurroo!!

His palace was thatched with straw;
   There he took all his meals and his glass;
And all his dominions he saw,
   When he sauntered along on his ass;
Hearty, simple, and free, to confide,
With no guard but "Dog Tray" would he ride
      By his side.

---

* *Spanchel*, noun-substantive,—a hay or straw rope, chiefly used for tying the legs together of cows or pigs, to hinder them, not from trespassing on their neighbour's property, but from roaming too far from home. *Spanchel*, verb,—to tie or fasten with a hay or straw rope.

† A felt hat of no particular shape.

Bryan's praise let us sing !
What a jolly good king
Was rattling ould Bryan O'Lynn !
    Hurroo ! !

The nation ne'er groan'd for his table,
    Though he drank rather fast, it is true ;
Says Bryan, " If my people are able
    To drink, sure I'll drink whiskey, too.
An income-tax, then, at each door,
A pint to each keg he would score,
        No more.
    Bryan's praise let us sing, &c.

'Mongst the darlings of gentle degree
    He was mighty polite ; and 'twas rather
Suspected his subjects could see
    Many reasons to call him their father.
Four days in the year, sometimes six,
To manœuvre the boys, he would fix,
        And their sticks.
    Bryan's praise let us sing, &c.

With the neighbours most friendly lived he,
    And sighed not his power to increase ;
If with Bryan all our kings would agree,
    The world would have comfort and peace !
When on high he was called to appear,
Sad Dalkey then shed its first tear
        On his bier.
    For his death let us cry,
    Let us cry, " Arrah, why,
Bryney, jewel, och ! why did you die ?
        Wirrasthrew ! ! !"

Bryan's phiz is preserved to this day,
   Hung out o'er a sheebeen-shop door,
Where those that are able to pay
   May drink of good whiskey galore.
The house is in Tandragee,
And it's kept by one Widow Magee,—
       D' ye see?
   Bryan's praise let us sing,
   What a jolly good king
Was rattling ould Bryan O'Lynn!
      Hurroo!

THE IRISH WHISKEY-DRINKER.

OLD TIME.

THERE's a mighty old spirit abroad in the air,
And his footsteps are visible everywhere.
He hath been on the mountain, all hoary with years,
And left it bedew'd in an ocean of tears;
He hath clamber'd o'er turret and battlement grey,
And wrapt them in mantles of silent decay;
He hath swept through the forest, and laid at a blow
The stalwart oak, chief of the leafy tribe, low.
In art, as in nature, the vast and sublime,
All speak of the visits of greybeard "*Time*."

He's a skeleton thing, with a countenance grim,
All toothless his gums, and his eyeballs dim;
A two-edged scythe in his lank, boney hand,
His scutcheon's a hatchment, and glass ebbing sand;
With tiar of jewels, worm-eaten and black,
And arrows armipotent slung at his back;
He leaps with the lightning, and mounts with the wind,
Destroying and scattering before and behind;
The sun-dial's shadow, and old abbey's chime,
Denote, with a warning, the mission of "*Time*."

He roameth, unwearied, by night and by day,
A daring old foot-pad, still tracking our way;
He feareth no dungeon, no judicial fate,
But plund'reth alike from the beggar'd and great;
He nestleth with youth in its valley of flowers,
And sporteth with love through the eagle-wing'd hours;
But the bald-pated laird and the tremulous knee
The most he delighteth with ever to be;
While the wounded in heart, and the deepest in crime,
Beg a call from the mighty physician, old " *Time.*"

He mindeth the traffic both early and late,
That lineth the road to eternity's gate,
And passeth none by, shod with earth's clayey mire,
But he taketh the body as toll for his hire.
The grandee may sit in his richly-carved chair,
And the life's blood of insects indignantly wear,—
And the monarch may rule as a god on his throne,
O'er the leasehold of "ashes" he maketh his own;
But the spoiler at last round their strongholds will climb,
And " six feet of earth" be the conquest of " *Time.*"

GEORGE LINNÆUS BANKS.

THE NORMAN PEASANT'S HYMN TO THE VIRGIN.

Hope of the faithful! behold us now bending,
　Submissive, contrite, at thy footstool of love ;
The tears of thy children repentant are blending,
　Oh! plead for their help in thy kingdom above !
　　　　Thou canst each bosom see,
　　　　May it more sinless be,
　　　　　Ave Maria,
　　　　To glorify thee !

We are defenceless without thy protection,
　To watch o'er our night, and to shield us by day ;
And 'tis to the warmth of thy care and affection
　Our thoughts are more hallow'd, our feet less astray.
　　　　Thou canst each bosom see,
　　　　May it more sinless be,
　　　　　Ave Maria,
　　　　To glorify thee!

Be thou our comfort, when shaded by sorrow,
　For weak are the tendrils we cling to below ;

As night is subdued in the dawn of a morrow.
  Illume with thy brightness the depths of our woe!
        Thou canst each bosom see,
        May it more sinless be,
          Ave Maria,
        To glorify thee!

Through the dim valley our vespers are pealing,
  Borne on the winds to a sunnier sphere ;
While yon star that lonely the skies are revealing
  Doth tell in its beaming thou hearest our prayer.
        Thou canst each bosom see,
        May it more sinless be,
          Ave Maria,
        To glorify thee!

                              WILLIAM JONES.

THE QUIET HOUR.

LISTEN, listen! sounds are stealing
  Tiptoe on the balmy air ;
Eve, her rainbow robe revealing,
  Blushes through the twilight fair ;
Whilst dreamy voices, touch'd with Pleasure's pain,
Hum their sweet incense through the yearning brain.

Listen, listen! hearts are beating
  To a soft yet dulcet tone ;
Speak not—breathe not,—eyes are meeting,
  Rich in light as jewell'd zone :
Echo enchanted sleeps—the fragrant breeze
Just fans the leaflets on the em'rald trees.

Listen, listen! streams are singing
  Down amid the amber glade ;
Fairies perfumed bells are ringing,
  The night-bird trills from out the shade.
Shall not our silent souls awake to move
In unison, when all around is love ?

T. J. OUSELEY.

THE CHRISTENING OF HER ROYAL HIGHNESS THE PRINCESS ALICE MAUDE.

MOLLY, my dear, did you ever hear
    The likes of me from Cork to Dover?
The girls all love me far and near,
    They're mad in love with " Pat the Rover."

Molly Machree, you didn't see
    The Princess Ailleen's royal christening;
You'll hear it every word from me,
    If you'll be only after listening.
To see the mighty grand affair
    The *Quality* got invitations;
And wasn't I myself just there,
With half-a-dozen blood relations?
               Molly, my dear, &c.

What lots of Ladies curtsied in,
    And Peers all powdhered free an aisy!
Miss Biddy Maginn, and Bryan O'Lynn,
    Katty Neil, and bould Corporal Casey.
Lord Clarendine, and Lord Glandine,
    Each buckled to a Maid of Honour,
The Queen of Spain, and Lord Castlemaine;
    The Queen of France, and King O'Connor,
               Molly, my dear, &c.

There was no lack, you may be sure,
   Of writers, and of rhetoricians,
Of Whigs and Tories, rich and poor,
   Priests, patriots, and politicians.
The next came in was Father Prout,
   With a fine ould dame from the Tunbridge waters,
And Dan O'Connell, bould and stout,
   Led in Rebecca and her Daughters.
                    Molly, my dear, &c.

Some came in pairs, some came in chairs,
   From foreign parts, and parts adjacent !
" Ochone ! I'm alone !" says the Widow Malone,
   " Is there nobody here to do the daycent ?"
There was Peggy O'Hara, from Cunnemara,
   And who her beau was I couldn't tell, sir ;
But the Duke of Buccleuch danced with Molly Carew,
   And Paddy from Cork with Fanny Ellsler !
                    Molly, my dear, &c.

We every one sat down to tay :
   The toast and muffins flew like winking ;
Before or since that blessed day
   I never saw such eating and drinking.
We had pigeon-pies, and puddings likewise ;
   We walk'd into the pastries after ;
We 'd D'Arcy's whiskey, and Guinness's stout,
   Impayrial pop, and soda-water !
                    Molly, my dear, &c.

And when there was no more to sup,
   The Prince cried, " Piper, rouse your chanter !"
The band of blind fiddlers then struck up,
   And scraped " God save the Queen" *instanter.*

Her Majesty she danced, d' ye see,
   An Irish hornpipe with Sir Bobby ;
We piled the chairs upon the stairs,
   And pitch'd the tables on the lobby.
                  Molly, my dear, &c.

The clargy then at last came in—
   Says he, "Ladies and gentlemen, will ye 's all be
     sayted ?"
" Faith," says I, " I wish you'd soon begin ;
   I long to see the job complayted."
And soon it was.   The young Princess
   Was stood for by my gossip's daughter ;
And didn't Father Mathew bless,
   And sprinkle her with holy water?
                  Molly, my dear, &c.
                   THE IRISH WHISKEY-DRINKER.

A LYRIC FOR CHRISTMAS.

WINTER has resumed his reign;
Snow envelopes hill and plain;
Sleep the summer flowers in earth,
And the birds refrain from mirth:
Yet mirth lightens every eye;
Every pulse is beating high;
Gladness smiles in cot and hall,
Like a winsome dame on all,
And the church-bells sweetly chime,—
'Tis the merry Christmas time.

From the holly-tree be brought
Boughs with ruby berries fraught;
Search the grey oak high and low
For the mystic misletoe;
Bid the ivy loose her rings
That round rock or ruin clings;
Deck the shrine with foliage green;
In each house be verdure seen,
Just as earth were in her prime,—
'Tis the cheerful Christmas time.

Pile the board with viands rare,
Savoury dishes—hearty fare;
Brawn of boar, and capon good,
Fowls from river, marsh, and wood;
Partridge plump, and pheasant wild,
Teal and duck by art beguiled;
Bid the huge sirloin smoke nigh,
Luscious pastry, fruit-stored pie,
Fruit that grew in Eastern clime,—
'Tis the festal Christmas time.

Quickly broach the oldest cask,
Bring the goblet, bring the flask;
Ale of England, wine from Spain,
Rhenish vintage, choice champagne:
Fill as wont the wassail bowl,
Let it round the circle trowl;
Whilst the yule-fire blazes bright,
Whilst the yule-torch lends its light,
Till we hear the morning chime—
'Tis the joyful Christmas time.

Feed the hungry, clothe the poor,
Chide no wanderer from the door;
Bounteous give, with thankful mind,
To the wretched of mankind.
This day throws the barrier down,
'Twixt the noble and the clown;
For an equal share have all
In its blessed festival,
Of each colour, class, and clime,—
'Tis the holy Christmas time.

As our fathers used of old
Still the solemn rites we hold,
And with season-hallow'd mirth
Celebrate our SAVIOUR's birth.
Chaunt those ancient carols well
That the wondrous story tell;
Call the jocund masquers in;
Bid the dancers' sport begin.
Blameless tale and cheerful song
Shall our merriment prolong,
Whilst around the church-bells chime
For the solemn Christmas time.

W. G. J. BARKER.

THE GENIUS OF THEOCRITUS.

" And with a tale, forsooth, he cometh to you—with a tale which
holdeth children from play, and old men from the chimney corner."

SIR PHILIP SIDNEY.

THEOCRITUS! Theocritus! ah! thou had'st pleasant
    dreams,
Of the crystal spring Burinna, and the Haleus' murm'ring
    streams ;
Of Physcus, and Neaethus, and fair Arethusa's fount,
Of Lacinion's beetling crag, and Latymnus' woody mount ;
Of the fretted rocks and antres hoar that overhang the
    sea,
And the sapphire sky and thymy plains of thy own sweet
    Sicily ;
And of the nymphs of Sicily, that dwelt in oak and pine—
Theocritus! Theocritus! what pleasant dreams were
    thine!

And of the merry rustics who tend the goats and sheep,
And the maids who trip to milk the cows at morning's
    dewy peep,
Of Clearista with her locks of brightest sunny hair,
And the saucy girl Eunica, and sweet Chloe kind and
    fair ;

And of those highly favoured ones, Endymion and Adonis,
Loved by Selena the divine, and the beauteous Dionis;
Of the silky-haired capella, and the gentle lowing kine—
Theocritus! Theocritus! what pleasant dreams were
 thine!

Of the spring time, and the summer, and the zephyr's
 balmy breeze;
Of the dainty flowers, and waving elms, and the yellow
 humming bees;
Of the rustling poplar and the oak, the tamarisk and the
 beech,
The dogrose and anemone,—thou had'st a dream of each!
Of the galingale and hyacinth, and the lily's snowy hue,
The couch-grass, and green maiden-hair, and celandine
 pale blue,
The gold-bedropt cassidony, the fern, and sweet wood-
 bine—
Theocritus! Theocritus! what pleasant dreams were
 thine!

Of the merry harvest-home, all beneath the good green
 tree,
The poppies and the spikes of corn, the shouting and the
 glee
Of the lads so blithe and healthy, and the girls so gay
 and neat,
And the dance they lead around the tree with ever
 twinkling feet;
And the bushy piles of lentisk to rest the aching brow,
And reach and pluck the damson down from the overladen
 bough,

And munch the roasted bean at ease, and quaff the
    Ptelean wine—
Theocritus! Theocritus! what pleasant dreams were
    thine!

And higher dreams were thine to dream—of Heracles
    the brave,
And Polydenkes good at need, and Castor strong to
    save;
Of Dionysus and the woe he wrought the Theban king;
And of Zeus the mighty centre of Olympus' glittering
    ring;
Of Tiresias, the blind old man, the famed Aonian seer;
Of Hecatè, and Cthonian Dis, whom all mankind revere;
And of Daphnis lying down to die beneath the leafy
    vine—
Theocritus! Theocritus! what pleasant dreams were
    thine!

But mostly sweet and soft thy dreams—of Cypris' loving
    kiss,
Of the dark-haired maids of Corinth, and the feasts of
    Sybaris;
Of alabaster vases of Assyrian perfume,
Of ebony, and gold, and pomp, and softly-curtained
    room;
Of Faunus piping in the woods to the Satyrs' noisy rout,
And the saucy Panisks mocking him with many a jeer
    and flout;
And of the tender-footed Hours, and Pieria's tuneful
    Nine—
Theocritus! Theocritus! what pleasant dreams were
    thine!

TO THE SPIRIT OF THE FLOWERS.

SPIRIT of floral beauty! where
Hast thou thy dwelling? In the air?
    Or in some flow'ret's cell?
Or lingerest thou in leafy bed,
Where the young violet droops its head,
Which on the breeze such fragrance shed,
    Or in the lily's bell?

Speak, fairy spirit! is thy form
With life instinct, with feeling warm?
    Or has all-bounteous heaven
A dewy essence from on high,
Invisible to mortal eye,
Yet sweeter than the west wind's sigh,
    To human weakness given?

Ah no! for angels loudly sung,
When first thy beauty's rays were flung
    On Eden's sinless bowers;
For in those joyous primal days
Both earth and heaven were join'd to raise
One universal hymn of praise,
    As sprung the laughing flowers!

When morn, with golden sandall'd feet,
Comes forth the dewy earth to greet,
    Thou floatest swift along,
And, by a sunbeam borne on high,
Careerest through the rosy sky,
Unmindful of the tempest nigh,
    To join the lark's sweet song!

Then through the long sweet summer hour
Thou wantonest from flower to flower,
    Unwearied as the bee;
The nectar'd honey-drops which dwell
Within the fair narcissus' bell,
Or in the woodbine's fragrant cell,
    He gladly shares with thee!

If chill the breeze of evening blows,
Thy form is folded in the rose,
    And through the livelong night,
On silken couch of beauty rare,
Curtain'd with crimson drapery fair,
Secure from harm thou slumberest there,
    'Mid dreams of soft delight.

Bright spirit! from my childhood's hour
A secret spell of soothing power
    Thou laid'st upon my heart;
And now that in maturer life
The storm and tempest still are rife,
And never-ending seems the strife,
    I could not say, "Depart!"

I woo'd thee in the sylvan glade,
Were hawthorn sweet a temple made
    For such as loved the spot,
And in the garden's trim retreat,
And by the winding hedge-row sweet,
Were carpet sprung beneath my feet
    Of blue " Forget-me-not."

And when the mighty forest-trees
Were bending in the autumn breeze,
    Oh ! then in greenhouse fair,
A cherish'd and a favour'd guest,
'Mid courtly beauties gaily drest,
In azure zone or crimson vest,
    Fair queen ! I sought thee there !

And thou cans't hallow'd feelings bring,
And softest recollections fling
    O'er pensive memory.
The rose-buds, stain'd with many a tear,
I laid upon each little bier
Of some, the beautiful, the dear,
    Too early lost to me !

Oh ! evermore in rural dell,
In flow'ry grot, in mossy cell,
    Wherever springs a flower,
An altar will I raise to thee,
And faithful bend a willing knee
At shrine of thy divinity,
    And own thy mystic power !

                      H. B. K.

A MERRY AND MARVELLOUS DITTY ON THE MOUNTAIN DEW.

Whiskey—drink divine!
  Why should driv'llers bore us
With the praise of wine,
  Whilst we 've thee before us?
Were it not a shame,
  Whilst we gaily fling thee
To our lips of flame,
  If we would not sing thee!

CHORUS.

Whiskey—drink divine!
  Why should driv'llers bore us
With the praise of wine,
  Whilst we 've thee before us?

Greek and Roman sung
  Chian and Falernian;
Shall no harp be strung
  To thy praise Hibernian?
Yes; let Erin's sons,
  Generous, brave, and frisky,
Tell the world at once
  They owe it to their whiskey!
      Whiskey—drink divine! &c.

AD ROREM MONTANUM. DITHYRAMBUS

VITÆ Ros divine!
  Vinum quis laudaret
Te præsente—quis
  Palmam Vino daret?
Proh pudor! immemores
  Tui, dum te libamus,
Ore flammato tuos
  Honores non canamus?

CHORUS.

Vitæ Ros divine!
  Vinum quis laudaret
Te præsente—quis
  Palmam vino daret?

Veteres Falernum
  Chiumque laudavêre;
De te nefas filios
  Hibernice silere!
Nam fortes et protervi
  Hibernice habentur;
Tibique has virtutes
  Debere confitentur.
      Vitæ Ros divine! &c.

If Anacreon, who
   Was the grapes' best poet,
Drank the Mountain Dew,
   How his verse would show it!
As the best then known,
   He to wine was civil;
Had he Innishowen
   He'd pitch wine to the *divil!*
       Whiskey—drink divine! &c.

Bright as Beauty's eye
   When no sorrow veils it;
Sweet as Beauty's sigh
   When Young Love inhales it;
Come thou, to my lip!
   Come, oh, rich in blisses!
Every drop I sip
   Seems a shower of kisses!
       Whiskey—drink divine! &c.

Could my feeble lays
   Half thy virtues number,
A whole grove of bays
   Should my brows encumber.
Be his name adored
   Who summ'd up thy merits
In one little word,
   When he called thee " SPERRITS !"
       Whiskey—drink divine! &c.

Send it gaily round;
   Life would be no pleasure
If we had not found
   This immortal treasure.

Teius Lyæi
  Cecinit honorem ;
Cecinisset dulcius
  Montanum ille Rorem !
HORDEARIUM si
  Forte libavisset !
Ad inferos Lyæum,
  Anacreon misisset !
        Vitæ Ros divine ! &c.

Clarior ocello
  Veneris ridente ;
Suavior suspirio,
  Cupidine præsente !
Liceat beatis
  Te labris applicare,
Imbrem et basiorum
  Guttatim delibare !
        Vitæ Ros divine ! &c.

Versibus pusillis
  Si satis te laudarem,
Lauro Apollinari
  Hæc tempora celarem.
Faustus ille semper
  Sit, et honoratus,
A quo " SPIRITUS" tu
  Meritò vocatus !
        Vitæ Ros divine ! &c.

Ordine potemus
  Festivo recumbentes,
ur vivere optemus
  Hoc munere egentes?

And when tyrant Death's
   Arrows shall transfix you,
Let your latest breaths
   Be " Whiskey ! whiskey !! whiskey !!!"

CHORUS.

Whiskey—drink divine !
   Why should driv'llers bore us
With the praise of wine,
   Whilst we 've thee before us?

THE IRISH WHISKEY-DRINKER.

Cum te Libitina
  Telo vulnerabit,
" Nectar ! Nectar !" spiritus
  Deficiens clamabit !

CHORUS.

Vitæ Ros divine !
  Vinum quis laudaret
Te præsente—quis
  Palmam vino daret ?

ENDURANCE.

FROM THE PROM VINC. OF ÆSCHYLUU.

OH ! air divine,
Breezes of fleetest wing !
Oh fountains clear,
When pearly rivers spring ;
Waves of the sea!
Whose countless twinklings tell of mirth ;
And thou benign
Parent of all,—dear mother earth !
Thou full-orb'd sun !
That shinest on
Whate'er thoughout the world hath birth ;
On you I call—behold ! and see
What evils I, Divinity,
From Deity must bear ;
Oh ! see me mock'd with bitter scorn,
Oh ! see me by rude insults torn,
And rackt by sleepless care.
For years on years no changes I shall see,
For years on years shall strive against my fate ;
So hard the chain that has been forged for me,
By heaven's new tyrant's unrelenting hate.

Ah me! I mourn the evils of to-day,
  I weep the perils of my future years!
The goals of sorrow, tell me, where are they?
  When will be dried the fountain of my tears?
    What say I? for my future doom
    Too well I know. No ill can come
Unknown to me. Oh! then, as best I may,
  I'll learn with firm, resigned soul,
My lot to bear. There has been found no way
  Whereby to shun necessity's control.

                  REV. W. B. FLOWER, B.A.

SPRING.

A RELIC OF PROVENÇAL LITERATURE.

ANGELIC choirs in upper air chaunt with their golden
    tongues
The praises of that mighty king to whom the world
    belongs;
Who bade the stars to shine in heaven; who severed land
    from sea;
Who gave the fishes to the deep, the cattle to the lea.
The beauteous Spring begins its reign; the woods are in
    their bloom;
The verdant trees put forth their leaves, the flowrets shed
    perfume;
The birds commence their twittering songs, and of the
    feather'd crowd,
The smallest has the notes that are the sweetest and most
    loud.
'Tis Philomel, who in the grove has sought the highest
    spray,
And thence pours forth sweet melody from eve to dawn
    of day.
Ah, gentle bird! incessantly why dost thou thus bewail?
Wouldst quell the sounds of lyre and harp by thy more
    plaintive tale?

The maid who strikes the timbrel stops to lend a willing
    ear,
And princes in attention stand thy thrilling song to hear.
Cease, gentle bird, to strain thy throat with notes so
    wild and deep,
And let the weary world at last resign itself to sleep.
Ah! wretched bird, thou wilt not cease, but through the
    livelong night,
Neglecting food, wilt persevere the listeners to delight.
All hear with joy, but in return none succour will afford,
Save He who gave the power of song, the all-preserving
    Lord.
But summer comes, the bird is hush'd, by parent's care
    engross'd,
Forgotten then, unknown he dies by chill of winter's
    frost.

W. C. TAYLOR.

SONNET FROM PETRARCH.

TRANSLATED BY LADY NUGENT.

I go lamenting o'er my days past by,
Those days consumed in love of mortal thing,
Without attempt to mount, I having wing
Perchance to soar and give example high.
Thou, who dost see my deep iniquity,
Invisible, immortal, heavenly King,
Aid the frail soul in her wild wandering,
In what defective form thy grace supply;
So I, with strife and storm wont to contend,
May thus in peace and haven die. I see
How vain the past, yet blameless be the end;
O'er that short span of life now left for me,
And at its close, thy saving hand extend—
Thou know'st I have no hope in aught but Thee.

OWED TO MY CREDITORS.

In vain I lament what is past,
   And pity their woe-begone looks ;
Though they grin at the credit they gave,
   I know I am in their best books.
To my *tailor* my *breaches* of faith,
   On my conscience now but lightly sit,
For such lengths in *his measures* he's gone,
   He has given me many *a fit.*
My bootmaker finding *at last,*
   That my *soul* was too stubborn to suit,
Waxed wroth when he found he had got
   Anything but *the length of my foot.*
My hatmaker cunningly *felt*
   He'd seen many like me before,
So *brimful* of insolence, vowed
   On credit he'd crown me no more.
My baker was crusty, and burnt,
   When he found himself quite overdone,
By a *fancy-bred* chap like myself—
   Ay, as *cross* as a *Good-Friday's bun.*
Next my laundress, who washed pretty clean,
   In behaviour was dirty and bad ;
For into hot water she popp'd
   All the shirts and the dickies I had.

Then my butcher who'd little *at stake*,
  Most surlily opened his *chops*,
And swore my affairs out of joint,
  So on to my carcase he pops.
In my lodgings exceedingly high,
  Though low in the rent to be sure,
Without warning my landlady seized,
  Took my things, and the key of the door.
Thus cruelly used by the world,
  In the Bench I can smile at its hate ;
For a time I must alter my stile,
  For I cannot get out of the Gate.

                          ALFRED CROWQUILL.

FAREWELL WINDS AND WINTRY WEATHER!

FAREWELL winds and wintry weather!
Mistress, let us go together
Forth into the fields, and pay
Due observance unto May.
On the breezy hills we go ;
For once no daily care shall find us;
Where the city sleeps below,
Wear and tear we leave behind us.

Stretch'd upon the springing grass,
Lazily the day we'll pass,
And, with half-shut, dreamy eye,
Look upon the cloudless sky ;
Or along the river side,
Through its silent meadows strolling,
Moralize till eventide,
As we mark its waters rolling.

If beneath a bank they flow,
Where the lowly spring-flowers blow,
While o'er head the eglantine
And the clustering maythorn twine,

On whose sprays the wind doth breathe,
Lover-like, with soft caresses,
There we'll linger while I wreathe
Garlands for thy sunny tresses.

And I'll sing thee many a rhyme,
Framed in honour of the time;
Or in thought I'll Arcite be;
Thou a fairer Emilie.
Or I'll crown thee Queen of May,
Though no village maids, advancing,
Greet thee with their joyous lay,
Or are round the May-pole dancing.

Thus in olden time they paid
Homage to the bounteous Spring,
And reviving Nature made
The object of their worshipping;
Thus they met her earliest smile,
Glad and thankful welcome giving,
And forgot life's load awhile,
In the mere delight of living.

THE IRISH WHISKEY-DRINKER.

FORGET ME NOT!

COME, Herman, soothe this hour of sadness,
　Come to thy Bertha's throbbing breast,
The breast which Love once filled with gladness
　Is now with darkest woes oppressed.
Too rapidly the moments stealing
　Demand obedience to thy lot,
Yet, ere the final hour is pealing,
　Receive my prayer, Forget me not!

No breast can ever love thee fonder!
　Forget not, then, thy faithful maid,
Who oft from home and friends would wander,
　To seek with thee the silent shade.
These eyes from thine would rapture borrow,
　No cloud then dimmed my happy lot;
But now my voice oppressed with sorrow,
　Can scarcely breathe, Forget me not!

This burning kiss shall be a token
　That years thy form shall ne'er efface;
Those solemn vows our lips have spoken
　Are sealed in this, our last embrace.
But, see! the emblem flow'rets wither
　That bloomed beneath my lowly cot;
And they, till thou returnest hither,
　Shall whisper still, Forget me not!

When shadowy branches wave before me,
   When murmuring zephyrs charm my ear,
Thy faithful form shall hover o'er me,
   And memory wake the silent tear.
Ah! then from yonder verdant willow—
   Our names record the sacred spot,—
The breeze shall waft across the billow
   My earnest prayer, Forget me not!

Ah! silent then yon weeping fountain,
   Ah! scentless then the flow'ret's bloom;
Dark shades will hang o'er vale and mountain,
   And heaven itself be wrapped in gloom.
The birds will greet the blushing morrow—
   Their amorous joyful notes forgot,
With tones that breathe in fruitless sorrow
   The longing wish, Forget me not!

When magic strains are round thee breathing,
   Ah! think on her who loves thee yet,
Though fairer maids thy flow'rets wreathing,
   May tempt thy spirit to forget.
May *her* afflictions never sadden,
   Her tears ne'er dim thy brighter lot;
Yet 'mid the joys thy manhood gladden,
   Thou happier one, Forget me not!

THE HEART'S MISGIVINGS.

LINES ON THE PICTURE BY FRANK STONE.

THERE'S a languor in the air,
   And a stillness all around,
The landscape wide and fair
   Is in dreamy silence drown'd
The sky is blue and bright,
   And all is fair to see ;
But the maiden sigheth sadly,
   " Ah ! he careth not for me !"

The royal sun goes down
   Like a bridegroom to his bower,
Flash from his golden crown
   Bright beams on tree and tower ;
But that scene of summer splendour,
   Though so beautiful to see,
She heeds not, but sighs sadly,
   " Ah ! he careth not for me !"

Like as snow her forehead white,
   Dark her hair as raven's wing,
Bright her eyes as stars of light,
   Sweet her lips as flowers of spring :

Quick her breathing heaves her bosom,
  Like the throbbings of the sea,
And she sighs again more sadly,
  " Ah ! he careth not for me !"

Against the old stone wall
  She leans with clasped hands,
Nought to her that castled hall,
  Nought to her these wide-spread lands;
For on the youth that 's near her
  She gazes fixedly ;
But she sighs, and thinketh sadly,
  " Ah! he careth not for me !"

He sits, while *she* doth stand,—
  He laughs, *her* eyes grow dim,
He sees that only on his hand,
  She sees but only him :—
A hawk is on his hand,
  And a dog is at his knee,
And the maiden sigheth sadly,
  " Ah ! he careth not for me !"

" No ! he careth not for me,
  Though my heart is all his own ;
Since I saw him ne'er 'twas free,
  And 'tis his, and his alone !
'Tis no slight thing or unstable,
  'Tis no trifle that I 've given !
For my *life* to him I 've trusted,
  And he is now my heaven !

" Pure as that sky above,
  With not a cloud to dim,
Is the pure and holy love
  That I have shrined in him ;
But he laughs whene'er I tell him
  That like this my love can be."
And once more she sighed sadly,
  " Ah ! he careth not for me !"

" Oh ! he little thinks the anguish
  His unconcern can bring,
Or deems the heart can languish
  In life's first early spring,
But thinks that merry girlhood
  Must *ever* thoughtless be."
And again she sighed sadly,
  " Ah ! he careth not for me !"

" When he speaks mine eyes do glisten,
  And I feel a burning glow
Come o'er me as I listen
  To the voice so well I know.
When he comes I know his footstep,
  And I thrill with ecstacy !
But"—she paused, and sighed sadly,
  " He careth not for me !"

" No ! his hound, his steed, his bird,
  To him are dearer far,
And no reproachful word
  Shall his youthful pleasures mar.

Yes! these my heart's misgivings
   Shall not damp his happy glee"—
But the maiden sighed sadly,
   "Ah! *would* he 'd care for me!"

Down went the royal sun,
   And the purple twilight came,
And the stars rose one by one,
   Still the maiden gazed the same!
But unmoved by twilight hour,
   That "hour of love," was he,
And the maiden sighed sadly,
   "Ah! he careth not for me!"

There's a languor in the air,
   All around's in dreamy rest,
And love is everywhere
   Save in *his* youthful breast:
More entranced with his hawk
   Than that maiden fair is he,
And her heart's misgiving is,
   "Ah! he careth not for me!"

CUTHBERT BEDE.

IRENE OF SESTOS.

THE EAGLE.

I.

CALMLY the dewy moonbeams sleep
Where Helle's restless billows sweep
Round Sestos' height ; the sky is clear,
And o'er that scene to love so dear
Broods silence, save for the low plash
Caused by the waters as they dash
Against the rocks with trembling motion,
Making soft music o'er old ocean.
Rich odours float upon the air
From groves of limes and citrons rare ;
And all the flowers asleep that lie
Send up sweet incense to the sky,
Whence many a planet's lambent glow
Showers influence o'er the world below.

II.

It is a spot from eldest time
In song renown'd through eastern clime,
Since Helle in her blooming age,
Flying to 'scape unnatural rage,

Found 'neath those waves her destined grave,
And to the strait a title gave.
And sadder still the interest thrown,
O'er sea and land, o'er cliff and stone,
By young Leander's fate, who died
Love's martyr in the storm-lash'd tide;
And her's who, having lit in vain
Her lamp, to guide through wind and rain
That hapless youth, beheld him borne
Lifeless beneath her tower at morn,
And faithful, chose the same dark doom,
Sharing alike his death and tomb.

III.

Yet not peculiar to that place,
Its clime serene, and classic race,
Are the sweet legends minstrels tell
Of lovers who but loved too well;
For every land beneath the sun
Can boast some tale of marvels done
By fond affection,—cape and bay,
Mainland and isle, through Beauty's sway
Have hallow'd been; and every clan
Of the wide scatter'd tribes of man,
How rude soe'er in all beside,
Still treasure up with jealous pride
Traditions sad, for ages kept,
O'er which long since their fathers wept;
Stories of young hearts' deep devotion—
   Love's ardent hopes, and words, and sighs;
That passion pure, whose true emotion
   Never save with existence dies.

IV.

On Sestos' towers the moonbeams rest,
  Casting a radiance solemn
Around each temple's sculptured walls,
  Carved frieze, and polish'd column :
The marble statues of the Gods,
  Lit by their silver streaming,
Resemble those celestial forms
  We only see when dreaming.
Amid the sombre cypress groves
  The light in circles glances,
On Juno's fountain's murmuring stream,
  As if in sport it dances.
Not brighter was that radiance shower'd
  When Night, with tardy pinion,
Saw Dian watch on Latmos mount
  The wakening of Endymion.

V.

Gaze not upon those sacred towers,
But rather turn, where girt with flowers,
A mansion stands of modest size,
Round which the dark green chestnuts rise;
Against the sky : there, in a room
Half shaded by the pleasant gloom
Of vine and clematis that twine
About its casement, and combine
Their tendrils sportively ; half lit
By beams that on its pavement flit
Like elvish visitants, is laid
In slumber deep a youthful maid,

Her ivory arm her rose-cheek pillows,
   That cheek is with a faint blush warm,
And floating down in raven billows,
   Her dark hair partly veils her form:
Amid its fragrant tresses lie
Sea-pearls, and blooms, whence scent and dye
Have hardly faded;—though repose
Has made those snowy eyelids close
On glorious orbs, whose tender light
Is as the evening planet bright,
Not all-unconscious is she now—
A smile illumes both lips and brow—
Her bosom heaves—one low-voiced word
She speaks, so soft 'tis scarcely heard.

VI.

Ah, truant Love! in sleep revealing
   The tender thoughts that maiden care,
Through the long sunshine hours concealing,
   Forbids the dearest friend to share:
In dreams thou still dost promise bliss,
Fitter for brighter worlds than this;
Painting with heaven's ethereal hues
The darkest scene thy votary views,
And kindling hopes which after-pain
Too late will prove were lit in vain.
Restraint may be around thee thrown
By day, but night is all thy own;
And 'twas thy purest, holiest flame,
That, when she murmur'd Cleon's name,
Called to Irene's cheek the blush
Mantling it yet with roseate flush.

VII.

Has Jove from high Olympus sent
  His own celestial bird
To guard the dreaming maiden's rest,
  And whisper some sweet word
In her entranced ear; and keep
Fantastic visions from her sleep ?
Or did an earthly eyry bear
The glorious eagle watching there
Beside her couch ? His flashing eyes
  Are partly closed, as if he slept;
And smooth each folded pinion lies,
  That late thro' storms unruffled swept—
Smooth as the wood-dove's silver wing
  Seen through the pine-bough's shadowing.

VIII.

Upon a lofty rock of Thrace
  To life that eagle sprung;
A youthful band assail'd the place,
Destroy'd the parents of the race,
  And seized their unfledg'd young.
One nestling Cleon proudly bare
In triumph to Irene fair,
And gave ;—love-gifts were prized of old
As much when slight as when of gold.
The gentle girl right tenderly
Nourish'd the helpless bird, for she
And Cleon loved ;—besides, the task
Was such as maiden care might ask ;
Pleased she beheld the white down shed
And sprouting plumage deck his head,

And saw each callow wing unfold
Its feathers bright of brown and gold:
The noble creature well repaid
The kind affection of the maid;
On pinions weak would round her fly,
Or haste to meet with joyous cry,
Striving how best he might express
The love he bore her tenderness;
And when at length the chase he sought,
   And slew the leveret or the quail,
Triumphantly his prize he brought,
   From rocky glen or fertile vale,
And laid it at Irene's feet,
So offering homage strange but meet.

IX.

The maiden joy'd to watch his flight,
   Upsoaring through the highest clouds,
As if to him belonged a right
   To pierce the azure veil that shrouds
The dwellings of the gods from sight,
And bask amid eternal light.
A thousand dreams her fancy blended
   Of bowers and bliss beyond those skies,
Till mark'd she, as the bird descended,
   The soften'd glories of his eyes;
Whilst downwards through pure ether stooping,
On wings that scarce her tresses fann'd,
Closely around his mistress swooping,
   Beside her he resumed his stand—
   Folding his pinions—as her hand
Would smooth each plume, and careful deck
With favourite flowers his glossy neck;

And his mute gestures eloquent
You well might deem responses meant
To her caresses.   When the sun
   Low in the western main was sinking,—
When beasts their lairs, and birds their nests
Sought, and the day-blooms dews were drinking—
When sweet repose upon her bed
Irene wooed,—above her head
His wings the eagle always spread,—
Like guardian from a better land,
An avatar of Heaven's bright band ;
And whilst in guiltless dreams she slept,
His watch and ward unwearied kept.
The tale was bruited, and some few,
Who almost more than mortals knew,
Said, JOVE upon that Eagle had conferr'd
High gifts, and deem'd him a celestial bird.

                      W. G. J. BARKER.

RAILWAY DACTYLS.

HERE we go off on the "London and Birmingham,"
　　Bidding adieu to the foggy metropolis!
Staying at home with the dumps, is confirming 'em ;—
　　Motion and mirth are a fillip to life.
Let us look out! Is there aught that is *see*-able?
　　Presto!—away!—what a vanishing spectacle!
Well! on the whole, it is vastly agreeable—
　　"Why, sir, perhaps it is all very well,"—
　　　　Tricketty, tracketty, tricketty, tracketty!
　　"*Barring* the noise, and the smoke, and the smell."

Now, with the company pack'd in the carriages,
　　Strange is the medley of voluble utterings,—
Comings and goings, deceases and marriages,—
　　Oh, what a clatter of matters is *there!*
History, politics, letters, morality,
　　Heraldry, botany, chemistry, cookery,
Poetry, physic, the stars, and legality,—
　　All in a loud opposition of tongues!
　　　　Tricketty, tracketty, tricketty, tracketty!
Never mind *that*—it is good for the lungs.

" All that 's remarkable, now, we may *stir* and see ;
    Free circulation—how huge are its benefits !"—
" Yet, sir, with all the improvement in *currency*,
    Great is the dread of *a run on the banks*."—
" *Fight* with *America !* Do but the folly see !
    Since unto *both*, sir, belongs the same *origin*."—
" What 's your opinion of Peel and his policy ?"—
    " What of the weather ?—and how is the wind ?"
        Tricketty, tracketty, tricketty, tracketty !
    " Oh ! that that *whistle* were far off as Ind !"

On, like a hurricane ! on, like a water-fall !
    Steam away ! scream away ! hissing and spluttering !
" Madam, beware lest your out-leaning daughter fall !"
    " Yes, sir, I will ; but her *life* is *insured*."—
" Cobden 's a-coming to mob and to rabble us !"—
    " Zounds ! sir, my *corn !* Do ye think I'm of adamant ?"—
" Oh, what an appetite ! Heliogabalus !
    That little fellow will eat himself *ill !*"
        Tricketty, tracketty, tricketty, tracketty !
    " When you 're at home again, give him a pill."

Oh, Mr. Hudson ! Macadam's extinguisher !
    Men are as boys in the grasp of thy *schoolery !*
Those who love England can no better *thing* wish her
    Than to have *thee* for her *Ruler of Lines !*
Praised as thy course is, to heighten the fame of it,
    I 'll give you a hint, without fee or expectancy :—
Write us a *book*—and let *this* be the name of it,
    " *Rail*-ways and *Snail*-ways ; or, Roads New and Old.'
        Tricketty, tracketty, tricketty, tracketty !
Won't such a volume in thousands be sold ?

Here we go on again, every link of us!
    Oh, what a chain! what a fly-away miracle!
Birds o' the firmament! what do ye think of us?
    Minutes! be steady, as *markers of miles!*
Well! of new greatness we now have the germ in us!
    But the *collector*, I see, coming hither is.
" Ladies and gentlemen—this is the *terminus*—
    Ticket, sir! ticket, sir!—end of the line!"
        Ricketty, racketty, ricketty, racketty!
    " Friends of velocity! now let us *dine!*"

                                       G. D.

A GAME AT ST. STEPHEN'S CHAPEL.

WHILE honest John Bull
   With sorrow brimfull,
Lamented his trusty friend Pitt,
   Some sharpers we're told
   In cheating grown old,
Thus tried all their *talents* and wit.

Let's invite him to play,
   John never says nay,
So they ask'd him what game he approv'd;
   John talk'd of All Fours,
   And Beat the Knave out of Doors,
The games of his youth which he lov'd.

Lord Howick spoke first,
   " In these games I'm not versed,
But they surely are old fashioned things,
   The best game *entre nous*
   Is the good game of Loo,
Where *knaves* get the better of *kings*."

Sam Whitbread rose next,
  By all Court Cards perplext,
Since at his trade they reckon no score;
  For at Cribbage tis known,
  That by Court Cards alone,
You can't make fifteen-two, fifteen-four.

Then Sheridan rose,
  Saying he should propose,
Tho' at all times he played upon tick,
  The good old game of Whist,
  For if honours he miss'd,
He was *sure to succeed* by the *trick*.

Now with blustering voice,
  Tierney roars out " My boys,
I approve none of all the selection;
  What I recommend
  To myself and my friend,
Is to play at the Game of Connection."

By his master respected,
  But by both sides suspected,
Telle est la fortune de la guerre
  Once the minister's *ombre*
  Now dejected and *sombre*,
The good Sidmouth preferred *solitaire*.

Next with perquisites stor'd
  Spoke Temple's good Lord,
(Whose wants are supplied by the nation,)
  " From our memory blot
  Pique, Repique, and Capot,
And practice our friend's Speculation."

Lord Grenville stood bye
  With considerate eye,
Which forbore e'en his thoughts to express;
  But Wyndham less mute,
  Own'd in each game in each suit,
He had play'd without any success.

  "Try again, sir, your skill,"
  Says Burdett "at Quadrille,
Then some of your friends may ask leave;
  As for calling a king
  I shall do no such thing,
But shall soon play alone, I believe."

  Braced with keen Yorkshire air,
  Young Lord Milton stood near,
Who improved in all talents of late,
  Said he feared not success
  In a bold game of chess,
And should soon give the king a check mate.

  "Hush," says Grenville, " young man
  I'll whisper my plan,
While professing great zeal for the throne,
  We may leave in the lurch
  Both the king and the church,
By encouraging slyly Pope Joan."

  In one hand a new dance,
  In the other Finance,
To throw on each subject new light;
  Young Petty appeared
  And begg'd to be heard,
In settling the game of the night.

" Cassino," he cries,
" Sure of all games supplies
Amusement unblended with strife,
     For the black, grey, or fair,
     With their fellows may pair,
And to all form a pleasure in life."

     Without further debate,
     Down to Cass they all sate;
But how strange is the game I record;
     The knaves were paired off,
     Of all Court Cards the scoff,
And in triumph the king cleared the board.

     John rubbing his eyes,
     At length with surprise,
Discovered the tricks of the crew;
     And gaining in sense
     What he had just lost in pence,
From the wolves in sheep's clothing withdrew.

                              GEORGE CANNING; 1803.

THE ENTHUSIAST DEAD.

I.

I KNEW a man that lived within the walls
    Of this un-eastern city, where I write;
Who breath'd that deathless hope, that never palls!
    But lives out for one all-immortal light!

II.

He did foretell,—he had a thoughtful mind,
    Too oe'r-inform'd by thought!—that wise worn man!—
That the Messiah's advent to mankind,—
    Was lighting on the years,—then in the van!

III.

He pass'd, in his believing prophecy,
    As many a wearied, dreaming man hath pass'd—
He died, before he found his faith must die;—
    Believing and predicting to the last!

IV.

Sweet in all 'haviour to his fellow-men,—
    Earnest in argument, profound in grief;—
Wise, and communicant to friend,—save when
    A doubt was shadow'd o'er his vast belief!

V.

Then, all the Jewish spirit fiercely rose !—
   And through his veins and eyes a firelight ran !
He saw a destined triumph o'er all woes !—
   And, in the Paul-like prophet, sank the man !

VI.

May his religious frenzy sleep at length !
   May he, beyond the power of earth, find rest !
His hopes, upborne, of an appalling strength,—
   Oh ! may they, in their high flight, find their nest !
      *   *   *   *   *

J. H. REYNOLDS.

KING CHARLES OF SPAIN.*

A GLOOM was on King Charles's brow,
   As pensive he sat, and lone,
In the gorgeous hall of the Escurial,
   On a high and stately throne.
None dared intrude on the monarch's mood
   When his spirit was thus o'ercast ;
But linger'd near, with a thrill of fear,
   Till the cloud from his soul had past.

He watch'd the shadows of evening fall
   On the treasures that lay around ;
Rare works in gold, of a cost untold,
   And gems through the world renown'd.

* The Archduke Charles, son of Leopold I., Emperor of Germany, and successor to Charles II. It is related of this prince, that towards the close of life he was tormented by hypochondriac fancies, during one of which he descended by torchlight into the cemetery of St. Lawrence, where reposed three generations of Castilian princes. There he had the massy chests which contained their relics opened, and gazed on the ghastly spectacle with little emotion, until the coffin of his first wife was unlocked, and she appeared before him—such had been the skill of the embalmer—in all her well-remembered beauty. This awful sight was too much for his already-shattered frame; and, leaving the Escurial, he retired to Madrid, where he died."—Lord Mahon's " *War of the Succession.*"

But they charm'd not him,—his eyes were dim,
  For sorrow had veil'd their light;
Death—death was the theme of his ev'ry dream,
  Nor left him by day or night!

Sudden he rose, and he cried aloud,
  " St. Lawrence hath chimed the hour
I fain would go to the vaults below,
  Where moulder the sons of power!
And mark them still, in their chamber chill,
  With banner and shroud o'erspread;
Why hasten ye not? 'Tis a goodly spot,
  The home of the ghostly dead!"

The torches shone with a fitful glare
  As they threaded the chapel aisle,
And pass'd the gate, where, in funereal state
  Lay the princes of old Castile!
The chiefs of his race! 'Twas a lonesome place,
  But meet for a monarch's rest,
For the sword and spear were gather'd there,
  And lay on each warrior's breast!

King Charles survey'd with an unchanged mien
  The chests where his sires reposed;
And said, as a smile lit his brow awhile,
  " Let the slumberers be unclosed.
Why paleth the cheek as the lids ye break?
  'Tis a glorious thing to see;
My heart is light, and welcomes the sight;
  No fears hath the grave for ME!"

And the same wild look his visage wore
 As they open'd the coffins wide,
And shew'd the dead in their ghastly bed,
 Despoil'd of their ancient pride!
The bones were bare, and wither'd in air,
 Like the dew 'neath the morning sun.
'Twas a fearful lot, but the King quail'd not,—
 It seem'd though his mind was gone.

The last remain'd—'twas a massive chest,
 That stood near a cross of black;
The bolts gave way, and the torches' ray
 Shone o'er—but the King drew back.
Why shudders his frame as he reads the name
 Inscribed on that iron chest?
Why droops his head as he marks the dead?
 And whom had he robb'd of rest?

'Twas she who had long been deeply mourn'd,
 The wife he had fondly loved;
And there she lay, untouch'd by decay,
 Not a tress of her hair removed!
Beautiful still, though palid and chill
 She seem'd, in her queen's attire;
The jewell'd zone on her forehead shone
 And lighted the eyes with fire!

One look—'twas enough—the monarch wept,
 As with hands upraised he cried,
" Oh, God of the just! soon, soon, I trust
 To lay by that dear one's side!"
With a slow, sad pace, he quitted the place,
 And though his spirit awoke
To its wonted pow'r—in that dread hour
 The heart of the King was broke!

A DYING WIFE TO HER HUSBAND.

THEY tell me I must die, love,
   That nought can stay my doom,—
A week! and I must lie, love,
   In yonder silent tomb.

They say it *must* be so, love,
   And yet I feel no pain;
And see, the healthful glow, love,
   Comes to my cheek again.

Our babe's first sleep is sound, love,
   Her arms around me twine;
With *life* her pulses bound, love,
   Can there be *death* in mine?
     *   *   *   *

Thy burning temples throb, love,
   Thy tears fall fast as rain;
I hear thy stifled sob, love!
   Alas! my hopes are vain.
     *   *   *   *

We fondly deem'd but now, love,
  Our early troubles past,
And Hope's prismatic bow, love,
  Seem'd o'er the future cast!

I feel that it is sad, love
  From this fair earth to part,
While still young life is glad, love,
  Nor griefs have chilled the heart.

And yet I would not sigh, love,
  This happy world to leave,
Were 't not that I must die, love,
  While you are left to grieve.

Oh! think not that I dream, love,
  Nor chide me that I rave,
If faith like ours I deem, love,
  May live beyond the grave.

THE CORAL CAVES.

Round and round the coral bower
  Fairies dance the live-long day,
Watchful, lest the water's power
  Bear some jutting reef away :
Now they whisper, now they sing,
  To the laughter of the waves,
As their welcome song they bring
  To the distant coral caves.

Now they enter, and prepare
  For the transports of the night,
Wreathing in their shining hair
  Coral branches snowy white.
Hark! an echo, low and sweet,
  As they press the sleeping waves
Makes soft music to their feet
  In the silent coral caves.

Once again their hands entwine,
  And the banquet feast is spread,
Till the white reef, stained with wine,
  Like a maiden, blushes red :—
Now the festal rite is o'er,
  Day has peep'd into the waves,
And the fairies dance once more
  Round about the coral caves.

G. Linnæus Banks.

SONG OF THE PEOPLE.

I.

ONCE on a time in England,
  The king o'er all did rule,
Whether he were a knave or knight,
  A wise man or a fool.
And the haughty barons feared him,
  And bent before the crown ;
Nor heeded then the stifled cry
  Of the people trampled down.

II.

When this king he went a hunting,
  He sent his merry men
To drive the farmer from the field,
  The shepherd from the glen ;
And they razed each poor man's cottage
  In all the country round ;
That this king might go a hunting,
  On a kingly hunting ground.

III.

He seized the strong man's castle,
   By the right of the more strong;
And neither priest nor womankind
   Was sacred from his wrong.
What reck'd he of a woman's tears,
   Or of a churchman's gown?
What heeded he the stifled cry
   Of the people trampled down?

IV.

But this king he had a quarrel
   With his cousin king of France,
So he called out all his merry men
   With sword and bow and lance;
And they fought full many a battle
   On many a bloody plain,
And only rested from their strife
   To strive the more again.

V.

Then the barons they grew bolder,
   And they met at Runnymede;
" Thou 'st taught us war, oh king!" they cried,
   " And now we must be freed."
So the king he quailed before them,
   Them and their stern appeal,
And he gave them Magna Charta,
   And sealed it with his seal.

VI.

Next these barons ruled in England
  With iron heart and hand ;
And sorer even than the king
  Did they oppress the land.
They fought full many a battle,
  With roses white and red,
That they might put a shadow's crown
  Upon an empty head.

VII.

And in their bitter striving,
  The red blood flowed like rain,
Till the flower of English manhood
  By English hands was slain.
And their wars spread woe and wailing
  In country and in town,
None heeded then the stifled cry
  Of the people trampled down.

VIII.

At length they ceased to battle
  And to cut their neighbours' throats,
And, as gentler Whigs and Tories,
  They bought each other's votes ;
And rich men only made the laws
  For country and for town,
None heeded yet the stifled cry
  Of the people trampled down.

IX.

At last there rose a murmur
  From out that patient crowd,
And the sound of million voices
  Swell'd like a tempest loud,
" Our rights! our rights!" they shouted,
  Till it thunder'd in the ears
Of the gentle Whigs and Tories,
  And the king and all his peers.

X.

Oh! the will of earnest millions
  None may withstand its might,
When strong in holy patience—
  Strong in a holy right!
So, with justice for their banner,
  And reason for their sword,
They won their bloodless battle,
  But wrong'd no squire nor lord.

XI.

Now there's right in merry England
  For the cottage and the throne,
The king he has his honours,
  And the poor man holds his own ;
And in our happy island,
  In country and in town,
Is heard no more the stifled cry
  Of the people trampled down.

I O N E.

Sad are the glances from thy deep blue eyes,
            Ione!
Soft as the mirror of the summer skies,
When twilight's shadows o'er its surface steal,
And twinkling stars their radiant orbs reveal:
            Why are they sad,
            Which were so glad,
                  Ione?
Have their rays bath'd in dewdrops 'mid the air,
And still the sparkling moisture trembles there?
            Then smile, for dewy tears
            Melt when the sun appears,
                  Ione!

Yet thou art very beautiful in sadness,
            Ione!
More beautiful e'en than in gladness!
And the sweet music of those gentle sighs
Comes like the language of thy speaking eyes.
            What do they say?
            Tell me their lay,
                  Ione!
Fain would I learn from thee what passing thought
Can with such plaintive melody be fraught.
            Ah! wherefore turn away?
            Stay! yet a little stay!
                  Ione!

                              W. R. C.

A LETTER FROM AN OLD COUNTRY HOUSE.

DEAR ARTHUR,

       'Tis so very slow,
  I can't tell what to do,
And so I've got a pen and ink,
  And mean to write to *you!*
You know how intervening space
  I reckon'd, bit by bit,
Until this time arrived : and now
  It has not proved a hit !

'Tis very well. The house is old,
  With an enormous hall ;
I think what learned architects
  Elizabethan call.
With mullion'd windows, shutters vast,
  And mystic double floors,
And hollow wainscots, creaking stairs,
  And four-horse-power doors.

And authors who could write a book
  Might subjects find in hosts—
Of civil wars, and wrongful heirs,
  And murders, bones, and ghosts.

And this you know 's all very well
   'Neath a bright noontide sun ;
But when the dismal nightfall comes,
   'Tis anything but fun.

I'll own,—but this is *entre nous*,—
   I was in such a fright
At my gaunt bed-room, that my eyes
   I never closed all night
When first I lay there : for each thing
   Associations brought
Of bygone crimes, and mouldy deeds,
   With frightful interest fraught.

'Twas like the room where Tennyson
   Made Mariana stay—
A chamber odorous with time,
   And damp, and chill decay.
The moon look'd in with ghastly stare
   On those who haply slept :
And 'gainst the casement all night long
   Some cypress branches swept.

And tapestry was on the walls—
   Dull work that did engage
Fair fingers, fleshless long ago,—
   Now dim and black with age.
And when I trod upon the floor,
   It groan'd and wheezed and creak'd,
And made such awful noises that
   One's very temples reek'd.

And in the middle of the night,
   Half dozing in my bed,
Although beneath the counterpane
   I buried deep my head,
I saw most ghastly phantom forms
   Of mildew'd men and girls ;
With axe-lopp'd heads, and steel-pierced breasts,
   And long gore-dabbled curls.

I was so glad when morning came,
   · For then all fear was o'er.
I slept 'till Fox had three times changed
   The water at my door.
And when I reach'd the breakfast-room,
   The eggs and game were gone,
And I was tied to marmalade
   And haddock all alone.

Now nothing can make up for this,
   Nor horse, nor game, nor gun ;
Nor yet charades, night after night,
   Until they lose their fun.
Nor Emily's contralto voice,
   And dark and floating eyes :
Nor that young Countess—*belle de nuit!*
   Nor Julia's smart replies.

I long to be in town again,
   For all the word recalls ;
The raptures of a private box,
   Or comfort of the stalls.

Those cozy dinners at the club ;
  Those rich *Regalia* fumes ;
A whirl at Weippert's ; or perchance
  A supper at our rooms.

So tell the boys I'm coming back,
  No more this year to roam,
(Don't send the birds to Collingwood ;
  He never dines at home).
The second dinner-bell has rung,
  I'll finish then forthwith,
And so

      Believe me to remain,

         Yours always,

            ALBERT SMITH.

THE PRAISES OF COLONOS.

I.

WELCOME, stranger! thou hast come
To the Gods' well-favour'd home,
Where Colonos rears on high
Its chalky cliffs unto the sky;
Listen, stranger, and I'll tell
All the joys that here do dwell!

II.

Here are horses, that with pride
E'en a king would deign to ride;
Here the sweet-voiced nightingales
Softly tell their mournful tales;
Where the purple ivy's bloom
Shrouds the vale in twilight gloom!

III.

Here's the leafy, pathless grove,
 Which the Wine-god deigns to love,
Where the mighty trees have made
Gloomy aisles of unpierced shade,
Where the tempest's raging breath
Stirs not e'en a leaf in death.

IV.

Here, within the leafy halls
Roam the joyous Bacchanals ;
The Nysian nymphs, who from the first
Never left the God they nurst,
But now with laugh and merry stir,
Crowd around the Reveller !

V.

Here, enrich'd by heavenly dew,
The golden crocus bursts to view,
And the sweet narcissus throws
All around its clustering shows ;
The holy flow'r which erst, 'tis said,
Wreath'd a mighty goddess' head.

VI.

Here, the sleepless fountains ever
Stream into Cephissus' river ;
Earth enriching in their flow,
Nomad-like, they wand'ring go,
Loved by all the Muses mighty
And by gold-rein'd Aphrodite.

VII.

Here, I've heard, too, is a tree,
Such as Asia ne'er did see,
Unplanted by man's hand, the fear
Of friendly and of hostile spear ;
For 'tis here the olive grows,
In the land where first it rose !

VIII.

Here, shall neither young nor old
E'er be impiously bold
To cut down the sacred grove,
For 'tis watch'd by Mosian Jovo,
And the great Minerva too,
With her eyes of melting blue!

IX.

Here, (and this I reckon most
For the Mother-City's boast,)
Here, 'twas first the Ocean King
Bade the stately steed to spring,
And with bits did curb him then,
To be useful unto men!

X.

Thus our city's reached the height
Where true Glory sheds her light:
She's the nurse of chivalry,
And the mistress of the sea;
And 'tis thou, O Saturn's son,
That this mighty work hast done!

XI.

Dashing through the briny sea,
The tall ship bounds on wondrously,
Tracking through the waste of waters
Nereus' hundred-footed daughters:
For our King is Saturn's son!
Stranger, now my tale is done!

CUTHBERT BEDE.

THE DANISH SEAMAN'S SONG.

KING CHRISTIAN stood by the high mast,
        In cloud and smoke,—
With his axe he hammer'd away so fast,
That helm and skull around he cast—
Sunk every foeman's yard and mast,
        In cloud and smoke.
" Fly !" cried he, " fly ! who now fly can !
Who stands for Denmark's Christian !
        In fight and smoke ?"

Niels Juel, to storm and cry gave heed—
        "Now is the hour !"
And hoisted up the flag blood-red,
Flew blow on blow—fell head on head—
As he shouted through the storm, " Give heed !
        Now is the hour !
Fly !" cried he, " fly ! who safety seek !
Who stands for Denmark's Juel now speak
        In fight this hour !"

O North Sea! how our lightnings rend
            Thy murky sky!—
There in thy lap chiefs seek their end—
For thence their shafts death—terror send,
—Shouts through the battle break, and rend
            Thy murky sky!
From Denmark flames thy " thunder-shield ;"
Then cast thyself on heaven and yield!—
            Or fly!

Thou Danish road to fame and power,
            Thou gloomy wave!
Oh, take thy friend, who ne'er will cower,
But danger dares, where'er it lower,
As proud as thou, in thy storm-power,
            Thou gloomy wave!
And quick through shouts of joy and woe,
And fight and victory, bear me to
            My grave!

OH! LET ME LOVE THEE!

Oh! let me love thee!
I ask not passion in return;
I ask but time, my love, to prove thee,
That my true heart thou wilt not spurn;
But let me love thee!

Oh! let me love thee!
Thy lightest word I will obey;
I'll own no sovereign above thee,
Ever obedient to thy sway,
Let me love thee!

Then let me love thee—
Thy every wish I will divine,
And if one smile from thee approve me,
That smile o'er all my life will shine,
So much I love thee!

M. A. B.

THE BOLD SEA WAVE.

Oh ! strong and brave, is the bold sea wave,
    And free as the wingless wind ;
With sunny tides o'er the deep it rides,
    And the white spray leaves behind :
Then the sun goes down, and his lordly crown
    We cease for a while to see ;
But the bold bright wave still tunes its stave
    In the deep ears of the sea.

When the storm comes out, and voices shout
    For help, o'er the gurgling main,
Till the stars that gave their light to the wave,
    Are frighten'd in again—
Then the bold wave 's heard, like a wild sea bird,
    Careering on its way,
Till it gains the shore, and raves the more,
    When its locks with rage turn grey.

Then here 's to the brave, the bold sea wave.
    That hath many a true heart borne,
And laid it low in the depth below,
    Like an infant newly born ;
While commerce brings to our ships' free wings
    The aid of a golden sail,
May its might increase, for truth and peace,
    Till the one mind shall prevail.

G. Linnæus Banks.

THE BROOK.

MID-JUNE is blazing in its fiercest might ;
    But what delicious coolness here ! its flowers
    The laurel shows from its thick glossy bowers ;
Trees twine an arbour o'er so dense, the sight
Sees the blue sky in speckles ; and the light
Dances like golden insects on the water.
The snowy lily, that most delicate daughter
Of all the graceful offspring of the brook,
Stoops to the hair-foot of the velvet bee ;
And now it dips, as from yon soft, dark nook
A furrow meets it by the wild duck's breast,
Raised as she launches dart-like from her nest
And seeks yon isle of water-cresses. See
Yon gleaming shape, the snowy crane out dashes
From the soft marge where he so long has stood
Poising his neck for prey ; his plumage flashes
An instant and is gone. How beautiful
    Yon sight ! the little timid musk-rat swimming
    By that smooth greensward the full current rimming ;
Nibbling yon plant, then giving hasty pull
    To the long vine that hangs down its green trimming.
But now his keen black beads of eyes have caught
My form, and he is gone. Most sweet the purl
Of this small waterbreak, one rising curl

A A 2

Of foam (a fairy Venus) from the plunge;
Whilst this sand-margin yields round like a sponge
Filling my tracks with silver.   Oh, how fraught
With lovely things is every part and spot
   Of nature! God hath made His world o'erflowing
   In beauty; and with heart and soul all glowing
To Him, our praise should rise and weary not.

ALFRED B. STREET

OLD GRUMBLETON.

Owld Grumbleton was a terrible Turk,
    As I 've yeard people zay,
And a zwore in an hour a'd do mwore work
    Than his wife wou'd do in a day:
" Wi' ael my heart," zays the good owld dame,
    " I'm agreeable, anyhow ;
Zo thee sha't bide at whoame to-day,
And I 'll gwo driv' the plough.

" But thee must veed the brindled zow,
    And the leetle pegs in th' sty,
And thee must milk the tiny cow,
    Or Tiney her 'll gwo dry ;
And thee must mind the hank o' yarn
    As I spun yesterday ;
And thee must watch the speckled hen,
    Or her 'll gwo lay astray :
And thee must zee to the dairy pans,
    Or the crame 'll be spwoilt therein,
And thee must mind to turn the malt
    That 's dryin' in the kiln."

The owld 'oman tuk the whip in her hand,
　And trudged to drive the plough ;
The owld man tuk the milking-pail,
　And tackled un to the cow :
But Tiney winced, and Tiney hunched,
　And Tiney cocked her nose,
And Tiney kicked the pail down,
　And the milk run auver his hose.
And 'tis " Oh, Tiney !" and " Wo ! Tiney !"
　And " drat th', cow, bide still !
If I milks zich a maggotty runt again,
　'T will be zore agin my will !"

And he vorgot the hank o' yarn,
　And the puppy-dog stole it away ;
And he vorgot the speckled hen,
　And zo her layd astray :
A went to veed the hungry pegs
　A-grunting in the sty,
A run his nose agin a pwoast,
　And amwoast knocked out his eye :
" A vine joke, my yead 's broke !
　A plague on the pegs and sty !
If they gets no vittles till Doomsday,
　They 'll never be zarved by _I_."

A left the crame to stand in the churm,
　And turnin' hizzelf about,
Lar' a massey haw ! there stood the zow
　A zlushin' in her snout !
A stoop'd to pick a swingein' stick,
　To gie th' owld zow her hire ;

Her run between his legs in a vright,
  And drowed un into the vire.
Oh drat thee now, vor a plaguy zow,
  A *zurprizin'* zow bist thee;
Thy snout it doos mwore harm in an hour
  Than I can mend in dree!"

In coomed th' owld 'oman a wringin' her hands,
  And thus in haste her spoke;
" The vore hos lays on his back in the pond,
  And the plough and stilts be broke;
And 'tis ' O Dobbin! my poor Dobbin!'
  And what an owld vool was I.
If I wears the breeches vor arr'n agen,
  I wishes as I med die!"

Owld Grumbleton zwore by the zun and the moon,
  And ael the green laves on the tree,
If his wife 'ou'd but take to her gear agen
  Her shou'd never be caddled by he.
And 'tis " oh zay no mwore, pray,
  Vor I hates to be called a vool;
But bustle to-night, and put ael thengs right,
  And I 'll gie thee lave to rule!"

DIRGE.*

WHEN on heaven's arch I gaze,
Deep through ether's azure blaze,
    Methinks her form I see!
Fair and pure that angel-form,
As a sunbeam through the storm,
    Sweetly smiling upon me!

When evening closes round,
Hush'd and tranquil ev'ry sound,
    In Nature's wide domain,
Still, one is near to me
Whom no other eye can see—
    One image doth remain!

When night darkly reigns,
And Philomel complains,
    Through the listening grove,
I hear in every tone,
One remembered voice alone,
    Now only heard above!

* From the German of Gustav Solling

When the stars, with sparkling eye,
Hang their golden lamps on high,
    She joins the glittering troop;
From the regions of the blest,
To soothe my aching breast,
    Methinks I see her stoop!

When around, returning Spring
Her emerald robe doth fling,
    And bids her blossoms glow,
Each flower appears to say,
" Thus bloomed, her short Spring-day,
    Your fair Sister, long ago!"

Ye flowers, softly weep,
O'er the grave where she doth sleep,
    Tears of gentle dew!
There, ye zephyrs mildly stray,
Ye moonbeams brightly play—
    She was mild and bright as you!

Heart! wherefore thus opprest?
Rather, envy her sweet rest;
    She hears thee not!
Though lost to mortal eye,
In her seraph-home on high
    May I share her blessed lot!

ETA.

A SONG OF COMO THE BEAUTIFUL.

An exiled daughter am I of that land,
  Where laurel-rose, and myrtle intertwine;
  Where, mid the wreathing foliage of the vine,
The zephyr's fragrant breath is pure and bland;
Where, at the twilight hour a happy band,
  Their voices soft and light guitars awake;
  In fairy barks glide o'er the purple lake,
While lovers sit apart, hand clasped in hand.
Some pluck the wilding lilies, and entwine
  A chaplet for their dark-eyed mistress' brow,
  Some chaunt the vesper hymn, and as they row
With every stroke the melody combine;
But to the ancient poets those most incline
With commune of the past in whispers low:
Sweet Como! where are all thy glories now?—

The Tuscan Medici,* with brow of snow,
  There last I saw, the loveliest of her race,
  She wore the charmed robe of native grace,
Rosebuds her lips, her soft hair's sunny glow

* The Madame de Medici, the most beautiful w..man in Florence, since deceased.

Hung round dark eyes, whence flew the shafts of Love
  In all the pitying softness of the dove,
Mid sun-kiss'd cheeks, black eyes, and raven hair,
Thou Tuscan Lily! fairest of the fair!
Yet, ah! *what* is she, and *where* is she now?
All coldly pale the marble of her brow,
And closed in death those bright and dove-like eyes,
Pillowed on stone that tender form now lies.
Yet from the tomb such beauty shall arise!
Vanished from earth that sweet, that seraph face,
Shall to an angel lend immortal grace.

Just where the lime-trees over-arching meet,
  Their fragrance pouring on the evening air,
An aged mother's† last and calm retreat
  Is by a daughter's love created there.
Rich jasmines by the tall mimosas climb,
  And there the orange stands in courtly rows,
  With golden fruit and green, it buds and blows.
Sweet mockery of seasons and of time!
Dewdrops, the pearls in Flora's diadem,
  Lie hid within the delicate musk rose;
The oleander waves its graceful stem,
  The scented night-flowers all their cups unclose.
The evening star now glittering like a gem,
Sheds on those marble forms a dewy light,
That, bowered in myrtles, shine all coldly bright.
See, where the willow's flexile boughs are hung,
  All weepingly enamoured of the wave,
Forth from the knotted roots and rocky cave,
  Safe anchorage! you tiny shallop sprung.

* Madame Pasta has built three beautiful villas, one expressly for
her mother.

Light is her prow, of fairy hue her sides,
　　And rosy red her silken streamer waves.
Down the transparent stream she gently glides,
　　And silently, her floating beauty laves.
Now, as she leaves the steep and rocky shore,
　　What female hand propels the bark along,
Poising with skill the light and dripping oar?
　　Medea's self! enchantress! Queen of Song!
Who erst in car of triumph dragons bore,
While Europe cried, exulting in her fame,
" Immortal as the Muse be Pasta's name!"

The fishermen still linger on the beach,
　　Breathing the fragrance of the loved cigar,
　　While to the tinkling of his old guitar,
A comrade sings, or frames his witty speech,
The Bergamasc, mid laughter heard from far.
How sweetly on the voice of echo borne,
　　Peals from its height the lonely convent bell;
How faintly sounds the goatherd's rustic horn,
　　Calling his stragglers from the chestnut fell!
Some pious few, in yonder sacred fane,
　　Lit by the silver lamps that palely shine,
　　All humbly kneel before Madonna's shrine,
　　And kiss the ground, nor shall they pray in vain,
Though homage of the heart, and tearful vow,
Be all the gifts these votaries can bestow.

The Queen of Night shines forth—she comes to make
　　A second day, more lovely than the first :
　　Beneath her beams what happy hopes are nurst,
When first Love dares his silence sweet to break.

When does the heart so soothingly o'erflow
   In its own commune, and with tears confess,
   And murmured sounds, its sense of happiness,
As when the moonlight sleeps on all below?
What youthful footsteps ever fall so light
   As those that dance beneath the starry queen?
   What palace pageant in their eyes so sheen,
As the green Treillis and the fireflies bright?
Earth's stars which gem the mantle of her night,
And glittering mid the vine leaves seem to say,
"Short as our life is your's—joy while you may."
Now peasant girls are clustering in the shade
   Of the acacia's sweet and pleasant grove,
   With eyes like night's, that seem to swim in love;
And jewelled ear, and darkly shining braid,
With silver bodkins crowned. And this the time
For childhood's gambols, sunny as its clime.

Alas! my glowing pulses beat too fast
   For these cold climes, where feeling withering dies,
   Where in each bowl of pleasure Caution lies
In wait, to dash it from man's lips at last.
Let me escape from these soul-chilling snows!
And may I, ere my latest sigh be past,   ·
Make on sweet Como's shore my mossy grave,
And sink beside those waters in repose,
While rose and cypress gently o'er me wave!

THERESA C. I. WEST.

ADVICE TO LOVERS.

LOVERS, who would your flame declare,
  Trust to the language of the eyes;
Truth ever is imprinted there,
  And the tongue's eloquence supplies.

No clever, well-turned phrases seek,
  List to the heart, and not the head;
Let the true heart its own words speak,
  And such will ever be well said.

Excess in words should caution raise:
  From chosen language true love shrinks;
And he who thinks of what he says,
  Says very rarely what he thinks.

M. A. B.

EMMA AND EGINARD.

A STORY OF THE DAYS OF CHARLEMAGNE.

Ho, butler mine! the goblet bring,
   And cross the brim with mystic wine!
Ho, Muses Nine! on airy wing
   Descend, and weave the fiery line!
Ho, gallant Pen! run merrily, and fling me forth a
   strain,
Right worthy of the noble theme that warms within my
   brain,
Of that great King of Christendom, the glorious Charle-
   magne!

Lord of the frozen Baltic, Lord of the German pines,
Lord of Italian valleys, and mountains thick with vines,
That look on Spanish headlands, where the dying day
   declines!

A thousand years are past and gone, yet long may poets
   sing,
What, to the base mechanic ear, much wonder yet may
   bring,
How the illustrious Charlemagne was "every inch a
   king!"

For nine foot four
He stood on the floor
(He couldn't of course have come in by the door);
And his toes, if you counted them, came rather more
Than the average number that gentlemen wore,
Even then, and we know there were giants of yore!
While, as for his sabre,
'Twould cost you less labour
To " put" the big stone or go " tossing the caber,"
Than vainly strive to poise and swing
The terrible blade of the strong old king!
His own right hand,
Alone in the land,
Might wield in the battle that ponderous brand,
Whose ruthless edge,
So legends allege
(Myself to that same I'd be sorry to pledge),
Could cleave a stout foeman of infidel breed
Through turban and breast-plate, thigh, saddle,
                              [and steed;
A feat which his aides-de-camp all were agreed
Was a capital way of confuting his creed!
Now, cracking the poll
Seems, on the whole,
But a roundabout way of assisting the soul;
Charlemagne didn't think so, and couldn't control
His zeal for the Church when him listed unrol
Her orthodox flag,
And continued to brag
Of multiplied converts brought safely to bag;
Of Saxon and Saracen,
Sent up to Paris, on

Purpose to have them baptized by the garrison,
Or church'd in a way that was quick by comparison ;
'Till superfine saints look'd immensely mysterious,
And the clergy pronounced him ' decidedly serious.'

Yet, woe to the great !
Since Envy and Fate
Have always conspired to libel their state :
Charlemagne, it is written in all of his lives,
Own'd a very extensive assortment of wives.
Some say three or four,
Some a dozen or more,
Which others in charity raise to a score ;
So, seeing in fact
One can't be exact,
Our muse has discover'd a sad want of tact,
In placing us all in a painful dilemma,
To choose a mamma for the beautiful Emma.

No matter ! such scandal we ought to forget ;
Why cloud the name of the sweet brunette ?
Enough to know
That, years ago,
A thousand at least—but chronology's low—
The exquisite eyes of the princess, our heroine,
Each gentleman's breast had at least put one arrow in !
As well they might,
For a pair so bright,
Set off with so charming a figure and height,
Don't flash every day, which is lucky and right,
Or Wakley 'd be sitting from morning to night !
And e'en in those days—for my tale, you're aware,
Dates back to the time when all maidens were fair,
And enchanted princesses weren't any way rare ;

B B

When Haroun was ruling in sunny Bagdad,
And all for the asking might beauty be had—
Even then there was not, on the world-wide horizon,
A star like our Emma whom all set their eyes on!

> Swaggering captains, cased in plate,
> Snorted sighs through helmet-grate;
> She liked them well—but bade them wait.

> Velvet courtiers, trim and neat,
> Pour'd their sorrows at her feet;
> She liked them too—they smelt so sweet.

> Sovereign princes fared no better;
> None could link the golden fetter;
> She only " wish'd that they might get her."

> " It was awkward to choose,
> It was hard to refuse!"
In short, her vagaries, that puzzle the muse,
> Made many a gent
> Express an intent
(Which something would always occur to prevent)
Of easing his mind by a desperate suicide,
And poking a carving-knife privately through his hide

> Now, the fiery Charlemagne,
> I need scarcely explain,
After all that I've said, had a pious disdain
Of every accomplishment idle and vain;
Spoke lightly of crochet, held worsted work low,
And dancing a vanity, music no go;—

And loved to declare,
  That a jewel so rare
Deserved to be set with unusual care,
For some brother-monarch to win and to wear!

Said he, "With your boarding-school simper and starch
  I cannot and will not away;
My daughter shall trip it in Intellect's march,
  A trifle ahead of her day!
Her dawning mind shall not be fill'd
  By any bleak old woman;
I'll have her drill'd by a tutor skill'd
  In learning quite uncommon!
Logic and Latin, and Greek, may be,
  Shall my own young chaplain teach her;
For he is a scholar of strange degree,
  And withal a wonderful preacher.
He reads by night, and he reads by day,
  Both Gradus and Delectus;
And she shall learn more, ere her years be a score,
  Than you'd put in a short prospectus!
So train her and teach her, my chaplain true,
  Much learning grave and stately;
For I were full fain that her scholarly strain,
  Should make men marvel greatly!"

Ho, chivalrous Macaulay!
  A boon, my liege, I claim:
You 've puzzled us so sorely,
  That you can't refuse the same!
Ho! did our fathers bully
  Their chaplains with such glee,
As you paint, so very coolly,
  To your famous Chapter III?

Did each man keep a curate,
  For his own especial snubbing,
At such a very poor rate
  As a ten-pound note with grub in?
       To fetch and to carry,
       And trundle a barry,
       And never to marry,
       And live in a garret
       On cow-beef and carrot;
Nail up the plums, and say grace like a parrot;
       And dub him 'young Levite?'
       Stuff! who 's to believe it?
Our Quarterly heretics will not receive it!
       They swear you 've perverted
       What Eachard asserted;
       And craftily told 'em
       What isn't in Oldham;
So, as to the scales, I'd be sorry to hold 'em!
       I've only to say
       That, in Charlemagne's day,
Good people knew better, and loved to display
Their zeal for the Church in a liberal way;
And blew out their chaplains with punch and tokay,
And cramm'd them with turtle and doubled their pay,
Delighted to see them both portly and gay!
       But pray don't suppose
       That here I propose
To paint a fat priest with a jolly red nose,
And a corpulent belly and corns on his toes!
       No! out on the bard
       Who could ever be hard
On that model pet-parson—the dear Eginard!

  O, Tea-tables of Cheltenham!
    O, spinster Saints of Bath!

What interest you'd have felt in him;
  How throng'd his primrose path!
For his words were, oh, so silky;
And his doctrine, oh, so milky;
And never, in a shrill key,
  Did he shriek out horrid things!
But so blandly he'd entreat you,
So benignly half way meet you,
That, really, in his seat you
  Saw an angel without wings!
And he did as other men did,
Lest the weak should be offended;
And, if he now and then did
  Awhile unbend the springs
Of life, and, waxing jolly,
Strike up with " Nix my dolly,"
People said it was no folly.

  In a chaplain of the King's!
They say " a little learning
  Is a dangerous sort of thing :"
Which useful hint returning,
  The muse begs leave to sing,
That a very little tutoring
  May work a man more woe,
Than all the downright suitoring
  He'll ever undergo!
If you doubt it or deny it,
  Choose a cousin bright and young;
For a fortnight fairly try it;
  Teach her some outlandish tongue :
Teach her Sanscrit,—teach her magic,
  Teach her anything you know,

'Till you find your tone grow tragic,
   And your bosom toss and glow ;
'Till you groan out ghastly adjec-
   tives in whispers hoarse and low ;
'Till your friends crack jokes ironic ;
   'Till you feel a weary wish
For a whiff of gas carbonic,
   Cooked in a charcoal dish :
'Till in short you learn how lightly
   Is the human heart divine
Fenced against eyes that brightly,
   Alas, too brightly, shine !
So shall you feel due sympathy
   For our reverend young beau,
If mazed in Cupid's dim path, he
   Shall chance at last on woe.
But, how he fared with Emma's eyes,
   We leave to Part the Second ;
Wherein his cast of blank or prize
   Shall all be duly reckoned.

PART THE SECOND.

Dear Alma Mater ! as in duty bound,
   I love thy grey old walls ! I love to tread
Thy voiceless cloisters, and to hear the sound
   Of my slow foot-fall echo over-head.
I love the sacred stream that floats around
   Those palaces of the immortal dead!
We spoke of mathematics, and I am
At once—in heart at least—beside the Cam !

To me, it 's idle ooze recals a time
   When one look'd out so bravely on the world ;
When hearts were free to fight, and hands to climb
   Its difficult heights, and thence to fling unfurl'd
The banner of their thought ; that young sublime !
   Alas, how tamely, in a nutshell curl'd,
Sleeps all its fiery promise !   Yes—of late,
Enthusiasm 's rather out of date !

We keep it bottled for a Pope's Aggression,
   Or grand new Cosmopolitan Bazaar ;
Perhaps its force increases by compression :
   And now I really wonder where we are ?
The man who can unravel this digression,
   And tell me how I ever stray'd so far
From aught and all in Part the First recorded,
Shall find himself most handsomely rewarded.

      And so—to proceed :
      Never, indeed,
Was a royal phenomenon train'd with such speed ;
For, long ere the sweet little princess was twenty,
She'd carol off, slick, the whole *As in præsenti*,
Had a competent knowledge of *Propria quæ*
Maribus, and much learning of lesser degree ;
So kindly, in short, did she take to her tutor,
She'd really no time to encourage a suitor :
      While her own royal father,
      Who, somehow, was rather
Behind with his writing, and hadn't got farther
Than high-shoulder'd pot-hooks, dropp'd in, now and then,
And became, by and by, quite a dab at his pen,
      Though others maintain,
      He tried, might and main,

That useful accomplishment ever to gain ;*
And haunted a school at the end of the lane,
Disguised as an elderly spinster so plain,
Six lessons to take, and it all was in vain
That he cramp'd his four fingers and puzzled his brain,
For trounced as a booby was haughty Charlemagne !

       Well ! it seems that the day,
       Between teaching and play,
Imperceptibly glided so quickly away,
That our exquisite tutor was forced to propose
To borrow a slice from the hours of repose :
       And, as teaching by night,
       By the merry lamp light,
In a lady's boudoir isn't orthodox quite,
And as Emma's apartment, so fragrant and gay,
Lay across the court-yard—in short over the way ;
Involving some nice points of ingress and egress, he
Thought it high time for a dim bit of secrecy.
       So, pointing out clearly
       The day wasn't nearly
So handy—if even for star-gazing, merely—
He proceeded to hint that, as folks would be shock'd
If he chanced to stay late and in consequence knock'd
People up, when the castle was all double-lock'd,
       He meant to crawl out
       Of his window,—no doubt,
He should very well find his way down by the spout :
And, if she'd let him in, why there wasn't a doubt
Her progress in Science would amply repay
For an ocean of obstacles braved by the way !

    * Eginard, in the biography of his royal patron, very frankly avows,
" tentabat et scribere .... sed parum prospere successit labor præposte-
rus et sero inchoatus !"

"O shocking imprudence!" I hear you exclaim:
"How could she, how dare she? oh, fie and for shame!
How can Mr. Bentley permit you to edit
Such scandal?" I 've only to say that I read it,
In Lauresheim's Annals,—they're quoted by Guizot,*
Whose remarks on the subject I trust will appease you.

    Heavily swayed the midnight bell,
    Counting slow its ponderous knell;
    Where through the lattice a taper had shone,
    Lattice was open and taper was gone:
        For the slim Eginard
        Hath tied a knot hard
In his reverend garters—the lattice unbarr'd,
And spun like a monkey-man into the yard:
        And, crawling and creeping,
        And craftily peeping
This way and that, though good people were sleeping,
        Warm in their beds,
        Nor troubling their heads
For a larky chaplain over the leads;
        He gains the boudoir,
        Taps at the door,
And—there let us leave him, till day-break, once more,
Dawns grey through the darkness on turret and shore!

    Merrily chimed the matin bell,
      At six o'clock in the morning:
    It broke up a loving and learned spell,
      With its unmistakable warning;
The tutor so grave and the pupil so shy
Just peep'd out once at the frosty sky,

      * Histoire de la Civilization en France, ii. 219.

As people will do, before wishing ' good-bye,'
   As a hint that it 's time to be going:
When poor Eginard, with a dismal cry,
Shriek'd, " Saints protect us—oh, my eye!
But here 's a kettle of fish to fry ;
   I 'm shot if it hasn't been snowing !
The ground 's as white as white can be ;
They 'll track my steps—it 's up to your knee ;
They 'll hunt me home with a villainous din,
'Twill be no use saying, you shan't come in !
They 'll chop my head off—close at the chin ;
And hammer it up at the gates to grin !
         Saints on high,
         Look down and try
If you couldn't, for once, let a gentleman fly ?
A pair of wings and a tail to match,
Across the yard, and never a batch,
Of candles blazed on an altar yet
Like those for which I'll be in your debt !"

        But never a word
        From Saint he heard :
It was clear that they thought it extremely absurd
Of a good beast to make an indifferent bird.
He felt before, and he felt behind,
But nothing unusual there could he find :
The startled princess wish'd him flown ;
It was very unpleasant to hear him groan :
At last she thought of a plan of her own.

" Listen to me, my tutor dear !"
Said she ; " there 's really nothing to fear

> One thing's clear,
>> You can't stay here,
> 'Till the beak and the feathers you talk of appear!
> Why, you mightn't be fledged by the end of the year!
> Jump on my shoulders!—it's not very far;
> I'll carry you over; and—there you are!
> My tiny print shall scarcely break
> The carpet of the crisping flake;
> And, if perchance my track be known,
> The trace is mine and mine alone;
> Scandal's self must own that here,
> Your innocence, at least, is clear.
>> No trifling, pray,
>> The only way
> To save us both is to do as I say:
>> If Dian the chaste
>> (Do, please, make haste),
> Could carry a beau on her shoulder braced,
>> Why shouldn't I?—
>> At all events try!
> It's no use your flapping—you never can fly!"

>> Small was the need
>> For the lady to plead;
> For the chaplain was very much frighten'd, indeed,
> And jump'd on her shoulders with singular speed;
>> Begg'd her to trot;
>> Cried that his lot
> Was a great deal too hard—he'd be hung on the spot!
> Now, couldn't she canter?—it wasn't so hot!

> The poor little princess was doing her best;
> She stumbled on, with a panting breast

(I wish I 'd been there;
'Tis vain to declare
How hard I 'd have kick'd the unmannerly bear!)
Stoutly and safely she carried him through,
'Till he clutch'd the string of his garters true;
Then kindly watch'd the lubberly lout,
Breaking his shins on the bricks and the spout;
Stopping half-way for a sprawl and a shout,
And yelling to know what the Saints were about,
To leave a man dangling in æther and doubt?
And so she watch'd and watch'd, until
She watch'd him over the window-sill.
Then, flush'd and breathless, homeward fled
The sweet princess, and only said,
"To judge by the way my dear tutor takes wing,
Learning is doubtless a dangerous thing!"

PART THE THIRD.

Charlemagne sat in his window,
    A-drinking early purl;
Twelve barbers stood behind him,
    The royal wig to curl;
Twelve paladins were kneeling
    Around him in a ring;
Twelve trumpeters were pealing
    At once, "God save the King!"
Twelve courtiers took their places,
    The royal jokes to praise;
To hand the royal braces,
    Or lace the royal stays.

All of a sudden he starts from his chair;
The very wig-royal flew straight in the air,
As he stagger'd and shouted, "Good gracious! look there!
Look, gentlemen, LOOK!!"

                    If the Exeter mail
Had run over the tip of Beelzebub's tail,
Accidentally drunk and asleep on the rail,
        Not Nick the Satanic,
        In pain and in panic,
Had bounced up with symptoms so loud and galvanic,
Or hurl'd such a broadside at stoker and guard,
As the furious Charlemagne at our poor Eginard!
And indeed, though a moralist, captious and slow,
Might have fancied his expletives rather *de trop;*
And prayed him, in nautical language, to " stow"
Certain pithy imperatives;—such a tableau
As a talented daughter, full trot through the snow,
With, perch'd on her shoulder, a dandy young beau,
Was rather what Cockneys define as a " go!"

        The courtiers grew
        Excessively blue;
They didn't know what upon earth to do.
        If pulling long faces,
        With frightful grimaces,
Were anyway useful in keeping their places,
Theirs were at least on a durable basis;
For they thump'd their breasts and roll'd their eyes,
And fill'd the roof with their dismal cries;
        Nay, one was seen,
        His shrieks between,
Indulging in anguish more dreadly serene,
For he buried his face in the tail of his coat,
And stuff'd his handkerchief down his throat!

Sharp thunder'd the King,
　　"Ho, gentlemen, bring
That parson pale and a penn'orth of string!
　　Turn out the guard
　　In the great court-yard,
And bid breakfast wait till we 've scragg'd Eginard!"

*　　　*　　　*　　　*　　　*　　　*

　　Charlemagne sat in his window,
　　　　Still drinking early purl;
　　His daughter stood before him,
　　　　Her hair was out of curl.
　　Her downcast eyes were counting
　　　　The tangled carpet-rushes;
　　The royal blood ran mounting
　　　　Through her cheeks in crimson blushes.
I would you had witnessed his majesty's grin,
As they kick'd the blubbering chaplain in,
　　　　His glowering scowl,
　　　　As he said, with a growl,
"Good youth, don't you see that it 's useless to howl?
What think you, my lords—shall we hang him or stick
　　　him,
Or, first of all, set a strong fellow to lick him?
How would your wisdoms advise us to slaughter
The rascal that dares to make love to our daughter?"

　　Then the spiteful courtiers gladly
　　　　Suggested sundry ways;
　　All which would hurt him sadly,
　　　　And bequeath to future days
　　Strong hints for those who madly
　　　　On a princess dared to gaze!
They talk'd of needles, they talk'd of pins,
Of singeing his whiskers and scraping his shins:

Of a rack, to crack
The small of his back;
Of drowning him slowly, done up in a sack;
Of toasting him gently—of boiling him hard,
Of a nice little fry with red pepper and lard;
Of a jolly Guy Fawkes in the tournament yard!
In short, how to pickle our poor Eginard,
With anything like a respectful regard
To his majesty's taste,
Which was cruelly chaste,
Was a problem they couldn't resolve in such haste.
They couldn't decide if a boil or a roast
Would turn, in a way that would worry him most,
A nice young curate into a ghost!

Perchance you 've watch'd a hungry bear,
Snarling over a bone:
If so, you may picture his majesty's glare,
And fancy his majesty's tone!
For in thunder roll'd his anger;
And the courtiers held their breath:
Emma thought he meant to hang her,
And she stood as white as death:
And her lover grew so funky,
He couldn't stand at all,
But, like a clock-work monkey,
Roll'd gibbering round the hall!

"Daughter mine,
You 've taken the shine
Out of our highly respectable line!
You have! you 've disgraced me.—I 'm cursedly hurt.
How could you—how dare you—go, vixen, and flirt

With a beggar? he 's scarcely a tail to his shirt!
Don't answer! I see you intend to be pert.
The shame and the scandal 't would only make worse,
Or I 'd send you together to church—in a hearse!
Now hear me and heed me—we won't, in our ire,
Roll out of the frying-pan into the fire;
We must act as a king—though we feel as a sire:
We pardon our daughter—for reasons of state:
Toward our chaplain we bid the wrath-royal abate:
Our courtiers we rather advise to relate
          What they 've seen of their tricks
          If they 're anxious to ' fix,'
A deuced long mile t'other side of the Styx,
Where Paris ain't half so well known as Old Nick's.
And finally, girl, since you 've chosen to carry him,
We'll stand no more nonsense; by jingo, you 'll marry
     him !"

        Then, smiling, spoke the courtiers,
           That stood before the King;
       " Though we talk'd of fire and tortures,
           We knew they were n't the thing!
       We knew your royal highness;
           And we knew your bosom ran
       With the cream of human kindness
           For this excellent young man:
       And we only spoke in joking,
           So please you, gracious King,
       When we said we 'd set him croaking,
           Or any such like thing!
       May our chaplain wax and flourish!
           May he wear the scarlet hat!
       May the princess yearly nourish.
           A churchling fair and fat!

May it ever be a lesson t' her,
  This blessed morning's fun !
Now how could we speak pleasanter
  Than what as how we 've done ?
And, if any of us mention
  Her charming little whim,
In traitorous intention,
  Or inuendo dim,
Why, strike him off his pension ;
  And strike his head off him !"

MY WINTER ROOM.

THE Winter wind is roaring in the air,
And crashing through the trees, upon the panes
A dull sound tells the beating of the snow,
And, now and then, a sharp quick tinkling where
The hail is smiting. Hark, how bitterly
The wild wind shrieks! and, as I glance from out
My casement, nothing but the black sky o'er,
And the pale ghastly snow beneath, I see.
Within, how warm and cosy is my room!
The broad bright blaze leaps, laughing, crackling up
The rumbling chimney, shedding round my walls
Its rosy radiance. Swarms of ruddy sparks,
Like dancing fire-flies, hover now below
The chimney's mouth, now stream up quietly
Its sable throat, and now right at my face
Dart swiftly, snapping out their testy lives.
The great swart andirons stand in sulky strength
Amidst the glowing redness. Now and then
A brand breaks up, and falls on either side,
Attended by a merrier dance of sparks.
And then the play of shadows. On the wall
The tongs has cast a straddling shape, with knob
Nodding so wisely, every chair has lined
Its giant frame-work all around. The tall

Quaint clock, which ticks with such industrious tongue,
Chiming harmonious with the silver chirp
Of the unceasing cricket, casts its high
And reaching figure up the wall, with breast
Bent to an angle, stretching half along
The ceiling, wavering to each mirthful fit
Of the glad firelight. How the cinder-blaze
Flashes upon the letters of my books,
Dances along the barrel of my gun
(Remainder of sweet Indian summer days
In the calm forest when the smoky air
Rang with its voice), and glittering on the joints
Of my long fishing-rod (awakener too
Of cool, dark forest streams, and leaping trout,
And dashing music, and of net-work gold
Dropped by low branches), glancing in the dark,
Smooth polish of my cane (that also tells
Of rambles in the fresh, green, pastoral hills
To view the summer sunset—through the glens
To while away the languid summer heat,
And by broad waters where the harvest-moon
Beheld its face reflected). Cheery nook,
Sweet cheery nook! how precious is thy peace
In my unquiet life! how gladly here
My heart expands in pure beatitude,
Feeling its storms all hushed in holy rest,
All tumults soothed—at sweet peace with itself—
In kindness with all kind. The mangling day,
Cares, disappointments, sorrows, may have brought,
But all have vanished. All the bitter things
Of being—unappreciated worth—
Wounded affection—barred ambition like
The Phœnix burning in the flames it fans

With its own pinions: hopes that, like old Rome,
Are strewed in wrecks, which tell how bright and grand
Their pristine shapes; all these roll off like mists,
And leave the crimsoned room a radiant shrine
Of blest contentment. Here the fancy, too,
Revels in its sweet dreaming, tracing things
Grotesque and beautiful from out the coals,
One glowing like a famished lion's eye
One cracking open like a maiden's lips
(So soft and rich their velvet ruddiness),
And melting one in ashes soft and grey,
Like sunset's rim, what time the sun hath sunk
Beneath it; and not only this, but lapped
In poetry, which dances now in sweet
And fairy music, as of harp and flute,
And marching now in stately phalanx on
To drum and trumpet. Glows the happy soul
Responsive, till the hours on downy feet
Have brought the time for slumber—then with prayer
To God, my head upon its pillow sinks,
And hearing, in the slow delicious creep
Of slumber o'er the frame, the stormy wind
And beating snow, I slide within the land,
The dim, mysterious, unknown land of dreams.

                                        ALFRED B. STREET.

THE DANE, AND HIS KING.

A PATRIOTIC SONG FOR DENMARK.

(A Sketch of February 11, 1659,) *from the Danish of Andersen.*

His white tent Winter spreads around,
In icy chains both Belts are bound ;
· But Denmark trusts in the Lord !

By Copenhagen camps the Swede,—
Trusts in his name, trusts in his deed ;—
But Denmark trusts in the Lord !

Sore, bitter Want rules village, town ;
And Hunger-death treads all men down :—
But Denmark trusts in the Lord !

The Faubourg all in ashes lies ;
From God's own house fierce flames arise ;—
But Denmark trusts in the Lord !

The Danish King from rampart calls ;—
The red-hot ball beside him falls,—
But Denmark trusts in the Lord !

Now holds the foe the Isle, and all,—
But Frederik swears that there he'll fall ;—
And Denmark trusts in the Lord !

All fight—what boots their place—who can,—
Each man's a god,—each maid a man !
And Denmark trusts in the Lord !

Shrouds, shrouds, the Swede now puts him on,
Like death-bands o'er the snows they're gone ;
But Denmark trusts in the Lord !

The living Snow-man comes like Death,
But melts before a woman's breath ;—
So Denmark trusts in the Lord !

On storms the Swede with shout and cry,
Soon in the snows a corpse to lie ;
For Denmark trusts in the Lord !

" Te Deum" speaks, as true hearts spoke,
And kneels the King with all his folk,
And thanks for all the Lord !

W.

THE WARDEN OF THE CINQUE PORTS.

A MIST was driving down the British Channel,
　　The day was just begun,
And through the window-panes, on floor and panel,
　　Streamed the red Autumn sun.

It glanced on flowing flag and rippling pennon,
　　And the white sails of ships;
And, from the frowning rampart, the black cannon
　　Hailed it with feverish lips.

Sandwich and Romney, Hastings, Hithe, and Dover
　　Were all alert that day,
To see the French war-steamers speeding over,
　　When the fog cleared away.

Sullen and silent, and like couchant lions,
　　Their cannon, through the night,
Holding their breath, had watched in grim defiance
　　The sea-coast opposite.

And now they roared at drum-beat from their stations
　　On every citadel;
Each answering each, with morning salutations,
　　That all was well!

And down the coast, all taking up the burden,
    Replied the distant forts,
As if to summon from his sleep the Warden
    And Lord of the Cinque Ports.

Him shall no sunshine from the fields of azure,
    No drum-beat from the wall,
No morning gun from the black fort's embrazure
    Awaken with their call !

No more surveying with an eye impartial
    The long line of the coast,
Shall the gaunt figure of the old Field-Marshal
    Be seen upon his post !

For in the night, unseen, a single warrior,
    In sombre harness mailed,
Dreaded of man, and surnamed the destroyer,
    The rampart wall has scaled.

He passed into the chamber of the sleeper,
    The dark and silent room ;
And as he entered, darker grew and deeper
    The silence and the gloom.

He did not pause to parley or dissemble,
    But smote the Warden hoar ;
Ah ! what a blow ! that made all England tremble
    And groan from shore to shore.

Meanwhile, without the surly cannon waited,
    The sun rose bright o'erhead ;
Nothing in Nature's aspect intimated
    That a great man was dead !

                                H. W. LONGFELLOW.

A POET'S LOVE.

WITH my love, so sweet and fair,
   None can compare;
With my love, so fair and sweet,
   None can compete!

Had I a hundred eyes
(Two my purpose serve but ill),
   Had I a hundred eyes,
I would gaze on her my fill!
     With my love, so sweet and fair,
       None can compare!
     With my love, so fair and sweet,
       None can compete!

Had I a hundred ears,
They would hear her slightest tone;
   Had I a hundred ears,
'They would list to her alone!
     With my love, so sweet and fair,
       None can compare!
     With my love, so fair and sweet,
       None can compete!

Had I a hundred tongues,
They would praise her night and day;
Had I a hundred tongues,
All together they would say,
    With my love, so sweet and fair,
    None can compare!
    With my love so fair and sweet,
    None can compete!

M. A. B.

THE GIPSEY.

ALONG the shaded banks of Wye
   Three sprightly sisters stray'd,
When lo ! a gipsey, passing by,
   Address'd each startled maid :—

"Ladies," she cried, "oh, turn to me,
   Your fortunes I can trace,
And show reflected to the three
   Each future husband's face."

The maidens laugh'd, the boon was given,
   To search the stream they flew,
And Wye, whose tide reflected heaven,
   Reflected beauty too.

"I see no unknown features," cried
   Each disappointed fair,
"My own I spy, and oft have spied,
   But no one else is there."

"Whene'er," replied the crafty crone,
   " Ye bless three happy men,
The features which are now your own,
   " Will be *your husbands'* then."

THE CLOUD IN THE HONEYMOON.

Know ye the road of sylvan notoriety,
　　Where close cabs stand, and omnibuses ply;
Which squares and crescents deck in gay variety,
　　And walled-up villas, hidden from the eye;
Which counts dramatic stars in its society,
　　In numbers that with Heaven's stars can vie;
Which boasts an hospital?—but wherefore prompt on?
The place you must have recognized, as Brompton.

Near this famed place, in a secluded spot,
　　By a small garden from the road divided;
A small house stood—a perfect rural cot,
　　In which, not many months ago, resided
A happy pair, contented with their lot;
　　Thinking all bliss, while they were not divided;
Asking kind Heaven for no further boon,—
'Tis true they still were in their honeymoon:

Yet, as good models for all constant lovers,
　　Joseph and Anna might have been displayed —
Each day, some brighter charm in her discovers
　　By fresh devotion on his part repaid—

One cloud alone in their horizon hovers ;—
   (The crumpling of the rose-leaf, I 'm afraid),
That horrid office !—every day, Poor Joe,
At nine o'clock is hurried off to go.

Short-sighted mortals ! why,—the separation
   Of those same eight hours out of twenty-four,
Adds to affection, zest and animation,
   Felt by the wife,—and by the husband more—
Returning from a long day's application,
   To find a sweet face smiling at the door,
A bright fire sparkling,—warmth, and joy, and peace ;
Does not the contrast home's true charms increase ?

" Don't be late back, love," Anna murmured, parting
   From Joseph, on the morn of the New Year ;
It almost paid the grievance of departing,
   Those tender words and gentle tones to hear.
So Joseph thought, while on his long walk starting,
   With Anna's sweet voice ringing in his ear.
He gave a sigh—then, quickening his gait,
Exclaimed, " Confound that watch ! I shall be late."

Elbowing, pushing, forcing on his way,
   At length a brother clerk he chanced to meet.
" Why, you are early from your work to-day !"
   Said Joseph, as he stopped, his friend to greet.
" Work !" said the other, " 'tis a holiday,
   " To us poor fellows a delightful treat."
" A holiday !" cried Joseph, " what a pleasure !
   " I 'll hasten home—what glad news for my treasure !"

How gaily now, his best exertions using,
　　Onwards to home and wife he quickly hies ;
With pleasant fancies, now, his mind amusing,
　　Anticipating Anna's glad surprise ;—
At other times, the length of way abusing ;—
　　At length the wished-for cottage meets his eyes—
He knocks once—twice—thrice, vainly at the door ;
The well-known raps strike heedless o'er and o'er.

At length, the door was opened ; and beside him
　　Stood Anna, in becoming agitation ;
She said, she from the window had descried him ;
　　And when he asked her, what her occupation
Was, that so long, an entrance she denied him ?
　　She blushed, and uttered with much perturbation,
Some faint excuse, which, with her shrinking eye
And changing tint, seemed very like a lie.

" Don't let us stand here in the cold to chatter,"
　　Said Joseph, in an accent somewhat stern,
His Anna would have asked, what was the matter ;
　　But feared lest her solicitude he 'd spurn :
Perhaps (my heroine I would not flatter),
　　Her busy conscience made her fair cheeks burn !
And thinking of the slip in her veracity,
Acted as a restraint on her loquacity.

But, by degrees, their spirits rose again,
　　And as they sat conversing, side by side,
With fond words Joseph tried to soothe the pain
　　His harsh tones must have caused his gentle bride.

"What could," he thought, "have made my silly brain
  "Form an idea against a love so tried?"
And quite convinced that *he* had been the offender,
He strove to make it up by words more tender.

What has occurred to make him, in a hurry,
  Draw back from Anna's slender waist his arm?
Can jealous thoughts again his fancy worry,
  And cause that sudden glance round of alarm?
Why does his look put Anna in a flurry?
  She rose, and murmuring, "'Tis very warm,"
Opened the window, and then left the room,
Leaving her husband sunk in deepest gloom.

Oh, jealousy! how much are to be pitied
  The victims of thy poisonous influence!
When once a mind is to thy power submitted,
  Farewell all hope, all reasoning, all sense!
Now art thou into Joseph's brain admitted,
  On what would seem too idle a pretence:
Those fears, those doubts, which all his pleasure mar,
Rise from the smell of an expired cigar!

"Now, who can have been smoking here?" thought
      Joseph:
  "There's no use asking Anna, I presume.
"She really might as well have got no nose, if
  "She can't perceive this evident perfume!
"She said she had no visitors—who knows if
  "I had not better ignorance assume?
"She *must* have smelt it, and, with guilty care,
"Opened the window, just to change the air.

" I 'll hide my doubts, and watch her every motion."
    Just then, his wife re-entered with a smile:
Her manner showed no traces of emotion,
    As, with gay talk, she strove the hours to wile;
Her merry laugh, her simple, fond devotion,
    Served, for a time, his fancies to beguile;
But still, that odour, floating in the air,
Contrived his coming gaiety to scare.

Vainly, dissimulation's aid invoking,
    The conversation round about he led;
Wished they had visitors—and said, half joking,
    That he had met a friend, who was ill-bred
Enough to want to come in, although smoking.
    Here he thought Anna's cheek grew very red;
But, as she answered with some slight remark,
He was obliged to leave off in the dark.

Next morning, Joseph lingers in his going,
    Although the clock his tardiness reproves;
Till Anna, with a smile, the hour hand showing,
    Presents him, as a hint, with hat and gloves.
" 'Tis but too clear! she 's quite impatient growing,"
    Thought he, as to the door he slowly moves,
" But, this time, in hypocrisy I 'll match her.
" As sure as I 'm alive, to-day I 'll catch her!"

Resolved to act with care and circumspection,
    He hid the bitter pain from which he smarted;
He said " good-bye!" with much assumed affection,
    Trying to hum an air, and look light-hearted.

His doubts thus safe from all fear of detection,
   Upon his fatal journey off he started,
With plans that gave this gay, good-humoured fellow
A wonderful resemblance to Othello.

" If," thought he, " I find something wrong about her,
   " No pains, no torments of revenge I'll spare!
"Yet, after all, it is unjust to doubt her
   " On a cause, literally, ' light as air.'
" What a blank would existence be without her
   " Kind looks and words, her tender, loving care!"
Here, as he melted fast into the lover,
He hastened back, the whole truth to discover.

Through the small garden, now behold him stealing,
   With beating heart, and footstep light and airy:
Fearing some chance, his quick return revealing,
   Should spoil his plot, he cast round glances wary.
At length, successfully his form concealing,
   He reached the house; and then, with anxious care, he
Crept to the parlour window, and peeped in,
Trembling at what he might behold within.

What sees he there?—each jealous fancy flies;
   Doubt and suspicion are for ever gone!
By the fireside, his Anna meets his eyes,
   Reclining in an arm-chair, and alone.
But what her occupation?—(his surprise
   Is justified by such a cause, we own).
A faint cloud issues from her lips, which are
Puffing away at an immense cigar!

D D

The exclamation, he could not repress,
    Startled the fair one from her meditation;
Trembling with wonder, and with fear no less,
    She spied her husband at his observation.
"Joseph!" she cried, in accents of distress.
    He waited for no further invitation,
But, quick as thought, the window ledge he gained,
And to his heart his faithful wife he strained!

I need not tell how Joseph, doubts forswearing,
    Was of his jealous whims for ever rid;
How Anna had been longing, yet not daring,
    To own the secret habit from him hid;
How, all his frantic jealousy declaring,
    He owned his fears deserving to be chid;
How he forgave, and joined his constant Anna
In quiet indulgence in a mild Havanna.

Moral.

Now, of this tale the moral I'll explain:
    A useful one to husband and to wife.
Wives, let no idle fears your truth restrain,
    For mystery will oft occasion strife.
Husbands, from causeless jealousy refrain,
    Lest you embitter all your wedded life,
For doubts which afterwards you would revoke,
And fears, which may, like Joseph's, end in *smoke!*

                                              M. A. B.

THE CHURCHYARD AT CAMBRIDGE.

In the village churchyard she lies,
Dust is in her beautiful eyes.
  Nor more she breathes, nor feels, nor stirs ;
At her feet and at her head
Lies a slave to attend the dead,
  But their dust is as white as hers.

Was she a lady of high degree,
So much in love with the vanity
  And foolish pomp of this world of ours ?
Or was it Christian Charity,
And lowliness and humility,
  The richest and rarest of all dowers ?

Who shall tell us ? No one speaks ;
No colour shoots into those cheeks,
  Either of anger or of pride,
At the rude question we have asked :
Nor will the mystery be unmasked
  By those who are sleeping at her side.

Hereafter ?—And do you think to look
On the terrible pages of that book,
   To find her failings, faults and errors?
Ah, you will then have other cares
In your own short-comings and despairs,
   In your own secret sins and terrors!

W. H. LONGFELLOW.

SONG FROM THE GAELIC.

"Love, will thou trust thyself with me?"
  Whispered a bold and gallant rover;
"In distant lands I thought of thee,
  And 'midst the wild cry of victory,
          Thou wert before me."

The lady's eyes so bright and blue
  Turned on the knight, but not in sorrow,—
"I ever knew thee leal and true,
  And I will wed thee, love, to-morrow,
          And love thee dearly."

W. H. Maxwell.

IN SARAM.

I.

ANTE alias splendet specie pulcherrima Sara,
    Formosas superans effigie egregiâ.
Urget amore mihi pectus mentemque puella, et
    Angustâ in Nostrâ vivit honesta Viâ.
Virgineo in cœtu nullas dulcedine Saræ,
    Nobilibus natas, invenias similes.
Implet amore mihi mentem pectusque puella, et
    Angustâ in Nostrâ vivit honesta Viâ.

II.

Institor huic pater est, portans qui caulibus apta
    Retia per vicos clamitat assiduè :
Digna viro est uxor, merces cui fimbria longa est
    Vendita, siqua velit fœmina compta emere.
At tales talem quam dulcis numina Sara
    (Nobilis est certè !) non generâsse sinunt.
Est mihi deliciæ cordi mentique puella, et
    Angustâ in Nostrâ vivit honesta Viâ.

III.

Adveniente illâ fabricam inceptosque labores
    Desero continuò, victus amore meo :

SALLY IN OUR ALLEY.

I.

Of all the girls that are so smart,
  There 's none like pretty Sally,
She is the darling of my heart,
  And she lives in Our Alley.
There 's not a lady in the land,
  That 's half so sweet as Sally,
She is the darling of my heart,
  And she lives in Our Alley.

II.

Her father, he makes cabbage-nets,
  And through the streets does cry 'em,
Her mother, she sells laces long,
  To such as please to buy 'em.
But sure, such folks could ne'er beget
  So sweet a girl as Sally ;
She is the darling of my heart,
  And she lives in Our Alley.

III.

When she is by, I leave my work,
  I love her so sincerely :

Tunc irâ fervens improvisusque magister,
  Ut Saracenus, adit, me baculo feriens.
At quamvis feriat donec satiabitur iste,
  Omnia pro Sarâ perfero, sic peramo.
Firmat amore mihi pectus mentemque puella, et
  Angustâ in Nostrâ vivit honesta Viâ.

IV.

Hebdomadæ ex omni spatio serieque dierum
  Solem unum expecto, suavis et est mihi lux.
Isque dies Lunæ imperium ac Saturnia regna
  Disjungit, veniens lumine propitio.
Tunc etenim spatior Sarâ comitatus amicè,
  Vestituque nitens, splendidiùs solito.
Fert mihi lenimen curæ dulcissima Sara, et
  Angustâ in Nostrâ vivit honesta Viâ.

V.

Ad templum Domini me ducit sæpe magister,
  Sæpe at nequitiam corripit ille meam:
Scilicet aufugio furtim falloque magistrum,
  Sacro argumento vix bene proposito.
Dum monet Orator populum hortaturque disertus,
  Ad Saram effugio, dulceque colloquium.
Implet amore mihi mentem pectusque puella, et
  Angustâ in Nostrâ vivit honesta Viâ.

VI.

Quum volvente anno Christi Natalitia orta
  Sint, nummûm mihi erunt in loculo cumuli.
Omnes servabo, atque ipsâ cum pyxide Saræ,
  Tempora quum veniant, melligenæ tribuam.

My master comes like any Turk,
  And bangs me most severely.
But let him bang his bellyful,
  I'll bear it all for Sally;
She is the darling of my heart,
  And she lives in Our Alley.

IV.

Of all the days that 's in the week,
  I dearly love but one day,
And that 's the day that comes between
  A Saturday and Monday.
For then I'm dress'd in all my best,
  To walk abroad with Sally;
She is the darling of my heart,
  And she lives in Our Alley.

V.

My master carries me to church,
  And often am I blamed,
Because I leave him in the lurch
  As soon as Text is named.
I leave the church in sermon-time,
  And slink away to Sally;
She is the darling of my heart,
  And she lives in Our Alley.

VI.

When Christmas comes about again,
  Oh! then I shall have money,—
I'll hoard it up, and—box and all—
  I'll give it to my honey.

Atque utinam innumeras mihi opes fortuna dedisset !
  Sara suo totas exciperet gremio.
Est mihi deliciæ cordi mentique puella, et
  Angustâ in Nostrâ vivit honesta Viâ.

VII.

Irrident flammam vicini atque ipse magister
  Quæ me illamque urit, ludificantque facem.
Sed, sine amore tuo, præstaret, SALLI, revinctum
  Servi me vitam remigio trahere.
Quum tamen elabens lentè confecerit annus
  Septimus orbiculum, Sara mihi uxor erit.
Tum vero thalamum celebrabimus atque hymenæos,
  At procul Angustâ ibimus usque Viâ.

G. K. GILLESPIE, A.M.

And, would it were ten thousand pounds,
  I'd give it all to Sally ;
She is the darling of my heart,
  And she lives in Our Alley.

VII.

My master, and the neighbours all,
  Make game of me and Sally,
And, but for her, I'd better be
  A slave, and row a galley.
But when my seven long years are out,
  Oh ! then, I'll marry Sally,
Oh ! then we'll wed, and then we'll bed,
  But not in Our Alley.

YES AND NO.

CHRISTMAS time,
　Poets' rhyme
Calls the best of seasons;
For the pref'rence they bestow,
Can we find good reasons?
　　No!

　Yet do we
　Disagree
With those who despise it;
Does not Christmas joys possess
For which we should prize it?
　　Yes!

　When, with cold,
　We behold,
Pinched and blue our faces,
Can we all complaints forego,
Or forbear grimaces?
　　No!

　But when night
　Brings firelight,
And our friends are near us;
While we round the fireside press,
Does not pleasure cheer us?
　　Yes!

Frost bereaves
Trees of leaves,
Robs flowers of their lustre;
Can the glitt'ring ice and snow
For their charms pass muster?
No!

But their place
Will replace
Christmas trees and holly;
Their bright tints to value less,
Would not that be folly?
Yes!

To our gates,
When the waits,
Postmen, servants, traders,
All for Christmas boxes go,
Do we bless the invaders?
No!

But when some
Fine things come
As a Christmas present,
All inscribed to *our* address,
Don't we find it pleasant?
Yes!

M. A. B.

A BALLAD OF SIR JOHN FRANKLIN.

O, WHITHER sail you, Sir John Franklin?
   Cried a whaler in Baffin's Bay.
To know if between the land and the pole
   I may find a broad sea-way.

I charge you back, Sir John Franklin,
   As you would live and thrive;
For between the land and the frozen pole
   No man may sail alive.

But lightly laughed the stout Sir John,
   And spoke unto his men:
Half England is wrong, if he is right;
   Bear off to westward then.

O, whither sail you, brave Englishman?
   Cried the little Esquimaux.
Between your land and the polar star
   My goodly vessels go.

Come down, if you would journey there,
   The little Indian said;
And change your cloth for fur clothing,
   Your vessel for a sled

But lightly laughed the stout Sir John,
   And the crew laughed with him too:—
A sailor to change from ship to sled,
   I ween, were something new!

All through the long, long polar day,
   The vessels westward sped ;
And wherever the sail of Sir John was blown,
   The ice gave way and fled:

Gave way with many a hollow groan,
   And with many a surly roar,
But it murmured and threatened on every side,
   And closed where he sailed before.

Ho! see ye not, my merry men,
   The broad and open sea?
Bethink ye what the whaler said,
Think of the little Indian's sled!
   The crew laughed out in glee.

Sir John, Sir John, 'tis bitter cold,
   The scud drives on the breeze,
The ice comes looming from the north,
   The very sunbeams freeze.

Bright summer goes, dark winter comes—
   We cannot rule the year ;
But long ere summer's sun goes down,
   On yonder sea we'll steer.

The dripping icebergs dipped and rose,
   And floundered down the gale ;
The ships were staid, the yards were manned,
   And furled the useless sail.

The summer's gone, the winter's come,
  We sail not on yonder sea :
Why sail we not, Sir John Franklin ?
  A silent man was he.

The summer goes, the winter comes—
  We cannot rule the year :
I ween, we cannot rule the ways,
  Sir John, wherein we 'd steer.

The cruel ice came floating on,
  And closed beneath the lee,
Till the thickening waters dashed no more;
'Twice ice around, behind, before—
  My God ! there is no sea !

What think you of the whaler now ?
  What of the Esquimaux ?
A sled were better than a ship,
  To cruise through ice and snow.

Down sank the baleful crimson sun,
  The northern light came out,
And glared upon the ice-bound ships,
  And shook its spears about.

The snow came down, storm breeding storm,
  And on the decks was laid ;
Till the weary sailor, sick at heart,
  Sank down beside his spade.

Sir John, the night is black and long,
  The hissing wind is bleak,
The hard, green ice is strong as death :—
  I prithee, Captain, speak !

The night is neither bright nor short,
　　The singing breeze is cold,
The ice is not so strong as hope—
　　The heart of man is bold!

What hope can scale this icy wall,
　　High over the main flag-staff?
Above the ridges the wolf and bear
Look down, with a patient, settled stare,
　　Look down on us and laugh.

The summer went, the winter came—
　　We could not rule the year;
But summer will melt the ice again,
And open a path to the sunny main,
　　Whereon our ships shall steer.

The winter went, the summer went,
　　The winter came around;
But the hard, green ice was strong as death,
And the voice of hope sank to a breath,
　　Yet caught at every sound.

Hark! heard you not the noise of guns?—
　　And there, and there, again?
'Tis some uneasy iceberg's roar,
　　As he turns in the frozen main.

Hurra! hurra! the Esquimaux
　　Across the ice-fields steal:
God give them grace for their charity!
　　Ye pray for the silly seal.

E E

Sir John, where are the English fields,
    And where are the English trees,
And where are the little English flowers
    That open in the breeze?

Be still, be still, my brave sailors!
    You shall see the fields again,
And smell the scent of the opening flowers,
    The grass, and the waving grain.

Oh! when shall I see my orphan child?
    My Mary waits for me.
Oh! when shall I see my old mother,
    And pray at her trembling knee?

Be still, be still, my brave sailors!
    Think not such thoughts again.
But a tear froze slowly on his cheek;
    He thought of Lady Jane.

Ah! bitter, bitter grows the cold,
    The ice grows more and more;
More settled stare the wolf and bear,
    More patient than before.

Oh! think you, good Sir John Franklin,
    We'll ever see the land?
'Twas cruel to send us here to starve,
    Without a helping hand.

'Twas cruel Sir John, to send us here,
　So far from help or home,
To starve and freeze on this lonely sea:
I ween, the Lords of the Admiralty
　Would rather send than come.

Oh! whether we starve to death alone,
　Or sail to our own country,
We have done what man has never done—
The truth is founded, the secret won—
　We passed the Northern Sea!

MY PORTRAIT.

Oh, young and richly gifted! born to claim
No vulgar place amidst the sons of fame;
With shapes of beauty haunting thee like dreams,
And skill to realize Art's loftiest themes,
How wearisome to thee the task must be.
To copy these coarse features painfully,
Faded by time, and paled by care, to trace
The dim complexion of this homely face,
And lend to a bent brow and anxious eye,
Thy holiest toil, thine art's high mystery.

Yet by that art almost, methinks, divine,
By hand, and colour, and the skilful line,
Which at a stroke can strengthen or refine,
And mostly by the invisible influence
Of thine own spirit, gleams of thought and sense
Shoot o'er the careworn forehead, and illume
The heavy eye, and break the leaden gloom.
Even as the sunbeams on the rudest ground
Fling their illusive glories wide around,
And make the dullest scene of nature bright
By the reflexion of their own pure light.

MARY RUSSELL MITFORD.

FIELD-PREACHING.

THE cassock'd priest's grave homily
    You rightly deem claims reverence;
For me, I own the heresy,
    Field-preaching has more eloquence.

A budding leaf, a blade of grass,
    A ripple on the stream, a reed,
A beam or shadow that may pass
    To me with holiest unction plead.

And therefore sometimes I am found,
    While close cathedral walls on you,
Where breeze and bird are chanting round,
    Where blossoms sparkle with the dew.

Or when within the pillar'd fane
    You view the decorated tomb,
Where effigy and record vain
    Adorn with pomp the common doom:

Some rural haunt displays to me
    Affecting types of life's decline,
The barren field, the naked tree,
    And many a grave and solemn sign.

And as the woodland path I tread,
    Where late the new-blown flowers were gay,
Where now the wither'd leaves are spread,
    Wise teachers meet me on the way.

Say not I break Divine commands!
    Say not I shun the house of prayer!
There is a house not made with hands,
    And there are hearts that worship there!

JULIA DAY.

SEMPRE LO STESSO.

EVER the same!—let this our watchword be
  Upon the dreary battlements of time,
With a clear soul I breathe it unto thee
  In tones whose fervour mocks this idle rhyme ;
Ever the same ;—how sweet to earn with pain
  The tested love that casteth out all fear,
And amid all we suffer, doubt and feign,
  To own one true and self-absorbing sphere!
Ever the same ;—as moons the waters draw,
  A simple presence calms all inward strife,
And by the sway of some benignant law,
  With high completeness fills the sense of life :
The Holy One this sacred thought confest
When leaned the fond disciple on his breast.

H. T. TUCKERMAN.

THE TWO ANGELS.

Two angels, one of Life and one of Death,
    Passed o'er the village as the morning broke;
The dawn was on their faces, and beneath,
    The sombre houses hearsed with plumes of smoke.

Their attitude and aspect were the same,
    Alike their features and their robes of white;
But one was crowned with amaranth, as with flame,
    And one with asphodels, like flakes of light.

I saw them pause on their celestial way;
    Then said I, with deep fear and doubt oppressed:
" Beat not so loud, my heart, lest thou betray
    The place where thy beloved are at rest!"

And he, who wore the crown of asphodels,
    Descending, at my door began to knock,
And my soul sank within me, as in wells
    The waters sink before an earthquake's shock.

I recognised the nameless agony,
    The terror and the tremor and the pain,
That oft before had filled and haunted me,
    And now returned with threefold strength again.

The door I opened to my heavenly guest,
   And listened, for I thought I heard God's voice;
And knowing whatsoe'er He sent was best,
   Dared neither to lament nor to rejoice.

Then with a smile, that filled the house with light,
   " My errand is not Death, but Life," he said;
And ere I answered, passing out of sight
   On his celestial embassy he sped.

'Twas at thy door, O friend! and not at mine,
   The angel with the amaranthine wreath,
Pausing descended, and with voice divine,
   Whispered a word that had a sound like Death.

Then fell upon the house a sudden gloom,
   A shadow on those features fair and thin;
And softly, from that hushed and darkened room,
   Two angels issued, where but one went in.

All is of God! If He but wave his hand
   The mists collect, the rain falls thick and loud,
Till with a smile of light on sea and land,
   Lo! He looks back from the departing cloud.

Angels of Life and Death alike are his;
   Without his leave they pass no threshold o'er;
Who, then, would wish or dare, believing this,
   Against his messengers to shut the door?

W. H. LONGFELLOW.

THE SHOE.

THERE's a great ball to-night at the castle;
There are knocks at the door all the day;
Every knock at the door brings a parcel,
Every parcel contains something gay.
My dress gives no room for complaining,
Flowers, trimmings, and gloves, all quite new;
And the only one thing now remaining,
Is to look for a pretty shaped shoe.

With great trouble, I make a selection,
For I must have a well-fitting pair :
At length, some appear quite perfection—
Their beauty will make the world stare!
My toilet thus fixed; to begin it,
I go very early, 'tis true;
But I wait for the very last minute,
To put on my beautiful shoe.

My dress I discover no faults in—
At eleven we start from the house;
And half-an-hour after, we 're waltzing,
In time, to the sweet airs of Strauss.

But that proverb, so frequently quoted,
Of the cup and the lip, proved quite true;
And the dancing, on which I so doted,
Was spoiled by my horrible shoe.

How could I have guessed, while admiring
Its beautiful form in the glass,
That the pleasure I'd been so desiring,
Would be quite ruined by it; alas!
But no sooner had I begun twirling,
Than my shoe took to doing so too;
And while in the gay dance, still whirling,
Off danced my detestable shoe;

In *l'Eté*, while I in a *chassé*,
My *vis-à-vis* hastened to meet,
I felt, on a sudden, quite *glacée*,
By something cold touching my feet.
A dreadful suspicion came o'er me!
I looked on the ground,—full in view
Of the crowds of spectators before me,
A yard or two off, lay my shoe!

This leads to a pause in my dancing;
To sit, sadly still, I'm reduced;
When I see our fair hostess advancing,
And I rise up to be introduced.
I return with a curtsey her greeting,
Then drew back,—when I found—fancy, do!
I had left at her feet, in retreating,
My hateful, my horrible shoe!

By these accidents fairly affrighted,
All hopes of a dance I renounced;
And I must own, I felt quite delighted,
When our carriage, at last, was announced.
But on mounting its step,— who can utter
My grief! some one pushed—Lord knows who!
And I found my foot right in the gutter,
Deserted, of course, by my shoe!

Left barefoot—(there could be no wearing
A thing covered with mud every inch);
I determined, next time, on preparing
A shoe that would serve at a *pinch*.
You may talk of the torture of squeezing,
What is that, pray, to being wet through?
Take my word, there is nothing more teazing,
Than to play hide and seek with your shoe!

M. A. B.

THE TOMB OF GLORY.

Hark to the solemn toll—the muffled drum !
Bearing the " mighty dead," behold they come !
A nation comes !—for all that long array
But *represents* a nation's grief to-day.
Its myriad souls unite in silent prayer—
In spirit, if not presence, ALL are there !
Unsullied laurels grace the warrior's bier,
And triumph's smile illumines sorrow's tear.
Though for a season deep regret may reign,
And solemn silence shrouds yon sable train—
Though for a moment glory sits in gloom,
Immortal radiance hovers o'er the tomb !

Greatest of modern Britons !—thou whose name
Shall henceforth be synonymous with FAME—
The second Arthur of our matchless isle—
On whom did virtue, valour, fortune, smile—
Whom pride is proud to honour—and whom state
Owns, in thy simple grandeur, truly great—
Soon to thy name the sculptured tomb shall rise,
And ART's high efforts tell where GLORY lies.
The graver's chisel, and the poet's lays,
For thee shall consecrate a nation's praise.

Yet oh! how feeble ev'n the loftiest art
To paint the feelings of a nation's heart.
That mighty heart, to which in true response,
Thine echoed once!—alas, that sad word ONCE!
Ah! vain is all the incense they can raise—
Sculpture's fair forms, and poesy's high praise.
'Tis but the taper glimmering in the sun,
The wreath superfluous, when the race is won.
Glory needs no memorial—born to live
In that best life its deeds or works can give.
With its own hand its monument it builds,
With its own light death's dark abode it gilds.
'Tis thus the name we would record shall last,
And time preserve it when the tomb is past.
That for the living, not the dead, we raise,
To bid them emulate the name they praise—
To tell to after ages *here doth lie*
All of immortal glory that can die—
To ask no idle sigh, nor transient tear,
But proudly tell that WELLINGTON sleeps here!

ETA.

THE COBBLER OF TOLEDO.

A LEGEND OF CASTILE.

You 've all of you heard, or you 've all of you read,
Of a little old cobbler whose dwelling is said
To have been nothing more than a stall or a shed,
Where he could n't stand up without bumping his head;
But which still, as the choicest authorities say,
Both served him for kitchen and *salle à manger*.

This same little cobbler— so fickle is Fame—
Has never yet figured in rhyme with *a name;*
And even the place of his birth or " location,"
His life, death and actions, his language and nation,
Are all alike left to our imagination.
      Yet, he lived and he died;
      He 'd a language beside,
And a mother of whom he was haply the pride.

I 've traced them all out with much trouble and pain,
And I 've taken a journey expressly to Spain
To search all the archives—I hope not in vain,—
As I found that this maker of shoes for " the million,"
Was born at Toledo—a thorough Castilian.

Toledo 's a city renowned through all ages,
In clerical tomes and historical pages,
For bishops and warriors, princes and sages,
And sword-blades, which even in these modern days
(When we 're giving up fighting and choleric ways)
Are confess'd to be matchless in " temper"—a rarity
Scarcely more known to our peace-men than charity.

In one of the streets of this city of steel—
This Sheffield and Birmingham store of Castile—
Stood a gloomy old mansion, with windows so few,
And so closely barred up, how the light could get through
Was a puzzle to all who beheld them the more,
As the street was so narrow and dismal before,
That no ray of the sunlight had ever been known
To wriggle its way down and burnish one stone.

Like a little excrescence below this great hall
Projected a queer little, black-looking, stall,
Whence the sound of a hammer assail'd you, together
With odours of beeswax and blacking and leather.
  And if you look'd *in*,
  In the midst of the din,
  And the gloom and the smell—
  And the dirt, too, as well—

You might see a small body, a very big head,
Two eyes very bright, and one nose very red,
Two hands very large and as grimy as soot,
And not the least sign of a leg or a foot.
  Don't fancy, I beg,
  That there *was n't* a leg—
But merely their owner, a cobbler at work,
Tuck'd them quite out of sight as he sat *a la* Turk.

And *this* is " the cobbler who lived in the stall
Which served him for kitchen and parlour and all :"
And this is the cobbler—Pedrillo by name—
Whose wonderful story my verses proclaim.

One day, as Pedrillo sat mending the sole
Of a shoe that its owner had worn to a hole,
And stitching, and waxing, and pegging, and thumping,
And filing, and smoothing, and ' clicking,' and ' clumping,'
He somehow got thinking on all sorts of things
And all sorts of persons, from cobblers to kings.
Pedrillo was not a philosopher, nor
Had he ever much practised at thinking before ;
Or, at least, I much doubt till that moment if ever he
Had made the remotest approach to a reverie.

 Yet, how charming a reverie *is*
  When the mind and the heart are at rest,
 When we shake off the clay of the world
  And we dream of some land of the blest !

How pleasant to loll at one's ease—
 Arms a-kimbo and eyes on the ceiling—
And shut out, in an opium trance,
 (If we can) ev'ry earthly-born feeling !

But we 're apt to do just the reverse—
 Begin thinking of every evil—
Our pains, and our debts, and our sins,
 Our long balance-sheet with the devil.

     F F

" Ah, Life thou 'rt at best but a dream !"
    Is a saying each dreamer well knows—
And oh, what a deuce of a nightmare
    Doth trouble some mortals' repose !

How we fret, and we fume, and we snore,
    How we kick off the clothes, how we quake—
How we fight with the phantoms we raise :
    And how stupid we look when we wake !

Yes—we 've taken a great deal of trouble
    To suffer a great deal of pain ;
And when we awake to our folly,
    We turn round and act it again.

It 's needless to point out our madness,
    We see it and feel it *within*—
But the spendthrift goes deepest in debt when
    The least he 's encumber'd with " tin."

        I don't mean to say
        'Twas at all in this way
The thoughts of Pedrillo attempted to stray.
        He thought of his life
        Of struggle and strife
'Gainst the pangs of Necessity, sharp as his knife.
        He thought how much Fate
        Had bless'd all the great
Who roll'd by his stall in their coaches of state.
        He thought of his soul—
        What a dark little hole
It was shut in, in *this* world—as blind as a mole.

He wished he was rich—
How quickly he 'd pitch
This shoe to the dev'—— here he made a false stitch.
He thought he could spend
Heaps of gold without end,
And wear more new boots than he e'er got to mend.
He thought how he 'd dine
And what oceans of wine
He 'd swallow of Spain and of France and the Rhine.

Till the very idea of extensive potation
Produced on his brain an uncommon sensation,
And made him feel dreamy and vicious ;—at least
He fancied he 'd like to try thrashing a priest !
And this terrible notion so tickled his brain
That he burst into laughter again and again,
As he thought of his reverence dancing with pain.

When a wicked idea gets into the head
There's no guessing the lengths into which it may spread ;
It expands ev'ry moment and gets more defined,
Till it seems to fill up ev'ry nook of the mind,
And leaves not a square inch of virtue behind.

And so with Pedrillo : each moment there fled
Some good little thought that remained in his head,
And its place was supplied by a bad one instead ;
Till at length, quite o'erwhelmed in the vortex of evil,
He cried, in the midst of his fanciful revel—
" I should like to have one little peep at the devil !"

Rat-tat-tat-tat—a whole shower of knocks
Come pattering down on his dark little box,

F F 2

And he starts from his day-dream and sees with amaze
A very tall man with a sinister gaze,
Who stands at his window, and lifting his foot
Shoves it in as he utters—" *there*—make me a boot."

Pedrillo feels sick—he 's half ready to faint,
His horror no language of mine could e'er paint
As he grasps—not a foot—but a hoof hard and thick,
Just such as tradition assigns to Old Nick!
While the owner cries, " Now then, you booby, be quick—
Take the measure at once, sir—what makes you so slow ?
Hang the fellow, my dinner 's all spoiling, I know—
I 've got a roast heretic waiting below."

Half dead with the fright which he 's trying to smother,
Pedrillo contrives in some manner or other,
To measure the hoof with his tape ; while the " gent "
Casts on him a glance of such evil intent
That cold perspiration commences to ooze
From the top of his head to the soles of his shoes.
" Now make that boot well, or you'll be in a mess,
And bring it home quickly, sir—*there 's my address :*"
And he throws down a card with a sulphurous smell,
And one word of four letters—I'd rather not tell
What it was, but the reader will guess pretty well.

———

'Tis now the merry month of May
And all Toledo's streets are gay.
The bells peal forth a merry chime
In honour of the joyful time :

From steeple tow'r and mansion-top
In graceful folds bright banners drop,
Shallop, and barge, and tiny boat,
Across the glittering Tagus float,
Bearing their smiling freights along
To mingle in the gladsome throng
That revel in each street.   The song,
The joyous laugh, the pleasant jest,
The strains of music—all attest,
Mid sighs of mirth and sounds of glee,
The noisy reign of Revelry.

Let 's follow in the motley train,
And listen to the blithesome strain
Yon maiden sings : how rich and clear
Each cadence strikes the list'ner's ear !

I.

Ye nobles and gentles come near,
    And list to the glee-maiden's lay ;
Fair ladies, approach ye and hear,
    The words from my lips as they stray :
'Tis Love is the theme of my song,
    Love's praises my verses proclaim,
And to *you* all his honours belong—
    For without you he is but a name.

II.

Say, is there a jewel on earth
    So brilliant, so priceless as this?
Does one hour of a lifetime give birth
    To a joy like the lover's pure bliss?

It glows like a furnace in youth;
   In manhood more constant its flame;
In age its companion is Truth—
   In each—'t is Love only—the same!

III.

'T is a gleam from some Angel-built sphere,
   The dowry our Maker hath given
To prove, while we're sojourning here,
   That we still have a portion of Heaven.
It knows not the leav'n of despond;
   It fears not the clouds that impend,
But sees the bright vista beyond,
   And vanquishes Fate in the end.

IV.

Let Wealth be your mistress alone—
   Let Glory allure you awhile—
Yet Love shall still claim you his own,
   You shall turn from all else for his smile.
You shall taste all the pleasures that fall
   From the bounty of Heaven above,
And confess you would barter them all
   For one moment of exquisite Love!

Now look to the right and you see a great crowd,
With a man in the centre who's bawling aloud
Some speech, or some verses, or songs, which appear
To please the rude folks who're collected to hear.
The language, you'll notice, is not over choice,
Nor sung in a very melodious voice;

And therefore, good reader, I strongly advise
That we move 'tother way.   Up yon narrow street lies
The Cathedral :—I fancy we'd better go there,
Because we're in Spain, and of course you're aware,
Whenever a "rumpus" takes place in that land,
For fun or for fighting, the Church bears a hand,
To help in the "scrimmage:" and mightily grand
Are the shows she gets up, though 't would puzzle to say
Where the deuce she can raise all the money to pay
For such costly affairs : but the utmost that *I* know
About it, is simply—she *does* get the "rhino."

And now I remember—I very much doubt
If I 've told what these holiday scenes are about.
It 's simply his Catholic Highness of Spain,
Who had buried one wife, has just married again ;
And so, all his people go mad for a day
And rejoice at the deed in an orthodox way.

We stand within the sacred pile –
The long broad nave, the narrow aisle,
E'en to the very altar's stone,
Scarcely one spot untrodden own.
Yet solemn silence reigns around,
Save when the silver bells' light sound
Proclaims the Host :—then bows each knee
Before the symbol'd Majesty
Of Christ Incarnate : each one there
Mutters his penitence and pray'r ;
While, pealing forth, the organ's note
Seems through the vaulted roof to float,
Rearing aloft its solemn tone
To bear its praise to God's high throne.

The hymns are sung, the mass is said
The crowd of worshippers has fled.
Deserted e'en by monk and priest
    The lofty temple's aisles are bare :
The gorgeous altar in the east—
    No suppliant form is kneeling there!

The motley crowd that whilome trod,
With silent step, the house of God,
Now dance the gay-deck'd streets along,
Or shouting join the ribald song.

And such is man! thus vain his mind
And fickle, as the veering wind :
Now Pleasure, and now Heav'n his text—
This hour a Saint—a satyr next!

In a dark little street is a "hullah-ba-loo,"
And shouting, and yelling, a precious "to-do ;"
            What hustling and rushing
            And running and crushing,
            And pulling and tearing,
            And laughing and swearing!
What masses of people all crowding to see
The fun or the fight, or whate'er it may be!
While each asks the other as fast as they run,
" Holloa—what's the row there? *do* tell us the fun :
What the deuce are they doing? do *you* know, or *you?*
Are they baiting a badger, or shaving a Jew?"

In that dark little street is the dark little stall,
Where our poor little cobbler 's at work with his awl—

At work when the rest of the city's at play—
At work on this glorious festival day!
The crowd are astounded—they can't make it out—
So they yell to the cobbler, and holloa, and shout,
And they bid him come forth and partake of the revel,
And pitch all his leather and tools to the devil.
"That's just *it!*" cried Pedrillo, as soon as he heard
The multitude utter that last naughty word.
"Just *it*, my old beeswax? just *what*, my old Turk?"
"Why—it's just for his worship, I mean, I'm at work."
"His worship—what worship? hang me if I know
What you mean." Why—his worship that lives *down
    below.*"
And here poor Pedrillo turned awfully white,
And even his nose grew pale with affright.
"He's mad," cried the mob—" pull him out of his hole."
"Oh mercy! not yet—I 've not finished the sole !"

In spite of his cries poor Pedrillo is seized,
And dragg'd from his hole, and most ruthlessly squeezed,
And carried in triumph, still grasping a shoe
Half-finished—not fit for a Christian or Jew ;
But a queer-looking thing, made I scarcely know how,
And exactly the shape of the hoof of a cow !
            Away they all run
            In the height of their fun,
            And bear off their prize
            Amid laughter and cries,
And huzzahs for the cobbler who, first of his trade,
A shoe for his evil-named Majesty made.

In the midst of their running they suddenly stop,
And cease from hurrahing ; and quietly drop

The load that they carry: then hasten away—
And, before the poor cobbler could manage to say
One word to his captors, they 'd left him alone,
With his comical shoe, sitting squat on a stone.

But, absorbed in one notion, he falls to his work
(Still seated, of course, as before—*à la* Turk)
And marks not the place where he 's left in the lurch—
Alas! 't is the porch of Saint Anthony's church!

    With stately step and solemn mien
    A black-rob'd priest is shortly seen
    Emerging from the door that lies
    Behind Pedrillo: and his eyes
    Rest on the cobbler in surprise!

    The latter stitches as before,
    Unconscious of his visitor,
    And heeding not the open'd door.
    The priest stands still in dumb amaze
    At the strange sight that meets his gaze—
    The cobbler with his absent air,
    And the queer shoe he 's making there.

    At length his holy indignation,
    At such an act of profanation,
    Burst forth in words—" Holloa! you hound,
    How dare you work on holy ground!"

    Pedrillo slowly raised his head,
    Not heeding what the priest had said,
    But slightly startled by the sound:
    And then he turn'd himself half round,

And saw, with supernatural fear,
A black-rob'd priest standing near.
In fact, he thought the figure must be
His most Satanic Majesty!

And so he cried—" What *shall* I do ?
I 've not quite done your worship's shoe ;
I 'm hard at work, sir—this is it—
Perhaps you 'll try how it will fit
Your worship's hoof—that is—I mean—
Your worship's foot—I 'd never seen
One like it till your worship came—
So, if I 've fail'd, you mustn't blame!''

Thus saying, he held out the cloven-hoof'd boot,
And gravely laid hold of his reverence's foot.

Then—oh for the pen of old Homer to trace
The passion that darken'd the holy man's face!
His eyes were half-red and his cheeks were half-black,
And he rush'd at the cobbler, and caught him a whack
With his toe on the nethermost point of his back,
That sent him a summerset, tumbling and sprawling,
Into the street, and with agony bawling.
            And before he could rise,
            Or had finished his cries,
Before the whole truth could have enter'd his mind,
Before he could rub where he smarted behind—
He was seiz'd on the spot, and with smart expedition,
Clapp'd into the jail of the fell Inquisition!

            Fair Spain, sweet Spain, the brightest gem
            In all Europa's diadem!

Land of the sun, the flow'r, the vine—
Land of a race once half-divine :
Land of fair scenes, and fairer ladies,
Whose forms, from Pyrenees to Cadiz,
May match with all the world can boast,
From Ind to Russia's ice-bound coast !
Land of romance—the rich, deep, store
Of poet's lay and monkish lore !
Birth-place of men whose ev'ry name,
Writ in the muster-roll of Fame,
To ev'ry age, 'neath ev'ry zone,
Attest their glory and thine own !

How art thou favor'd, glorious land !
What gifts thou hast at Nature's hand—
Climate and soil, and hills and vales,
And flowing streams—all that avails
To charm the eye or glad the heart,
Or sense of gratitude impart
To God above, whose hand benign
Hath bless'd thee thus—all, all are thine !

And yet, what art thou ?—lost, debased—
Thine annals past in glory traced—
Thy present but a wretched blank,
Or viler stain ! Where shalt thou rank
Among the nations of the earth ? Ay—thou,
Once crown'd with honour—sunken now
Below the meanest state enslaved
Where once thy flag victorious waved !

And why is this? what spell hath wrought
   A change so fatal to thy fame?
What sad reverse, with ruin fraught,
   Hath swept away thine ancient fame?

Alas! within thy bosom cherish'd,
   The deadly canker-worm hath grown,
And day by day thy weal hath perish'd
   'Neath his corroding sting alone.

Yes! History's impartial page,
   Thy glory and thy fall that tells,
Shall point to ev'ry future age—
   "The land is cursed where Priestcraft dwells."

In a dark dismal dungeon, where never a ray
Of sunlight has ever been tempted to stray;
Where the walls are all damp and all mildew'd, and where
An uncommonly scanty supply of fresh air
Is deem'd quite enough to supply the vitality
Of any imprison'd remains of mortality;
Where a heap of foul straw is to serve as a bed,
While the rats, by the dozen, run over your head,
And tickle your visage with tail and with claw,
Or vary the pleasure by taking a gnaw
At your toes, when they're hungry; where lizards and toads
Crawl out from the chinks of the pavement by loads—
In this highly-delectable tenement, all
That remains of Pedrillo lies chain'd to the wall.

Poor fellow! a visage so hollow and wan,
Scarce ever belonged to the form of a man.

His eyeballs so glazed, and his eyelids so blue,
And his skin of a greenish and yellowish hue ;
His hands were so bony, so long and so thin,
So grizzled the beard that hung down from his chin ;
So wasted his limbs, and his round little nose
So completely deprived of its *couleur de rose*—
That no eye could have ever detected, at all,
The poor little cobbler who lived in the stall,
Except that one hand, to its " cunning" yet true,
Still grasp'd the remains of an odd-looking shoe.

Pedrillo 'd been tried for the wicked pretence
Of mistaking a priest for Old Nick—an offence
Pronounced, with veracity, quite " diabolical"
By the holy Inquisitors—meek Apostolical
Lambs, who 've been famed, in all countries and ages,
As patterns of Christians and virtuous sages.
The verdict was " Guilty," of course—'t would n't " pay"
To let a man off when they 'd bagg'd him—to say
That they 'd made a mistake : and besides, just of late
They 'd been scarce of offenders in Church or in State,
And wanted a Jew or a heretic sadly—
And so poor Pedrillo was pounced upon gladly.

A little discussion between them took place,
Regarding the punishment due to his case.
Some voted for roasting—some hinted at flaying—
Which others declared to be trifling and playing.
The President would n't agree to the roasting,
And seized the occasion for modestly boasting
How mild and how gentle *his* sentiments were.
The fact is, his house stood just facing the square

Where the stake was erected when sinners were burnt,
And from many a past sad example he 'd learnt
That the smell of a roast was so highly unpleasant—
He 'd the strongest objection to try one at present.

And so, in the end, they decided on " mercy"—
Or, rather, what *I* should call just *vice versâ*—
That is—" out of care for his poor sinful soul,"
They left him to die, like a rat, in a hole.

    And thus our poor Pedrillo lay,
    Wasting his wretched life away :
    Dying by inches—dying slowly—
    Condemn'd by wretches self-styled " holy."

    Oh, God! and can thy lightnings spare
        The impious creatures who profane
    The sacred livery they wear,
        And take Thy holy name in vain,
    To sanctify a deed of blood,
    And name that deed " Religious, good !"

    How vain the question ! look, weak man,
    Beyond thy frail life's little span—
    See Retribution's work begun—
    God's name avenged—and Justice done !

In a dark little street is a dark little stall,
And a plump little cobbler at work with his awl.
Who is it ? Pedrillo ? by Jove it 's the same !
How on earth did he get there ? What influence came

To set him at liberty? see him at work,
Sitting just as before on his board *à la* Turk!
And he 's stitching with vigour, he 's making a boot—
Not a cloven hoof'd thing, but one fit for a foot.
And how happy he looks! and how plump and how red!
How punchy his body, how shiny his head!
And he sticks to his trade like an honest Castilian—
Making highlows and mending the soles of the million.

Now touching his freedom :—it chanced one fine day
That some two dozen Jews were all sentenced to pay
A very large sum for some very bad deed,
Regarding some matter of conscience and creed;
And finding the prison was rather too small
(In addition to those it contain'd) for them all,
A "weeding" took place—and 'mongst others, Pedrillo
To a Hebrew in trouble relinquish'd his pillow.

And such—without varnish, invention, or mystery—
Is the true, undeniable, record and history
Of the "little old cobbler who liv'd in a stall
Which served him for kitchen and parlour and all."

Moral.

There 's a saying so stale that it 's grown to an epigram—
Of course you all know it well—" *Ne sutor crepidam
Ultra :*" And some sleepy folks may opine
That such is the moral of *this* tale of mine.
They 're mistaken : such "morals" belong to the past—
They wont do for these days—we 're a great deal too fast
For such slow-coach old maxims. What! " stick to our
      last ?"

Nail the doctor to physic, the lawyer to law,
The parson to preaching!—a pretty fine saw
For this age of progression!—when ev'ry man's head
Is so full of the things he has heard, seen, and read—
It 's not easy to say where our knowledge *can* stop
When our brain is as full as a pawnbroker's shop.

No, no—I 've got something much better—much truer—
Much more to the purpose—and certainly newer
To tell you.   It 's this :—if you ever give way
To an evil-born thought—if you let your mind stray
In a naughty direction, don't think me uncivil
If I say that *you* 're making a boot for the devil.
And that very same boot—when your virtue 's clean gone—
You'll see him some day when he 's " trying it on."

AS I LAYE A-THYNKYNGE.

THE LAST LINES OF THOMAS INGOLDSBY.

As I laye a-thynkynge, a-thynkynge, a-thynkynge,
   Merrie sang the Birde as she sat upon the spraye;
     There came a noble Knyghte,
     With his hauberke shynynge brighte,
     And his gallant heart was lyghte,
       Free and gaye;
As I laye a-thynkynge, he rode upon his waye.

As I laye a-thynkynge, a-thynkynge, a-thynkynge,
Sadly sang the Birde as she sat upon the tree!
     There seem'd a crimson plain,
     Where a gallant Knyghte lay slayne,
     And a steed with broken rein
       Ran free,
As I laye a-thynkynge, most pitiful to see!

As I laye a-thynkynge, a-thynkynge, a-thynkynge,
Merrie sang the Birde as she sat upon the boughe;
     A lovely Mayde came bye,
     And a gentil youth was nyghe,
     And he breathed many a syghe
       And a vowe;
As I laye a-thynkynge, her hearte was gladsome now.

As I lay a-thynkynge, a-thynkynge, a-thynkynge,
Sadly sang the Birde as she sat upon the thorne ;
  No more a youth was there,
  But a Maiden rent her haire,
  And cried in sad despaire,
   ' That I was borne !'
As I laye a-thynkynge, she perished forlorne.

As I lay a-thynkynge, a-thynkynge, a-thynkynge,
Sweetly sang the Birde as she sat upon the briar ;
  There came a lovely Childe,
  And his face was meek and mild,
  Yet joyously he smiled
   On his sire ;
As I laye a-thynkynge, a Cherub mote admire.

But I laye a-thynkynge, a-thynkynge, a-thynkynge,
And sadly sang the Birde as it perch'd upon a bier ;
  That joyous smile was gone,
  And the face was white and wan,
  As the downe upon the Swan
   Doth appear,
As I lay a-thynkynge—oh! bitter flow'd the tear!

As I laye a-thynkynge, the golden sun was sinking,
O merrie sang that Birde as it glitter'd on her breast
  With a thousand gorgeous dyes,
  While soaring to the skies,
  'Mid the stars she seem'd to rise.
   As to her nest ;

As I laye a-thynkynge, her meaning was exprest :—
    ' Follow, follow me away,
    It boots not to delay,'—
    'Twas so she seem'd to saye,
      ' HERE IS REST !'

THOMAS INGOLDSBY.

THE END.

LONDON :
Printed by A. Schulze, 13, Poland Street.

www.ingramcontent.com/pod-product-compliance
Lightning Source LLC
Chambersburg PA
CBHW022016110726
47901CB00006B/1553